The Forgotten Ones

by

Kimberlee R. Mendoza

The Forgotten Ones

Cover Art by *Kimberlee R. Mendoza*

The Wild Rose Press, Inc.
PO Box 708
Adams Basin, NY 14410-0708
Visit us at www.thewildrosepress.com

Publishing History
First Crimson Rose Edition, 2013
Print ISBN 978-1-61217-860-8
Digital ISBN 978-1-61217-861-5

Published in the United States of America

An explosion rocked the desert floor.

Laura Black hit the sand, coughing against the smoke that consumed the air. Glass and rocks pelted her leather flak jacket. Jamming the rifle against her shoulder, she darted for a better position, ready to fire again.

Masked enemies, armed with AK-47s, scampered to her right, both ducking behind a deserted sedan.

Laura fired.

One of the targets dropped.

Heart racing, Laura crawled behind a beat-up sedan and peeked through the window. Except for dust and smoke, the horizon appeared empty. But she could sense them.

An automatic gun sprayed in her direction. Shards of glass showered her black cavalier helmet.

The radio clicked in her ear. "We're bugging out, now!" Agent Harding yelled. "That's an order from command."

Finally! Laura glanced around for an opening in the chaos. Her partner, Harding, climbed a ladder to the top of one of the few erect buildings. The helicopter would land there. She started to inch to his position, but stopped. Bullets pelted against the car bumper. She spun around and studied her exit points—a store window a few yards away and a hillside that dropped about thirty feet down.

A rocket grenade barreled toward her.

No time. She lunged for the store window. The blast launched her against a metal shelf, a rough corner slicing her skin. She swallowed against the pain and ran to the back of the store.

Just another day at the office.

Dedication

In Memory of Ashley Sampier
May you always be in our hearts.

Prologue

According to the BBC*, there are currently an estimated three hundred thousand child soldiers in the world, most in places like Sierra Leone, Liberia, Congo, Sudan, Sri Lanka, Afghanistan, and Burma.

For two decades in Uganda, ninety percent of the soldiers who fought in their various wars were children. Children are small and can infiltrate tight spaces undetected. Children seem innocent and are less likely to be a target. Children can be taught, blackmailed, and brainwashed. And in some cultures, children are unimportant and expendable.

In 1989, a former C.I.A. agent, Mel Greenstone returned from Africa with an epiphany for a black ops unit like none the U.S. Government had ever seen. However, he wasn't able to convince several high-ranking officials to implement his plan—to recruit orphans and young criminals to a secret organization and train them as special agents. He decided to take matters into his own hands. With a few financial backers, he created S.I.U.—the Secret Intelligence Unit.

In Greenstone's words, "Young people without a real future will be given one as the next generation of soldiers."

*http://www.bbc.co.uk/worldservice/people/features/childrensrights/childrenofconflict/soldier.shtml

Chapter One

An explosion rocked the desert floor.

Laura Black hit the sand, coughing against smoke that consumed the air. Glass and rocks pelted her leather flak jacket. Jamming the rifle against her shoulder, she darted for a better position, ready to fire again.

Masked enemies, armed with AK-47s, scampered to her right, both ducking behind a deserted sedan.

Laura fired.

One of the targets dropped.

Heart racing, Laura crawled behind a beat-up sedan and peeked through the window. Except for dust and smoke, the horizon appeared empty. But she could sense them.

An automatic gun sprayed in her direction. Shards of glass showered her black cavalier helmet.

The radio clicked in her ear. "We're bugging out, now!" Agent Harding yelled. "That's an order from command."

Finally! Laura glanced around for an opening in the chaos. Her partner, Harding, climbed a ladder to the top of one of the few erect buildings. The helicopter would land there. She started to inch to his position, but stopped. Bullets pelted against the car bumper. She spun around and studied her exit points—a store window a few yards away and a hillside that dropped about thirty feet down.

A rocket grenade barreled toward her.

No time. She lunged for the store window. The blast launched her against a metal shelf, a rough corner slicing her skin. She swallowed against the pain and ran to the back of the store.

Behind her, men yelled in Arabic. Guns rattled. Sparks popped inches from her skull. She didn't stop. A door lay open to her right. She darted for it. It led to a dirty alleyway. An agency chopper hovered above. She reached in her leg pocket and ripped out a flare, popped it open, and held the smoke over her head.

Several men sprinted around the corner, guns blazing.

One of her agents fell a few yards away.

Laura tossed the flare and fired.

Both pursuers crumpled to the sandy earth.

A rope ladder dropped a foot from her position. She grasped hold of it and lifted from the ground.

Just another day at the office.

****

Twelve hours later, Laura walked from the parking garage to a metal door, punched in her code, and waited. It clicked, creaked, and swung wide. On the other side, two armed guards greeted her, with hands on their hips and stoic expressions. She tossed a leather briefcase on a conveyor belt, then stepped to a red X painted on the left. A laser beam scanned her body, projecting an image on a monitor a few feet away. Her short, dark hair looked matted and disheveled in the depiction. Still covered in soot, filthy and sweaty, she longed for a shower.

A guard pushed a button on his computer, and the inner door slid open, revealing their headquarters. She inhaled and smiled. *Home!*

"Good morning, Agent Black," said Mr. Greenstone, the head of the agency, a bald, crotchety man with a salt-and-pepper goatee and a malicious disposition. He motioned for her to follow him to the briefing room. His sardonic smile exuded evil that intimidated most. "Please take a seat. We have a new crop coming in. I've picked you to run them."

With a hand to her lips, she held back a smile and nodded at the huge honor. "I just came off a mission." She removed a cavalier belt and hung it on the back of the conference room chair. "I'm supposed to debrief this afternoon, and you can tell I need a shower."

"You'll have time. I need a manager for this new group; I believe you're ready." Greenstone clicked the remote on the glass table and a monitor flipped over from the wall. Several mug shots appeared on the screen. "Being in the field may seem easier than training these people, but you'll do fine."

"Are you sure a more experienced agent wouldn't be the better choice?"

"If you're referring to age, no."

Of course. At twenty-six, Laura was practically a senior citizen. Most agents didn't make it to their eighteenth birthday. "No, I meant I haven't been in a teaching position before."

"You're one of the best, Black. It's time you shared your skills with others."

She walked around the table, her boots squeaking on the tiled floor, and stepped close to the monitors. "Tell me about them then."

The computer mouse scrolled across the page. It blinked and the picture of an African-American male popped to the forefront. He glared out behind dreadlocks, his expression cold; his eyes void of any joy, only visible anger.

"Meet Myers Luther. Age seventeen. He was arrested for armed robbery, larceny, and illegal selling. Had we not intervened, he would have been tried as an adult."

"He doesn't seem like our usual find." Laura glanced back at Mr. Greenstone. "He sounds like nothing more than a common thug."

Her boss shook his head. "He's a genius, a regular entrepreneur. When they searched his home, they found records for almost a million dollars in Swiss bank accounts." The picture faded into the background. "He's a con artist, business man. He'll come in handy."

Laura pursed her lips. "Not a very good con artist if he got caught."

"He wasn't caught because of a con. He got arrested for helping a friend boost a computer store."

Yeah, that's genius. She sighed and returned her attention to the screen.

A beautiful Asian girl smiled from the monitor. "Eri Lee Young. Age sixteen. Recently orphaned. The famous martial artist Chou Young was her uncle."

"Was?"

"He died last week in an accident, making her an orphan. She's well trained—a black belt by the age of six."

"But she's not a criminal?"

"No."

Big breath. Laura dug deep to block out her

emotions. She couldn't allow herself to feel connected to these kids. Most of the students who came through the agency died in combat, so getting attached would only hurt. The girl in front of her had dreams that would surely end here. "Next."

"Charlie Smyth. Age fifteen." A boy with dirty-blond, shoulder-length hair and a smirk appeared on the screen. "A.k.a. The Dark Hat."

She nodded, recalling that a *black hat* often referred to a criminal hacker. "Computer guy."

"Yes, he can infiltrate almost anything with code. He has a bit of an attitude, but he's brilliant. The feds are aware of his activities, but we want to pick him up before they do."

A girl with purple-tinted, black hair and ivory skin flipped to the front. "Denise Kruger. Age sixteen. Thespian by day, klepto by night. She is a master of disguise and a professional pick pocket."

"Only sixteen, a professional?" She tried to hold back the sarcasm, but this challenge was a game. Laura enjoyed toying with her boss. "How good can she be if she was arrested?"

"Not caught lifting. A friend turned her in."

"Nice friend."

Another face pushed to the front. Laura sat straighter. "He looks like a man, not a boy." Dark hair, intense blue eyes, firm jaw—she cleared her throat, hoping there was no hint of emotion in her voice. "Who is he?"

"Meet Bryce Chappelle. Age twenty-four."

Her eyes swung to her leader. "Twenty-four? We don't usually take them that old."

"In his case, we do."

She stared back at the screen. Her eyes mesmerized by his intense stare. Trying to ignore her accelerated pulse, she cleared her throat. "And what makes him special?"

The screen blackened and she spun around to face her boss.

"He's a trained Army ranger, top of his class." Her boss took a seat at the head of the table and opened a red folder. "He was on his way to prison when I intervened."

Sliding into the chair next to him, she said, "So we get a screw up? That doesn't sound right."

"The reason is top secret, but I assure you he's nothing more than a scapegoat. He has almost a sixth sense when it comes to finding the enemy. Only one week in Iraq, and he sniffed out the wrong thing. Someone wanted him gone."

"Will he be a problem? A detective type here could get ugly."

A sick smile crept on Greenstone's face. "You're missing the point, my dear. We want him to get dirt on the enemy. Blackmail can come in handy in our line of work. You know that."

"Doesn't sound like he'll play ball."

Greenstone's grin dissipated into a scowl. "He will or he'll be terminated."

Of course. "So, when do I meet this notorious brood?"

"In the morning." He slid the folder across the table. "Be careful, Agent."

She raised an eyebrow. It wasn't like him to offer such sentiments. "Careful? I think I can handle five students."

"Like this?"

She'd seen worse. "Was I all that nice when I first came to S.I.U.?"

"Imagine five of you."

That registered. When Laura entered the Secret Intelligence Unit, she bit, spat, hit, and spouted off to everyone in charge. They eventually teamed her up with a no-nonsense woman who put a gun to her head and said, "Give me one reason to pull the trigger. I beg you." Laura got the message and had played along since.

"Well, if that's all, I'll turn in." She scooted the chair back and stood.

"Of course."

She grabbed her coat and walked down the dimly lit hall to the science center. Her mind reeled with the possibilities of running her own team. Maybe she could make a difference. Train soldiers to care, instead of just fight. But as soon as the thought came, it drifted.

Who am I kidding? This place had one end—kill until you die.

The huge, technical warehouse housed more than two hundred black ops agents. Most of them trained before puberty. Laura was no exception, only thirteen when they found her living on the street. They brought her in, trained her, and sent her into the field to execute those they felt deserved it. More than a decade later, she was the best. Retirement didn't happen here, only elimination. The youth brought into S.I.U. were orphans, criminals, or runaways—people society wouldn't miss. They were the "forgotten ones."

Chapter Two

SUBJECT'S NAME: *Myers Luther*
AGE: *17*
STATUS: *Incarcerated*
SPECIALITY/OCCUPATION: *Con Artist/ Entrepreneur*
LOCATION: *Orange County Juvenile Hall*

Myers Luther stared down at his dark brown hands. They shook. What did he know about juvenile hall? He'd never been in trouble. Not that he was a saint. The arresting officer called him a white criminal. Myers had laughed. "You're obviously not referring to my skin color."

"I'm referring to your choice of crime," the officer said.

The computer was his vehicle and the Internet his freeway to the good life. *Well, was.*

His mind wandered to two days ago.

Myers opened his bedroom door, flipped the light switch, and jumped. A friend of his, Brody Parks lay sprawled on his bed. "Man, what're you doing in here? I about had a heart attack."

"Your foster brother let me in." He crossed his ankles. "Besides, you said I could crash here anytime I wanted."

Myers shook his head. "I don't think that's what I said."

Brody propped up on his elbows and scowled. "Don't knock a brother down, dude. Things are rough. My old man is drinking again, and I needed a place to crash."

Not like Myers ever said "no" to his buddies. His nerdy cousin once called Myer's good heart his own "kryptonite." Basically, his undoing. "Fine. One night. Then you're out of here. If my foster mom finds out you were in here, she'll kill me."

A big smile flashed on Brody's face. He kicked his dirty high-tops on the floor and stretched. "I don't know why she doesn't like me. I'm a good influence on you."

Myers blew a raspberry-sound with his lips. "Yeah, right."

"Hey, that hurts, man."

"I'm sure you'll live." Myers sat at his desk and booted up his computer. A chime sounded and the monitor flickered on. "You need to be quiet, got that? I have some major work to do."

"And you're worried about your mom finding out about *me*. Man, she'd shoot you if she knew your real business."

Myers twirled around in his chair and glared at his friend. "She better not find out. Got that?"

Brody lifted his hands in surrender. "Sure man. Totally."

"Good." Myers faced back to the screen and scrolled the mouse over an icon that housed his current projects.

"I'm just wondering—"

"What's that?" Myers said dryly, not looking back.

"Do you like the color orange?"

"Not really."

"Then don't get caught, or you'll be sporting a nice jumpsuit in your least favorite color." Brody grabbed his stomach and doubled over laughing.

So stupid. "Shut up, man. You're not even funny."

He quieted down and cleared his throat. "Not sure why you bother. You need a respectable job like stealing cars."

Myers laughed. "I think being behind this keyboard is better than boosting a car."

"Not in my book. Besides, both will get you ten-to-twenty. What are you going to tell your cellmates? Yeah, man, I got stuck in here for typing." Brody yawned and pulled a pillow onto his chest. "Sounds like a wasted life to me."

With the exception of his snoring friend, the room finally fell silent. Myers double clicked his mouse over an icon and a document opened.

"I have a question, or rather a favor, to ask you," Brody said.

Myers let out an exasperated gust of air and looked at him. "I thought you fell asleep."

"I woke up." Brody scooted to the edge of the mattress and smiled. "What if I had a way to make a ton of money and get you a better computer in the process?"

A warning sign flashed in Myer's head. *Deter him quickly.* "There's nothing wrong with this computer."

"It's like two years behind, man."

Myers crossed his arms, but didn't respond.

"Okay, look. I have a friend who's got the 4-1-1 about a large shipment of computers coming in this weekend. He said it is like the easiest gig ever."

"I don't need the money or the computer."

Brody held up a hand. "Hear me out."

Myers sighed.

"It's worth a lot of money, bro, and if I don't do it, I'm in big trouble."

That did it. How Myers hated his weakness for lost causes. "What kind of trouble?"

"I kind of borrowed money from Louie Patron."

Myers's eyes went wide. "Are you stupid?"

"I know. Dumb, right?"

"Ya think?"

Brody flopped back on the bed and raised his hands toward the ceiling. "I know I'm a bad friend to ask, but I need your help. I can't possibly pull this off by myself and everyone else I've asked—"

"Were all smart and said 'no.' Am I right?"

"Yeah," Brody whispered.

Myers squeezed his eyes shut. *How do I always get roped into having such loser friends?* He knew he'd say yes, because if he didn't and Brody got hurt, he'd never forgive himself. "Fine. What is it?"

"Really?"

Reluctantly, Myers nodded.

Brody leapt to his feet and pumped his fist. "Yes! Here's the plan."

****

For over two days, Myers had endured evil stares and the other inmates chanting "fish" every time he walked down the corridor. Apparently, the word "fish" meant new inmate. He had no idea how they equated the two.

Whatever. He lay down on the bottom bunk and

stared up at the mattress above him. Stains swirled in mustard-yellow and brown patterns. He imagined a tugboat, a woman's head, and a finger pointing. *Disgusting.* His mattress was probably the same. But it wasn't like he had a choice; he was stuck here.

"Hey, fish," a man yelled from behind the wall in the cell next to him.

Myers stood up and walked to the bars. "Name's Myers. What do you want?"

The guy laughed a husky baritone that made Myers imagine a big brute. "Can't wait to meet you, fish. We're going to have some real fun."

Myers retreated to his bunk, flopped down, and closed his eyes. If his lawyer didn't do something fast, he'd probably either die at the hand of the husky baritone or go insane.

"Hey, Luther."

His heart leapt. He glanced toward the bars and sighed with relief. It was a security guard.

"Yeah?"

The man unlocked the door. "You're out of here."

He jumped from the bunk, wide-eyed, not sure if he heard him right. "You're kidding?"

The officer just shrugged and led him down the hall. When they reached the front, the man undid his handcuffs and led him outside. A gorgeous woman dressed all in black, with short, dark hair and hazel eyes, met him behind an armored car.

"Hey, gorgeous." Myers winked at her.

She didn't flinch, her expression serious. "You will refer to me as Agent Black or not at all."

He swayed from one foot to the other, smiling. "Yeah, okay, sweetheart."

She nodded over his shoulder.

A man stepped up and shoved a dark hood over his head.

Myers panicked and tried to flail, but before he could do anything, something smashed against his head and he felt his body go limp as the world went dark.

Chapter Three

SUBJECT'S NAME: *Eri Lee Young*
AGE: *16*
STATUS: *Orphaned*
SPECIALITY/OCCUPATION: *Black Belt in Judo*
LOCATION: *Chinatown, Los Angeles County*

Eri posed with her legs apart and her arms ready for her attacker.

Black belt, Jane Chu rushed her, screaming.

Prepared, Eri grabbed Jane's left arm and swung her to the mat.

The young girl somersaulted to a standing position and charged again.

Eri blocked.

They sparred for a few minutes, when Uncle Chou entered.

Jane stepped back and bowed.

Eri returned her bow and faced her elder. "Uncle San. Are you okay? You look a little pale," she said in Chinese.

"I'm not feeling well, child."

She grabbed a chair and brought it to him. "Can I get you some tea?"

He shook his head. His white hair appeared thinner than before, his skin almost translucent against the purple rings under his eyes. "I need to talk to you."

"Of course." She knelt at his side.

"The doctors say I will leave you soon. I need you to know how much I love you. I am so proud of you."

A tear cascaded down her cheek, her throat tightened to the point she almost couldn't speak. "Please, uncle, don't say that."

He placed a shaky frail hand on her head and grinned. "All in timing, young one. But you will be okay. I will see you get a good family."

She didn't want to hear this. Her uncle, in so many ways, was like her father.

"My lawyer will be here tomorrow to draw up the will. Who would you like to live with?"

Who? She wasn't aware of any family. Both her parents were gone. And friends weren't readily available. Most of her days were spent home schooling so she could care for her uncle. "I don't know."

He patted her head. "Not to worry. I will figure that out in good time."

Eri helped him stand and walk back to his room.

He lay in his bed, and Eri covered him with a thick gold quilt. "You are so beautiful, like your mother," he said, then closed his eyes and let out a loud gurgling sound.

"Uncle?"

His body seemed so still.

"Uncle?" Eri reached down and touched his cheek.

He did not respond.

Panic rose in her throat. "Uncle!" She touched her hands to his neck. No pulse. "No! Not yet." She glanced around the room, not sure what to do next. She couldn't stop crying to focus. Her head spun. She couldn't lose him. She needed him. "Uncle," she sobbed. "Please don't leave me."

****

Eri walked to her uncle's coffin and laid a rose on top of the others. Soft organ music played in the background, but she barely heard it. Neither did she completely remember who had attended today. The faces in the room had appeared blurred, distant. Maybe due to the hundreds of tears that had poured from her eyes. Only five years ago, she lost her parents. This week—her uncle. She was completely alone.

Eri stared at the casket, unsure how to feel. Her uncle's face appeared vacant, surreal. Tiny brown stitches were visible at his eyelids and mouth. His once amber skin now looked peach, almost mannequin-like. His brilliant smile now fell flat and somber. No longer did his soul reside here. It made her numb, empty.

Most of the guests had gone home hours ago, only a few of her uncle's dojo members remained. *Why can't I leave his side?*

Someone walked next to her, but Eri didn't look to see who it was. She figured the housekeeper wished to take her home, but Eri didn't want to leave. *Not yet.*

"Eri Lee?" a woman said.

She didn't recognize the voice. Eri dabbed her eyes with the tissue and glanced at the most stunning woman she'd ever seen. *Who is she?* Certainly not one of her uncle's friends. Most of them were old or Asian.

"Yes?" Eri whispered.

"I really am sorry to bother you during your time of grief, but it is most important you come with me."

Eri peered around the empty funeral hall, then back to the coffin. "Now?"

17

"Yes, I'm afraid so."

Her heart skipped. "Is there something wrong?"

"I'll explain in the foyer. Please."

She didn't want to, but the woman appeared determined. Eri glanced at her, then to her uncle, and nodded. They stepped through a side door and into a hallway that led outside.

"Who are you?" Eri asked.

"My name is Agent Laura Black. I've been sent by my agency to bring you in."

Eri took a step back. "Bring me in? Like jail?"

The woman didn't respond.

"There must be some mistake. I'm a good girl. I haven't done anything wrong." She pointed to the coffin inside. "Besides, my uncle needs me now."

Laura shook her head. "He doesn't need you anymore. We do."

She stared at Laura. "I don't understand."

"Since you have no living relatives, or a will that says otherwise, you are automatically a ward of the state. The State of California planned to place you in foster care, but my agency intervened. We adopted you. You are now under my custody."

Eri swallowed. She had to go with this woman?

"I will give you a chance to say goodbye to your uncle. We've already collected your things." Laura stepped toward the exit. "I'll expect you outside in ten minutes."

"What agency?"

"All in time, dear. Now hurry." The sound of her heels clicked on the tile, and she disappeared out the back door.

Eri felt lost. Confused. Deadened. Adopted by an

agency? She crossed back to the casket and sighed.

A hand on her shoulder, she jumped.

"Eri? Are you okay?" her uncle's long-time friend, Morey asked.

She faced him, and a volcano of hot tears erupted down her cheeks. "I've been adopted."

"I know." He opened his arms and she fell into them.

Her shoulders shook as she sobbed, hard. There were too many emotions to know which one caused this torrent of saltwater to emerge. Her uncle died. That was enough.

When she quieted, Morey held her shoulders back and offered a slight smile. "Goodbye, child. Come see me when you can. I'm sure your new mommy will be good to you."

Eri grimaced. She thought of the stern woman who spoke to her in the hall. Somehow she guessed baking cookies would be out of the question. "Goodbye, Morey." She then turned to the casket and sighed. "Goodbye, Uncle."

Chapter Four

SUBJECT'S NAME: *Charlie Smyth*
AGE: *15*
STATUS: *Under Investigation*
SPECIALITY/OCCUPATION: *Computer Hacker*
LOCATION: *San Diego, CA*

Twenty-four hours ago
Charlie stretched out and tried to get comfortable. The sleeping bag did little to comfort his back on the cement walkway. He glanced at his buddy, Steve, who rested his head on a bundled jacket. "How many minutes left?"

Steve snapped open his cell and hooted. "Less than ten minutes to midnight."

A bolt of adrenaline fed Charlie's heart. In only a few minutes, he'd have the coveted expansion to *Omega Battle-X* in his hand. Every computer geek in America vied for the same piece of technology, and only the dedicated few would take it home tonight. *Dedicated meaning sleeping in front of a computer store for two days.* Charlie cracked his stiff neck and sighed. Truth be told, however, as stupid as it seemed, he would do it again without hesitation. Gaming was a very serious venture.

"They're opening!" a girl at the front of the line

yelled.

Like backward dominoes, the crowd stood with excited chatter.

Charlie rolled his sleeping bag back into a bundle, pulled his bag over his shoulder, and inhaled deep. *This is it.* If he weren't so exhausted, he'd probably hop around like a child on a sugar high.

"You stoked, man?" Steve asked, rubbing his hands together.

"Beyond. This will take me to a whole new level." Charlie pushed his shaggy hair out of his eyes and stepped forward.

An employee was asking people for their claim ticket at the door.

Charlie pulled his out. Nothing could keep him from this now. Suddenly, the *Star Wars* theme song cut through the air. *Not now.* He fumed as his cell phone continued to ring. He glanced at his full hands. *Now what? I should ignore it. Let it go to voicemail.* But he knew it was most likely one of his clients. All-important—because money was important. He stuck his sleeping bag between his legs, his ticket in his mouth, and dug it out of his back pocket.

The line moved forward.

He waddled with it and hit the green answer button on his phone. "Yeah?" he mumbled through the paper in his mouth.

"Dark Hat?"

Charlie recognized the voice as Bart Zimmerman. No idea what the guy did for a living professionally, but Charlie didn't really want to know. As long as the man had cash, that was enough.

"Yep."

"You still want that job we talked about?"

Charlie's heart accelerated. *Finally!* "Absolutely! When, where, and I'm there."

"Meet me in twenty minutes. You know where."

Charlie looked to the dozen or so people in front of him. "Can it wait until six or so? I'm kind of busy right now."

"Twenty minutes, or I give it to someone else."

"Shoot!" Charlie yelled with the mouthpiece covered, letting his ticket float to the ground. The job was worth ten grand. He couldn't give that up, not even for *Omega Battle-X*. Not that he would want to give up the job anyway. It was the challenge every hacker would kill to attempt—the top-secret kind that could land him in jail, but make him a legend. *Yeah, I'm in.*

"Fine. Twenty minutes." He ended the call and jammed the phone into his pocket before scowling at Steve. "I've got to go."

"What? You're joking, right?" He waved his hand toward the closing space to the entrance. "It's like right there, man. Please tell me you're joking."

"I wish. Later." He headed toward the parking lot, ignoring Steve's taunting of insanity. *Two days wasted.* But with this new chunk of change, he would get his expansion anyway. He'd have enough money to treat everyone on his block to a copy. A smile tugged at his lips as he started the car.

Yeah, it's worth it. I'm going to be legend. A rich legend.

****

Charlie slammed the mini-refrigerator door closed, popped the cap off a bottle of orange soda, and swiveled in his chair to face his desk. He took a swig of

22

soda, set it down, and smiled. He was done playing games. He adjusted the beanie on his head, cracked his knuckles, and leered at the screen. This computer program had kicked his butt for three days, but today, he would kick back. Only about an hour left and he'd have it.

Someone pounded on the door.

He rolled his eyes and looked back to the monitor. "Not now, Michael. I'm busy." His twenty-year-old brother had been left to raise Charlie when their single mother took off with some guy. Though it was cool to have someone to count on, Mike could be a real pain sometimes.

The person banged on the door again.

"Busy! Go away."

"Charlie Smyth. Open up."

His pulse quickened. *Cops?* His eyes darted over the CDs that lined his desktop. He tossed them in the garbage and then jammed a virus CD in the slot on his computer. He felt sick. All those hours wasted and now he'd have to destroy his work. *This is so bogus.* But if they caught him with all this stuff, they toss him away until he could vote.

The door flew open, sending splinters across the room. Two armed men entered, followed by one hot-looking woman.

Charlie placed his hand over the keyboard with the intent to press return. He glanced at them. One keystroke and all evidence would be destroyed.

A gun fired and his keyboard shattered.

He jumped away, hands up. "Okay, I get it. Cool. Don't shoot! Please."

The woman stepped forward. "My name is Agent

Laura Black."

"FBI?"

She produced a tight smile, but didn't answer. Her eyes scanned the room. "Gather everything you can find," she said to one of the other men. "The Intel is likely useful. Greenstone will want it."

"Look, I haven't done anything wrong. I'm just messing around. I promise."

Laura glanced back at him with pursed lips. "I hope not, Charlie. I'd be very disappointed."

He furrowed his brow. *Who is this woman*?

She pointed her gun at him, eye level, and motioned with her head to the door. "Let's go."

He was too stunned to move.

One of the other men grabbed the back of Charlie's shirt and shoved him out the door. Perspiration beaded on Charlie's forehead and ran into his eyes. His heart thundered in his chest. What would happen to him?

Oh, why didn't I just stay in line for Omega Battle-X?

Chapter Five

SUBJECT'S NAME: *Denise Kruger*
AGE: *16*
STATUS: *Incarcerated*
SPECIALITY/OCCUPATION: *Master of Disguise/Pick Pocket*
LOCATION: *Phoenix, AZ*

Denise scowled at herself in the mirror. Blonde ringlets framed her face, and her soft pale lips made her want to gag.

"Interesting style," her roommate, Vanessa said as she tossed a grocery bag on the counter. "I just might have to call your folks and kick you out."

"Shut up, Ness. It's for a job." Denise peered at her friend's leather jacket, pink hair and combat boots. What she wouldn't give to get out of this flowered dress and look like that right now. She felt ridiculous. "And don't even joke…I'm not going back."

"Well, blonde is obviously not your color." Vanessa, an eighteen-year-old punker, had shown compassion to Denise by letting her stay.

"Yeah, I'll say." Usually it was black, with a hint of some color. This week, it was blue.

Vanessa pulled a box of store-bought donuts out of a bag and ripped open the lid. The smell of chocolate drifted through the air. "So, what's the big moneymaker this time?"

Denise slid her lip ring out and sighed. "You know I don't share those kinds of things."

"You should really reconsider that, you know?" Her roommate smiled, brown frosting covering her teeth. "I could be a great asset to you."

Is it possible? To trust someone. Denise had always acted alone. Only two months ago, she had finally agreed to move in with someone, and only because she was sick and didn't have the money to get better on the streets. When the economy slowed, so did the amounts in people's wallets. No one carried cash anymore. Sometimes she could get something for credit cards, but not usually. And risk using them—never. That was suicide.

Vanessa gave her food and shelter. And in return, Denise cleaned up and gave her money when possible.

"You haven't paid me in a while, so I'm guessing you aren't making enough right now."

Bingo. "I'm fine."

"You need a partner."

Denise eyed her suspiciously. *What do I really know about Vanessa?* The girl was originally a runaway, like Denise. She came from someplace like Idaho or Nebraska. *Who knew?* Though she'd been on her own for five years, she'd found work in some office right away. She'd never struggled like Denise. One thing for certain—Vanessa lacked street smarts. Sure, she looked tough with her "punked out" style, but the naivety was evident the minute she talked. *How could she ever pull off a heist?*

"I work alone."

"Why?"

"Because, it's just better that way."

Vanessa pushed her breakfast away and stood. "I'm bored. Let me help. Just give me one job, and I'll never ask you again."

The childlike innocence in Vanessa's eyes made Denise uncomfortable. Maybe she should take her roommate just this once. Harden her a little bit. If nothing else, get the girl off her case. "Fine. But you've got to change your clothes."

****

Denise stood at the cosmetic counter pretending to look for the perfect lipstick shade. Out of the corner of her eye, she could see Vanessa talking to a sales lady.

Bring her this way.

Slowly, Vanessa moved around the counter as if deciding which one to have the woman pull out.

Perfect.

When the lady noticed Denise, she smiled. "I'll be right with you."

"Sure, no problem."

The woman glanced back at Vanessa. "Have you decided?"

Here we go. Denise rolled her eyes back and let her body fall limp to the tiled floor.

"Oh my!" Vanessa said like an actress meant to do this.

Denise peered under the counter. Just like she thought. Two purses. She stuck out two fingers for Vanessa to see—the code she'd shared with her earlier. If the purses were there, Vanessa was supposed to get the woman to walk to the phone and call 9-1-1. That would be just enough time for Denise to grab them and be gone.

"Can you call 9-1-1?" Vanessa pretended to search her purse. "I can't find my phone."

The woman's eyes were wide. She nodded and ran for the phone in back.

Denise smiled and leapt for the bags. "You were awesome. Ready?" She turned around and her smile disappeared.

Vanessa held a gun in one hand and a badge in the other. "Denise Kruger, you are under arrest."

Her face fell. This wasn't happening. "You're kidding, right?"

The traitor shook her head. "I'm afraid not. We've been investigating you for six months."

"Investigating? Me?"

Vanessa grabbed Denise's shoulder and forced her to turn around. "Place your hands on the counter."

Denise reluctantly obeyed.

"For such a young girl, you've got quite a reputation." Vanessa patted Denise's body for weapons. "You have the right to remain silent—"

Denise didn't hear the rest of her rights. Her mind reeled with the clues Vanessa was a cop. They were so obvious—now. And yet, Denise got suckered in.

"Let's go." Vanessa yanked Denise's arm and led her outside to a black and white car, now parked at the curb.

"I knew I shouldn't have trusted you." Denise spat before ducking down. "After everything I've told you about my past, how you could do this to me?"

"It's my job." She shrugged. Any ounce of decency lost. Vanessa didn't look like her friend anymore. Indeed, she was a just cop.

"How old are you, anyways?"

"Twenty-five." Vanessa smiled, then slammed the door closed, and hit the top of the car.

Denise stared out the window as the car rolled forward. Her wrists hurt from the metal "bracelets." She shifted in the seat, trying to get comfortable, but to no avail. Didn't matter. This was not the torture she feared. Nor was prison. Her worst nightmare—being sent home.

****

Denise pulled off the blonde wig, clawed her fingers through her dark blue hair, shifted in the metal chair, and glanced around the holding room. The mint green walls were scratched and smudged with fifth. A large mirror hung to her right. She'd watched enough detective shows to know someone was probably watching her.

A fish in a bowl, she thought. *I could kill Vanessa.* Who knew the girl was an undercover cop? *I knew I should never have trusted her.* Denise grimaced. *Never trust anyone.* A mantra that had served her well so far. *Break the rules, pay the consequences.*

After she shared her story, they said they might not send her home. So she no longer feared her situation. Maybe because she'd been able to talk herself out of almost everything in her entire life. Men always fell for her charm. Surely, she could sweet talk a policeman.

The door opened and a dark haired woman entered. Her face stern, her eyes hard.

Or not?

"Miss Kruger, it appears you've got yourself in quite a lot of trouble."

"Where's the good cop?"

"I'm sorry?"

Denise glanced at the door. "You know, good cop/bad cop. I assume you're the latter."

"I am neither. I'll tell you more later, but for now, you're coming with me."

"Who are you?"

"Agent Laura Black." She reached for Denise's arm and yanked her up. "Let's go."

"Agent? Like with the FBI? Am I that screwed?"

The woman didn't answer her, just escorted her down the narrow hall, outside to a dark van.

She opened the back door, "Get in."

Three people sat inside, two of them mirrored how she felt; the other had a hood over his face.

Denise stepped back, shaking her head. "What's going on?"

Agent Black leaned down so that her mouth was inches from Denise's ear. "See the guy with the hood?"

Denise nodded.

"If you don't want to be transported like him, I suggest you not make a scene and get in the back now."

This didn't feel right. Denise glanced around, weighing her options.

A man with an automatic rifle stepped out from behind the van door.

Options—none.

Denise looked back inside the vehicle and stepped up.

The door swung closed, and the space went black.

"Should I be afraid?" she whispered.

The Asian girl next to her answered, "I know I am."

Chapter Six

The plane touched down in a large dirt field surrounded by tropical vegetation. Laura was the first out of the cabin. She searched the runway for their ride. Almost on cue, a black limo sped around the corner, forming a dust cloud behind it. It screeched to a halt about two feet from the aircraft's steps. Two men sporting AK-47s stepped from the vehicle and stood guard.

The young adults descended the metal steps to the ground, their eyes big as cats. No one spoke, just kept their focus on the armed men.

Their trip to "hell" was almost complete. Laura sensed their fear, but trying to quiet it would be counter-productive. She needed them scared. It was the only way to save their lives and make them good soldiers. In the end, they would thank her. She opened the limo door and pointed. "Get in."

They glanced at one another, and then, one-by-one followed her orders.

Laura's partner, Agent Harding, exited the passenger's seat and walked to her side. She noticed his spiked, blond hair looked closer to the scalp than usual. He pushed his sunglasses higher on his nose and glanced around the lot, probably making sure no one was watching them. "We're running late. Greenstone will be upset."

"Yeah." Laura leaned in the car and handed out black hoods. "Put these on."

"Why?" Charlie asked.

She cocked a gun and aimed it at his head. "I give an order, you follow it. This is the last time we have this discussion."

Eri's hands visibly trembled as she pulled hers on. The others complied, but not without shooting her with death stares first.

"You know, kidnapping is an illegal act in all fifty states, a punishable crime," Charlie said from under the hood.

"You're not being kidnapped." Laura slid in the seat next to him and slammed the door closed.

"You could have fooled me," he said, his voice muffled. "You came into my house and took me. I believe that's the definition of kidnapped."

"We have all of you legally. Now be quiet." Laura sighed and stared out the window at the dark sky. A tropical storm hovered on the horizon. They needed to go.

The limo finally started to roll forward.

Soft sobs came from under Eri's hood.

Laura squeezed her eyes shut and tried to focus her thoughts. She hated having her motives questioned. She didn't really approve of S.I.U.'s method of confiscating their workforce but had no choice. Sure the initial acquisition was "legal," but what happened after that could be labeled abuse. If the U.S. government had full knowledge about what happened at their agency, they'd all be arrested. Of course, Greenstone lied. He claimed the U.S. had full disclosure. Laura knew better. Some agents believed the lies. But that was dumb. No minor should be treated this way. Laura glanced at the four teenagers wearing hoods. *And it will only get worse.*

They had about an hour drive to the base. Laura closed her eyes and tried to get some rest. She'd been awake for almost twenty-two hours. It would likely be another ten before she closed her eyes for the night.

Finally, the vehicle turned onto a surface road, and the familiar rock-covered gate slid open. They drove about thirty feet, and dogs and armed guards met them. The driver rolled down the window and passed out his badge.

Laura rolled down the rear window and did the same.

"Mission number?" a guard said, leaning in Laura's window.

"Bravo ten sixty-three. Mission, to pick up four new recruits from the west coast," Laura said.

The man punched the code in a handheld electronic device and nodded. "Cleared." He stood up and waved them through. A second gate slid open.

"You may remove the hoods," Laura said.

The four yanked them off in unison and then turned their eyes to the windows.

"Where are we?" Myers said.

"In time." Laura pointed to a two-story warehouse on the end of the lot. Most of the facilities were located underground, but the training buildings lay on the surface. Short palm trees, birds of paradise, banana plants, and tropical foliage surrounded the entire property. If it weren't for the electric fences that surrounded the land, one might think it a paradise vacation spot. "We're here."

The car stopped and Laura jumped out. "Line up in front of the building."

The four shuffled forward, brooding.

"I started here when I was thirteen years old. I'm now a senior officer. Do well and you too might lead your own squad someday."

"Squad? I'm sorry, where are we?" Charlie asked.

"What I'm about to tell you is classified. If you ever breathe it to another soul outside these walls, you'll be killed. No second chances."

The teens exchanged wide-eyed looks.

"Do you think you could keep it to yourself then?" Charlie asked. "I kind of like my body as is—you know, breathing."

She ignored him. "You now belong to a covert operation called the Secret Intelligence Unit or S.I.U. We're a private agency that trains tomorrow's generation to be assassins. We help eliminate the bad guys who the government doesn't feel is in their best interest to take out themselves."

Myers held up his hand, shaking his head erratically. "No, no. Wait. You're telling us that you're going to train us to be murderers?"

"For the good of the country—yes."

"I don't buy that the U.S. government would approve tax-dollars to go to a company like this," Charlie said. "I may have some conspiracy tendencies, but come on."

He'd be right, but she couldn't say that. "You don't need to buy it; it's free. So take it, and be quiet."

They started mumbling, shaking their heads. Myers walked backward, then turned, and started to run.

Laura didn't hesitate. She pulled her gun from the

holster and fired a warning shot, hitting a branch a few inches from his head.

He slid to a stop and lifted his hands. "Okay."

She waited for him to join them before continuing. "There are a few things you need to know. They won't help you sleep at night but they will save your life for now."

The group shifted.

"You're surrounded by electrified fences and trip wires that are set to explode. The guards are ordered to kill anything outside the safe zone. That includes you." She met every eye before continuing. "You belong to us now. All of you. The only way out of the company is in a body bag, so you might as well come to grips with it now. Save yourself some unnecessary heartache."

"Why us?" Eri rasped, her eyes swollen and red, her expression grim.

Laura fought the urge to join in the tear fest. Sure, she pretended to be hard, but inside her heart melted. "I will explain more later. Right now, I need to grab one more recruit." She waved to her partner. "Agent Harding will show you to your barracks."

They trudged forward and Laura turned for the prison entrance. It was time to get Bryce Chappelle.

Chapter Seven

SUBJECT'S NAME: *SGT Bryce Chappelle*
AGE: *24*
STATUS: *Incarcerated*
SPECIALTY/OCCUPATION: *Special Forces/ Sleuth Skills*
LOCATION: *S.I.U. Holding Facility*

About a month ago
Bryce heard his mother coming up the stairs, most likely to shoo his father off to work. But that couldn't happen yet. There was news to share, information that would likely hurt them both.

"Luis, hurry up. You'll be late," Bryce heard her say down the hall.

He tucked his hat under his arm and picked up his duffel bag. *Here it goes.* He snuck past her and down the stairway to the bottom landing. It didn't appear she had heard him. He tossed his bag in the corner by the door and went to breakfast. His mother had the usual egg dish—boiled eggs mashed up in rich, white gravy, smothering enormous buttermilk biscuits. His mouth watered. It would be the last time he ate this for a while. *Back to eating green eggs and dehydrated MREs (meals-ready-to-eat).*

The doorbell rang.

He already knew who stood on the front patio. His girlfriend, Shawna. She would be devastated. He couldn't stand the emotion this news would cause, and to bear it more than once would be too much. He chose to call them together for one outpouring of regret.

"Shawna?" his mother said at the door. "Why are you here so early?"

She giggled. Something she did all the time. "Bryce asked me to come over. Said he had important news."

"He did?"

He imagined Shawna's blonde bob bouncing, as she nodded, and his mother's wide eyes. Likely assuming a wedding date lingered in the near future. It made him feel worse.

"Well, come on in. We've just sat down for breakfast." His mother entered first, followed a second later by his girlfriend. Her hair was pulled up in the front, the way he liked it. The smell of rose wafted around her.

He smiled. "Hi."

She bent down and kissed his cheek, then quickly rubbed any evidence away. "So, I'm here. What's this…?" Her eyes fixed on his uniform. "Why are you dressed like that? Do you have weekend duty this week? I thought you just had it."

He glanced down at his desert camouflage sleeve. "Where's Dad?"

"Here." His dad, a large man with more hair on his face than head, scooted in at the end of the table, fork poised, ready to eat. "Well, hello, Shawna. Haven't had you over for breakfast in a long time."

"Hello, Mr. Chappelle."

He patted her hand. "I've told you before, sweetheart, Luis is fine."

She giggled.

Bryce swallowed. Sweat collected in his palm and on his back. The smell of boiled eggs began to turn his stomach. The yellow room seemed to push in. Why did his mother think retro mustard-colored paint was a good decorating idea for the dining room? He stared at a glass butterfly that hung on the wall. Not that he really noticed its detail; he just needed to get his bearings.

"You okay, hon?" His mother sat next to him and touched his shoulder. "You look pale."

"I need to talk to you."

A look of concern passed over her expression. "Okay."

"What is it, son?" his father asked.

Bryce let his gaze meet each one of them in turn. He tried to swallow. The people he cared about stared at him, wide-eyed, like they knew what was coming.

"I, um, just got orders. I'm leaving for Iraq."

His mother leapt from the table, her face two shades whiter than usual. "No!"

"Alisha, wait," his father said.

"You call them back and say you can't go."

Bryce stood and wrapped his arm around her slender waist. "Mom, I can't."

"You just got back." A tear streaked her makeup. "They can't send you."

"I have to go." He kissed her cheek. "I'm sorry. I knew this break would be short."

"You're leaving today," his dad said. It wasn't a question. His father knew. After two tours in Vietnam, he understood.

"Yes."

Shawna sniffed, reminding him she was there.

Bryce crossed to her. "Can we talk outside?"

She nodded.

"Mom, we'll be back in a moment. I don't leave for a few hours."

She pressed her lips together and sat at the table.

Shawna stood and followed Bryce onto the back porch.

He didn't know what to say. They'd been unofficially engaged for quite a while. He wasn't sure why he hadn't set a date for their wedding yet. He knew she wanted that, and it would matter more than ever now. She needed to know he would return ready to spend a lifetime together. She had hinted plenty of times. He wasn't sure why he put it off. Now it was too late to walk down the aisle, but maybe he could comfort her somehow.

"If something happens to you..." she started to say, but clamped her mouth shut, apparently unable to finish her thought.

No mystery followed her incomplete statement. He wrapped his arms around her and pulled her close. Her body shook against his chest. "I'm sorry I haven't married you yet."

"I know."

"But I'll return to you, and we'll have that dream wedding someday."

"How do you know?"

He drew back from her and forced a smile. "Because I know you're waiting for me."

She touched her lips to his and exhaled. "Promise."

"Promise. With all my heart."

****

Around a week ago

Two men, believed to be terrorists, lifted their hands in surrender. Bryce glanced at the sergeant, awaiting orders.

"Round them up," Sergeant Tuttle said.

Bryce stepped out from behind the armored vehicle and waved his gun, indicating they should stand. They kept their hands in the air as they stood, then shuffled forward, and climbed in the back of the Jeep. Bryce joined them and let the flap drop. Reaching under the seat, he withdrew some restraints for their hands.

Outside, he heard muffled voices between the captain and Tuttle. Their tone indicated a hint of anger.

"Get them out," Tuttle said.

Bryce peeked. "Why? What are you doing?"

Tuttle spat in the dirt and cussed. "There's no way we're taking these guys back to the base. Get them out of the truck, now!"

Bryce climbed out, confused. "What are you talking about?"

"They killed five of our men, including my brother Ross, and wounded two others. There's no way we're letting them get some kind of green light to kill again."

Captain Saylors met them at the bumper. "He's right. We've watched that happen too much lately."

This can't be a serious discussion. Not with an officer. "What are you two talking about?" Bryce asked again, afraid of their answer. Denial seemed to be his only defense. But he needed to hear them say it before he could believe it to be true.

"Killing them, of course." A big smile lit Tuttle's face, revealing a gold tooth. Something he was very proud of.

"But what about the Geneva Conven—"

Saylors cut him off. "This isn't about that. This is about justice. The brass will just assume we killed them in a fight."

No way. A sudden urge took hold of Bryce to defend these men. "But they surrendered and are unarmed."

Tuttle's white face changed to tomato red, his jaw tight, his fists clenched. "Look, kid, my brother is oozing blood from his kidney because these two men thought it would be okay to shove a grenade in his side. Ross deserved better." He stood close enough that Bryce smelled tobacco on his breath. "There is no way we're letting them go. Do you understand?"

"Who said anything about letting them go?" Bryce's voice raised an octave. "They're prisoners of war, guilty of war crimes. They'll get what is coming to them."

Saylors shook his head. "Nah, Tuttle's right. Those four guys who almost killed me with a bomb last week, the Army let them go. You saw it. Two feet closer, and my wife would have been standing over my flag-covered coffin right about now."

Bryce paced away from him. He couldn't condone murdering any man. Since being here, he'd fired his gun once, and missed. Joining the military was the dumbest decision he'd ever made, but in reality, he hadn't realized he couldn't shoot anyone until he was faced with the decision.

The minute he got back to base, he would tell the colonel he'd made a mistake. Killing wasn't something he could do. Not in good conscience. Especially like this. "I can't do it. Be a part of this. You pull the trigger, and I'll have to let them know."

The two soldiers glared at Bryce.

Tuttle poked a finger at Bryce's chest. "You say one word and it'll be your last."

Fear enveloped Bryce because he believed him. Tuttle would have no problem pulling the trigger. Bryce knew the type well. Some men went into the Army for a job or college money; Tuttle went in to fire his weapon. Killing made it all worthwhile.

Bryce stood back and watched as Tuttle pulled the men from the back of the truck and tossed them to the ground.

This isn't happening. This can't be real.

One of them pleaded in Arabic with folded hands.

But Tuttle and Saylors wouldn't hear him. Their minds were set. Vengeance was theirs. Both fired, and the men crumpled to the ground.

Tuttle cursed, then spit on their bodies, laughing. "Good riddance."

This wasn't what Bryce signed up for. His stomach twisted in disgust as blood pooled like red wine in the dust by their heads.

"Chappelle!"

Bryce met Saylors' stare. "Yes, sir?"

"One word and you're history." He nodded for him to get back in the vehicle.

Bryce's legs wobbled beneath him as he climbed in. How could he keep what happened quiet? He let out a moan sopped with anguish. He couldn't. The blade would drop. He would tell the truth.

****

Hours later, Bryce picked at a freeze-dried pork

patty in his lap and sighed. His conscience would not allow him to walk away. No threats were good enough.

"Chappelle?"

Bryce glanced up at the mention of his name.

"Colonel wants to see you," Saylors said with a sardonic grin.

He gulped. Not good. Bryce stuffed his trash back in a dark brown bag and placed it in one of his pants' pockets. A few yards away, he noticed Tuttle cleaning his weapon, eyeing him. The look in his eyes wasn't fear, but justice.

Bryce walked to the big tent at the end of the lot and ducked under the flap. The colonel stood next to two military police officers. Though Bryce already suspected this wasn't going to go well, their presence confirmed his suspicions.

"Sir?"

The colonel pursed his lips and stepped forward. His white mustache twitched. "I'm very disappointed in you, Sergeant Chappelle. I was under the impression you were a good man."

"I am, Sir."

The officer locked eyes with him. "Good men don't slaughter people, no matter what their crime."

"I would agree. If only I could explain what happened…"

He folded his arms and nodded.

"I wanted to let those men go, but Captain Saylors and Sergeant Tuttle thought differently."

Colonel Manning raised an eyebrow, an amused expression on his face.

"It's true, sir."

"I'm sure it is." He nodded to the M.P.s.

"Don't you care? I did nothing wrong."

He sidled up next to Bryce, his expression stern. "Captain Saylors and I go way back. I know him. I believe him. He said you would say something ridiculous like this to divert the attention away from the massacre you created out there." He waved his hand. "Until an official investigation can be conducted, I want you out of my sight."

An M.P. grabbed each of Bryce's arms and yanked him outside.

Bryce tried to fight them off, but they were too strong. Reluctantly, he relaxed his grip and allowed them to drag him away.

Tuttle and Saylors made sure he caught their smirks as he passed. What had they told the colonel? What lie did they conjure up to save themselves?

It didn't matter now. It was done.

As am I.

****

Bryce sat on cold cement staring into space. For two or so days, he'd been locked in a gray room with no bed, only a toilet. Why'd he have to be such a good guy? In this case, good guys finished last. If only he didn't care about innocent life, maybe he'd still be hiking it across the Iraqi desert, instead of being locked up in here.

He missed his girlfriend and his mother. He wanted out of this place. *Wherever this place is.* All he knew was they transported him by plane, but where, he had no idea. He could be anywhere in the world.

The door handle shifted down and the door swung open. He squinted. The bright light from outside blinded him from seeing who had entered.

"Hello, Mr. Chappelle," a female's voice said. She closed the door and a woman with dark, short hair; high cheekbones; and amazing eyes smiled at him. For some reason, he felt like he'd seen her before in a dream, and his heart fluttered. She was beautiful. "I'm Agent Laura Black, your handler. I will be helping you through your training."

"My training?" He slid forward and stood.

"Your time with the U.S. Army is over, but your service to your country is not." She walked to the door. "If you'll come with me, I'll show you to your room."

He didn't understand, but anything had to be better than this cement box. He followed her outside and covered his eyes to block the bright sun. The air smelled of rain and wild ginger. Once his eyes adjusted to the light, he glanced around. They appeared to be in the middle of a jungle. Lush tropical plants surrounded the clearing. Animals and birds called to one another in shrill chirps and screeches. An apple-green lizard scuttled by, licking at the air, ignorant of the humans that surrounded him.

"This way." She brushed past a banana plant and led him inside a white warehouse. A green light flickered overhead. They walked down a narrow passageway to a metal gate. She punched in a code and the door slid open. They strode down two more hallways until they entered a huge bay filled with military equipment. Four other people lounged in the center of the room, on a pair of leather couches, not talking, looking slightly frightened.

"Everyone, this is Bryce Chappelle. He will be the leader of your squad, but he is also one of you." She quickly said all their names and then pointed to a metal chair. "Have a seat."

He obeyed.

"Miss Lee asked earlier why you were all chosen." Laura revealed a manila envelope. "There are two reasons. The first, each of you has a gift that will benefit this team. Second, not one of you will be missed by society."

Bryce leapt up. "That's hardly true. I have family."

Laura handed him a newspaper clipping with a picture of him in basic training and a headline that read, "Hero dies in action in the Middle East."

"Better than the clipping that could have occurred, right Mr. Chappelle? It could have read how you were a traitor to the Army. We have done you a huge favor. This way, you save face with your family, while working off your debt by serving your country."

She passed articles out to the rest of them, each one either placed them in prison for life or six-feet under. "No one knows you're here. No one will come looking for you. We pick our recruits very carefully."

"My family grieves my uncle and now me?" A tear rolled down Eri's cheek. "How can you do this?"

"You don't have a family, Ms. Young."

"You're sick," Myers spat.

Laura narrowed her eyes. "And soon you will be, too. I was in your shoes once, Mr. Luther. You're no better than me. You think you'll get away, but I promise, everybody who has tried is dead."

"This is insane." Charlie punched his fist into the mattress he sat on. "So we're still prisoners."

"Except for Miss Lee, all of you were going to prison anyway. Instead of a life filled with making license plates, you get to serve your country. Do something worthwhile for a change."

"By killing people," Bryce said.

Laura turned to him and crossed her arms. "You were going to do that anyway, Mr. Chappelle. Or did you forget you're a trained military soldier who was pulled out of Iraq?"

"I'm not killing anybody." Eri sniffed. "It's not in me."

"Why did you become a black belt, Miss Lee?"

"To protect myself."

"You are a weapon. Did you ever think that if you had to defend yourself, you might kill the other person?"

She shook her head.

"The people you'll be sent to take out will kill millions unless we intervene. We aren't monsters, but heroes."

They all glared at her.

No way did Bryce buy the load Laura was dropping on them. He'd joined the military to protect America from the very person he was to become. A terrorist? *No way.*

"Guys, your room is to the left of the hall. Girls to the right. Your stuff has already been placed in both. Not that you were allowed too much contraband." She glanced at her watch. "I suggest getting some sleep. It won't be long until we start your training, and you're going to need it." She nodded once and left.

The door slammed shut and a bolt locked in place. They were officially in their "cell."

"Can you believe her?" Myers stood and paced. "That chick is insane."

"What's insane is that *I'm* stuck here." Eri wiped

her eyes. "I'm not even a criminal like the rest of you."

Denise crossed to her with balled fists. "You think you're somehow superior to us because you weren't arrested?"

"I…just meant…I'm not a criminal. I wasn't going to jail. I don't belong here."

"None of us belong here." Bryce clenched his jaws. "Just get over it and get used to it. We're not going anywhere." He'd been in these sorts of situations before. It was just better to obey orders and not make waves. He'd seen what going against the flow got him—a week in a military prison and now here. Here was better—for now.

Chapter Eight

A soft whimper drifted from across the room. Denise knew she should try and comfort Eri, but she'd never been known for her compassion. Sure, she was great with people, but it was all an act. A part of her drama-queen mentality. Fool the audience, make them love you, then rob them when they aren't looking. It wasn't the best behavior, but a runaway has to eat somehow.

She shuttered at the memory of the news clipping the agent showed her today. *Runaway murdered by a homeless man.* Her dad and wicked step-monster would now have closure to their search. *Denise is dead, let's party.* She frowned and ran a hand over her own damp eyes.

Maybe home hadn't been so bad. When her mother died, Denise found solace in the dark, writing poetry and song lyrics. She had never been close to her dad, mainly because he was a workaholic. But her mom's passing made that gap erode into a gaping canyon. When he remarried, a vast ocean.

The new "mom" enjoyed slapping her and threatened to ship her to a boarding school. So Denise ran away. It made sense. However, stealing was probably stupid. Dumb enough to land her in a prison camp. That's what this place was—a military bunker where they'd be broken and forced to do awful things.

Eri sniffed and her sobs increased.

Denise didn't feel sorry for her. They were in the same boat. But they could console each other. She flipped back the sheet and walked to her side. "Hey, you okay?"

"No," she said, her voice barely audible.

"Scoot over." Denise lay next to her and handed her a wad of toilet paper she'd snagged earlier. "It's not so bad. You can't let them get to you."

"Did you live on the street before coming here?"

"Yeah, sometimes."

Eri rolled to face her. "Not me. I'm an orphan, but have always lived with family. I am not spoiled, but I'm not streetwise either. I'm really scared."

Scared? It didn't matter that Denise was "streetwise." Fear would only be natural in this situation. But for Eri's sake, she pretended to be strong. "Agent Black might act like she's on your side, but she's not. Everything the people in this place do is all a game. They can't break you if you never let what's happening in."

"I don't know." Eri sniffed hard and then swallowed. "It sounds like this is it for us."

No way could Denise begin to entertain that idea. "We have to be strong, Eri. Together, we'll find a way out. I promise."

"I don't think that's a possibility. You heard Agent Black." She sniffed again. "We're stuck here forever."

Denise stared up at the shadowed ceiling. Light from the hall bounced against the furniture in the room, creating what looked like a bunny jumping. "I refuse to believe we're stuck here forever, and I'll do whatever it takes to make sure we're not."

"Really?"

"I don't believe in giving up."

"What would you do differently? I mean, if you could get out of here, what would you do now?" Eri asked.

Good question. Though home seemed reasonable, she doubted that would ever be in the cards again. "I think I'd try to get a normal job. One that will keep me out of jail."

"What kind of job?"

Boy, this girl asks a lot of questions. One thing on the street, no one ever talked about themselves. It was better that way. But secretly, Denise, like anyone else, liked talking about herself. It was a nice change. "This may sound stupid, but I'd love to be one of those characters who walk around at amusement parks."

Eri laughed. "I could see you as Snow White."

Denise smiled. "Yeah, I guess. Though as a kid, I always wanted to be Cinderella. I think it fits my story more."

"But Beauty's dress is the prettiest."

"Agreed." Denise sighed. "So, what about you? What would you do?"

"Run my uncle's dojo."

Denise shook her head in the dark. "No, it has to be something where the agency can't find you."

Eri didn't say anything for a moment, and then let out a soft whimper.

"I'm sorry."

"I guess I just realized, you're right. Whether we're free or not, this is it. No going back."

No going back. Sounded so final. Though that was

a good thing for Denise, it probably wasn't the status quo of the rest of her team. She didn't want Eri dwelling on it though. "So, all dreams wide open. What would you do?"

Silence.

"Eri?"

"Maybe open my own dojo somewhere. It's all I know, and something I'm very good at."

"I bet you can kick some—"

"Yes," she said, laughing. "Most definitely."

"You'll have to show me."

Eri touched her shoulder. "If…I mean, when…we get out of here, you can take lessons at my dojo for free."

"It's a deal."

****

Laura sat in the control room, staring at the green-lit monitor. Denise and Eri lay in the dark, planning a future on the outside—a future that would never come.

Those days weren't so long gone for her. Laura remembered dreaming of hope and blissful prospects of escape. She frowned. Empty dreams, now void. Several scars marked her body, reminding her that hope in this place was a death warrant. Many times, stubbornness had almost cost Laura her life.

"How are they doing?" Greenstone asked at the door.

Laura jumped, grabbing her chest. "Fine, sir. They're just settling in."

"Let them fall asleep for about twenty minutes, then wake them up for drills."

"Yes, sir."

"Night," Greenstone said.

And to her relief, he exited.

Though she'd been under his care for almost nine years, he still made her nervous. Possibly because with one stroke of a pen he could finish her. He signed orders to terminate people almost every day. Many of them had been her friends. Not that she had friends anymore. *What's the point?*

Laura focused her attention back on the screen.

The monitor to Laura's right showed vitals. She would wait for REM sleep, then clock twenty minutes.

The boys, on the other hand, fell asleep right away. It wasn't fair. They'd get almost a full hour. But nothing was fair about this place. It was all about breaking them.

****

Charlie opened his eyes. A thick haze lingered around his desk. Maybe he'd overslept and couldn't clear his head. He turned to his computer and clicked the mouse. A tunnel appeared on the monitor. He was in. He did it. Months of trying to break into the Feds' database finally paid off.

Suddenly, a siren sounded.

Oh, no! His eyes darted to the door. Red lights flashed. Someone yelled his name. The door began to swell, like it might explode. The sound pulsed in his ears. He glanced back to his hard work. It was over. He'd have to delete it all. His biggest accomplishment flushed down the proverbial toilet.

"Charlie Smyth!"

He turned to the desktop, dropped his find into the trash, and then punched "delete." A bar appeared on the screen. Within seconds, his work vanished into a cyber-abyss.

"Charlie!"

The door busted open, but he couldn't see anything. Wait, his eyes were closed. He opened them.

Myers stood over him. "Wake up, man!"

It was only a dream? A siren blared in the warehouse. He covered his ears. "What's going on?" he yelled.

Bryce sat on the bunk next to him, lacing up his boots. "Get dressed," he yelled over the noise. "Some kind of drill."

Charlie tried to clear his head by shaking it. He slipped on the black T-shirt and cargo pants that were issued to him. Though they were given black painters hats, he donned his beanie instead.

Laura entered and the siren subsided.

A second later, the girls appeared, also in uniform.

"How long were we asleep?" Eri whispered.

"Not long enough." Denise yawned.

"Well, I'm glad you're all up and dressed. We're running an obstacle course," Laura said.

They all groaned.

She glanced at her wrist. Since the agency confiscated all their watches, only Laura knew what time it was. "You have one hour to run the course and be back in your beds. If you don't make it, you don't sleep tonight."

"Where's the course?" Charlie asked.

Laura handed them each a map. "Night goggles and gloves are in the lockers at the end of each bunk. There are four points with numbers along the course. We'll know you've reached them when you punch your code in a box found at each point on the map. Good luck. Your time starts now." She clicked a button on the side of her watch and it beeped.

The five of them exchanged looks, then rushed to their lockers, removed their supplies, and ran out the door.

The sticky night air made it hard to breath, instantly making Charlie sweat, but the adrenaline pumping through his body propelled him forward. He could do this, he hoped. Exercise wasn't something he got a lot of back home. He lived a pretty sedentary lifestyle. Most of his days were spent sitting in a chair behind a computer keyboard or at a video game console.

He started to check his map, when Bryce ran to his left. Forget the map, he'd follow the Army ranger. Seems the rest of them saw that wisdom and charged in his direction.

They ran up a steep incline that landed them at the top of a ridge. Bryce slipped the night goggles on and peered around. "We've got to keep going up. The first station is less than thirty clicks to the north, but to get to it, we have to climb that wall."

Charlie stared through the night. He didn't see a wall, nor did he have any idea what a "click" was. He slipped on the goggles and the inky black turned green. A faint outline of a brick wall lay ahead.

They took off, most panting as they ran up the extremely steep incline to the destination point.

"How do we get over it?" Denise said, wheezing, holding her side.

"Here," Bryce interlaced his fingers and placed them at the base of the wall. "Step in my hand."

Denise stared at him for a moment.

"Trust me."

Her expression revealed that trusting was obviously a foreign concept to her.

Eri pushed forward and slid her boot in his cupped hands. He lifted her and she scrambled up the wall, grabbed hold of what looked like a branch, and lifted herself to the top.

"What do you see?" Bryce asked.

"The box Laura told us about…it's on the other side."

"Can you jump down?"

"I think so."

"Good." Bryce said. "Next."

Charlie stepped forward and into his palm, placing a hand on Bryce's shoulder, he pushed up. He grabbed hold of a tree limb above and hoisted to his seat. The drop wasn't that bad. He jumped down and ran to the keypad. The numbers glowed in the dark. He had memorized his personal code. Four-two-D-A-R-K-H-A-T-Seven. It registered then cleared.

Denise jumped next to him and lightly shoved him out of the way. Eri waited a few feet away, gnawing on her fingernails.

Finally, Myers keyed in and Bryce joined them.

"This way." The soldier pointed down a dark path, then sprinted forward.

They all followed. The road dropped down and as they picked up speed.

Charlie's chest heaved. He really needed to get in shape. Somehow, he had a feeling this place would help him achieve that goal.

They ran down an incline that ended at a stream of water. It flowed at least ten feet across in both directions.

"There's a bridge on this map. Look for it!" Bryce said.

The five of them spanned out, running up and down the bank.

"I think I found it," Myers yelled a ways down the bank. "It's not big though."

Charlie ran behind him and frowned. A wood plank, no more than an inch wider than a yardstick lay across the water. Its length would get them across, but it didn't look stable. "No way. We'll fall in."

"We have to try," Myers said. "I'm tired. I have to sleep."

Eri pushed passed them and started walking across. She kept her arms out from her sides, balancing. A few times she wobbled, but she successfully made it across. The other three made it without a hitch. Now it was Charlie's turn. Big problem if he fell, he couldn't swim.

"Come on, Charlie," Eri said. "You can do it."

He licked his lips. The dark, rushing water made his stomach turn. He slowly placed his foot on the board. It felt slippery. He reached out to his sides and took a deep breath. Cautiously, he inched forward. Each of his team punched in their code on the other side. Only Eri watched him.

Charlie glanced at the water and felt himself sway. He leaned to the right to keep from falling, but over extended. His feet slipped, plunging his body into the water. The cold jolted his system. His heart thundered. He slapped at the surface, panicked. *I'm going to die.*

"I can't swim!" His head thrust under the surface. He breathed in water and started coughing. The river dragged him away. Rocks scraped his legs. He reached out. Slapping at the river. Searching to find something to hold onto. Nothing. *This is it.*

"Give me your hand," Bryce yelled from the bank.

But Charlie couldn't see it. His body shivered. First test and it was over.

Suddenly, a hand grasped his wrist and yanked him on the shore. Charlie trembled and coughed.

"Are you okay?" Bryce asked.

He pushed up from the ground and nodded, his teeth chattering. "Well, at least I'm not hot anymore."

"Hurry up and punch in your code," Myers said.

Charlie hands were wet. He shook them a few times, then pressed the buttons on the screen. It clicked over.

Water sloshed in his boots and his pants and his shirt clung to him, but he was alive.

"No way." Myers stopped. "Tell me we don't have to climb that?"

Bryce hit Myer's back and offered a closed-mouth grin. "I'm afraid so."

Charlie stared at the thirty-foot rope-spider web thankful it wasn't another water task. He could do this. He slid his boot into the lowest hole and balanced himself. Then reached for one higher. Slowly, he climbed. Bryce made it to the top first, followed by Eri, then him and Myers. Denise struggled below.

Twice she fell.

"She'll never make it. We should leave her," Myers said.

Bryce shook his head. "Never leave a man behind."

"This isn't the Army, soldier. This is every man for himself, and I intend to sleep tonight." Myers jumped to the ground, punched in his code, and ran off.

Eri glanced at Charlie, probably wondering if they

should follow Myers or stick with the ranger? After his dip in the river, he was flypaper to Bryce, no matter what.

"I'm going to go down and get her," Bryce said. "When I get her high enough, you both grab her."

"Okay," they said in unison.

He climbed down and whispered something to her. She nodded and together they climbed. When they approached the top, Charlie put out his hand. She grasped it and he pulled hard. He wedged his foot in the last rope to keep from falling and she made it.

The four jumped to the ground and punched in their codes.

"Where's Myers?" Denise asked.

"Selfish jerk took off." Eri kicked the dirt with her boot, sending a rock skidding into the trees.

Bryce studied the map, then nodded to their left. "Let's go. One last hurdle and we sleep."

Charlie's eyes stung and he could think of nothing better. They ran through some brush and stopped. The distinct sound of gunfire sounded overhead.

"Drop!" Bryce fell to the ground.

Charlie and the others followed suit.

Ahead lay a net of wires horizontal to the ground. Bryce inched forward on his belly and under the mesh. Charlie followed and the girls tailed him.

Twice the metal barb caught on Charlie's shirt. He'd have to dig more into the ground to keep from snagging it again. He still had to crawl another five feet. Bullets whizzed overhead. Each one made him flinch.

Finally, he reached the other side.

Denise and Eri met him and entered their codes. He wondered if Myers knew to duck.

They ran down an embankment to a large wooden fence. "I thought there were only four hurdles," Charlie said.

"Boost me up," Bryce said.

Charlie cupped his hands and placed them at the base.

The solider pushed up and looked over. "This isn't a hurdle. It's home. Come on." He reached down and Eri took his hand and pulled up. Then Denise and Charlie. They dropped to the ground and ran for the warehouse.

Bryce reached it first and yanked on the door. It didn't open. He tried again. Nothing.

"They're playing with us," Eri said.

"Ya'think?" Denise shook her head. "Jerks. Now what?"

Bryce stepped out and peered at the building. "Come on." They followed him to the end to a lone window. He picked up a rock and tossed it at the glass. It shattered. He smiled. "Sleep anyone?"

They all piled in the hole that dropped into a medical office, and then ran out the door, down the hall, to their room.

Laura sat on Charlie's bed, her eyes on the stopwatch. They ran to her and stopped, out of breath. She looked up, but didn't smile. "You're short a man."

"He chose to do his own thing," Denise said.

She pursed her lips. "I see."

Charlie glanced down the hall. He hoped nothing happened to Myers. Though the guy could be a jerk, he didn't deserve to be shot in some silly game either.

Laura stood. "You've earned five hours. Lights out."

"What about Myers?" Charlie asked.

Her eyes met Charlie's, but she didn't answer. She turned on her heel, flipped off the light, and disappeared down the corridor.

Chapter Nine

Myers held the goggles to his eyes and peered around. His breathing echoed loud in his ears. *Why didn't I stay with the group?* He glanced down at the map, unable to decipher one landmark from another. *I can create a business, run a successful scam, make thousands of dollars in an hour, and I'm too stupid to get out of the dumb forest.* He kicked at a rock.

Over the hill, a faint glow emerged. Daybreak. This was insane. His shirt hung wet from perspiration, his muscles ached, and his eyes burned from a lack of sleep. He trudged on, unsure where to go next. Twice, he'd tried to backtrack to where he'd left the group, but every bush looked alike. Every hill mirrored the last.

Something shimmered in the dark. *That's different.* He ran ahead. Shots fired overhead. He dropped to the ground. *Is someone shooting at me?*

A horizontal barbed-wired covering lay just ahead. Maybe this was it—the next phase. He crawled forward. The closer he got, the more bullets whizzed over his head. Though it seemed stupid to move in the direction of the firing maniac, it felt logical. He ducked under and maneuvered like an inchworm to the other side. When he got to the end, the firing stopped. He spotted the keypad. He could have kissed it. He logged in his numbers and ran forward. He had to be close.

A rock wall lay just ahead. He stopped. Home was probably just on the other side. But how would he get over? Once again, a good reason to have stayed with the group. Not that being a team player was likely. Listening to others just wasn't something he did well. An orphan early in life, he found solace in calling his own shots. He started his own company and hardly ever delegated—a self-made millionaire, not usually one to partner. And face it—the last time he listened to a friend, he'd ended up in prison.

Ahead, he spotted a tree. He jogged to it. Yeah, he'd climb that. He stuffed his goggles in his pocket and leapt for the lowest branch. He caught hold of it and swung his legs up. Like a kid on the monkey bars, he managed to end upright. He saw the warehouse. *Yes. I'm almost there.* He shimmed to the wall, then dropped down.

He ran to the door and tried the handle. It didn't budge. *Great.* They'd locked him out. Maybe there was a door on the other side. He ran around the building, but saw nothing.

He knew knocking wouldn't do any good. This building was locked with a code. Earlier that evening, Laura had logged one in before they went to bed. He folded to the ground and closed his eyes. Maybe he'd catch some sleep here.

****

Laura stared at the monitor, a slight smile on her face. So, Myers had found his way home. Unfortunately for him, he quit. Not finishing the mission meant a miserable twenty-four hours. Greenstone would see to it.

A part of her wanted to go let him in. Pretend this

never happened. But she knew better. Besides the fact it would make him weak later; it also would be recorded. Everything at the ranch was under a watchful eye.

No, he would learn the hard way to depend on his team.

The phone on the wall buzzed.

She picked it up. "Agent Black."

"Black, why is there a recruit sitting in front of the warehouse?" Greenstone asked.

Laura pinched her eyes shut. "Because, Sir, he didn't stick with the team and made it back only a few minutes ago."

"Not a team player?"

"No, Sir."

There was silence on the other end. That only meant one thing; Greenstone was contemplating a serious repercussion.

"You've read his file?"

"Yes, Sir."

"What is he afraid of?"

Laura hated that question. She knew it was how the man operated. Vile acts, the devil himself would be proud. "Apparently, his missionary mother was killed due to an infected spider bite she got in an African jungle. He's got arachnophobia in the worst way."

"Marvelous." She pictured Greenstone rubbing his hands together, drooling. "See to it that he spends his day in the pit."

She balled her free hand, trying to subdue her feelings. "Yes, Sir."

The line fell dead.

The pit. On his second day? There were agents who had been here for over a year, had gone through

P.O.W. training, and still couldn't withstand the pit. It was filled with all sorts of repulsive and scary creatures. A cement cellar, thirty feet down, about twenty-feet wide filled with rats, spiders, roaches, and who knew what else. She'd never been admitted, but those who had came out with all sorts of wounds, not to mention psychological scars. Laura feared for the young man's sanity and health.

Lord, be with him. Funny that she'd pray now. She hadn't done that in over eight years. Not even when they tortured her. Call it survival. How could any good God-fearing person live in a place like this? They couldn't. So, it was easier to consider herself an atheist, than deal with the alternative—guilt.

She walked down the dark corridor toward the front entrance. Snoring echoed down the hall from the rooms. She wished Myers joined them in their nightly song. Instead, he was about to live out his worst nightmare.

The keypad was against the door. She punched in the code and the door slid open.

Myers jumped to his feet. "Am I glad to see you, I'm sorry, I got separated…"

She held up a hand, not cracking a smile, and motioned for him to follow her. The best strength that any of the agents had was silence. She knew respect came from her not showing any emotion no matter what they said. They would follow her, because they had no way to gauge how she felt. This was something taught to agents very early on. She saved her tears for her pillow at night.

About fifty feet from the compound in the heart of jungle, she led him down a flight of cement steps to the pit's entrance. A thick metal door swung out like a hatch on a submarine. Grabbing the handle, she unwound the lid and yanked it open. The rusty lid creaked in complaint.

"What's this place?" Myers said, alarm clear in his voice.

"We call it the pit."

Myers visibly trembled. "Look, I'm real sorry. I learned my lesson. I'll be a team player from now on. I promise. Please."

"I'm sure you will." Laura waved at the dark opening. "Inside."

He stared down the hole and shook his head. "No way, lady."

"This isn't a negotiation." She withdrew her gun. "Inside."

"Please, I promise it won't happen again."

"I believe you." She pointed to the metal ladder with her pistol. "Go on. Get in."

"Please, ma'am." His voice wavered. "I can't do this."

"I know." She swallowed back the emotion that threatened to reveal her true feelings. "But you have to go. This isn't my call. It came from Greenstone. If you don't do it, there is only one alternative. Either way, you're going into a dark hole."

He stared at her a moment, obviously assessing if she meant it. His wide-eyes filled with tears.

She nodded to the ladder.

He shifted onto his belly and swung his legs to the ladder. Slowly, he went down, sobbing like a young kid.

What could she say that would help him? Nothing

came to mind. "I'll be back before sunset."

He disappeared into the darkness. She pulled the gated lid over the top and latched it closed. *I hate my job.*

A scream echoed from the other side of the closed lid.

I hope he'll be all right.

****

Myers turned around in the dark, but didn't step to the ground. Instead, he sat on the third rung from the bottom of the ladder. Below he heard movement. Maybe he'd wait for his eyes to adjust. Then he'd know what he was up against. His skin crawled and horror clutched his throat. He couldn't remember being more afraid.

If only he could stop shaking. His eyes adjusted some. The floor appeared to be moving. His heart skipped. No way would he go any further. No matter how numb his legs got sitting on the metal bar, he wouldn't step down there.

He pulled his arms tight around his torso, closed his eyes, and hummed a song that one of the attendants in the orphanage used to sing when he had nightmares.

He wished he could remember the words. Something about the fiery furnace and lions' jaws. He hummed some more, trying hard to remember. "Hmmm…God was in the fiery furnace, and held the lions' jaws…hmmm…God brought them out of Egypt and to the Promised Land…"

He hummed a few more bars. He smiled as he recalled the rest of the song. He sang it again, this time louder. Each verse soothed him. Though he'd never been religious, there was something soothing about singing and praying. And right now, he'd never been so grateful for knowing them.

For hours, he'd sing the song.

And just maybe, survive this day.

Chapter Ten

Laura stared at the monitors. The women now slept in their own beds, both looking peaceful. She glanced over to the men's room and her breath caught. Bryce's blanket rested at his waist. His ripped chest and strong muscles clearly showed. Her cheeks warmed. *I should look away.* But her eyes wouldn't budge. He was gorgeous. She blinked. *What am I saying?* She knew better. Fraternizing during training was always frowned upon, but relationships between trainer and recruit—absolutely forbidden. Of course, the agent in her position was usually five years older and the recruit several years younger. Not two years apart.

She rested her chin on her palm and leaned forward. His chest moved in and out. He had stirred something in her the minute she saw his mug shot. Maybe it was because she'd never met anyone so attractive. Or maybe because until now, she'd always been so busy trying not to die there hadn't been a moment to notice the men around her. Whatever the reason, she had to get her feelings in check. Liking Chappelle would endanger them both.

The phone buzzed.

"Agent Black," she said after she picked it up.

"Have you been watching the pit?"

Greenstone. She frowned. *Don't you ever sleep?*

"No. I didn't know I could."

"Far right monitor. Switch it on."

She leaned over and hit the red button below. The scene came into view. Myers sat on the ladder, his eyes closed, singing. A light seemed to be coming from somewhere, but it was unclear where.

"He's not scared," Greenstone said with disappointment in his tone.

"He was going in. I assure you."

"Well, it's time to wake up the recruits. Get him out and have him train with the rest of them." Greenstone coughed. "He's obviously stronger than we thought. We'll have to try to break him another way."

Laura nodded, as if he could see her.

The phone buzzed in her ear.

She smiled. "I don't know what you did, Myers. But you just saved yourself hours of torture."

****

The gate clanked above his head. Music to Myers' ears.

"You okay in there?" Laura said.

"I am now." He turned around and placed both his feet on the rung. His legs wobbled beneath him and his rear felt numb, but he was ready to go. He slowly climbed up and squinted against the light above.

"What were you singing?"

He cocked his head to the side. "Singing?"

She grabbed his arm and helped lift him out. "Yeah, we could hear you in the monitor."

"A song from Sunday school."

She gave him a tight smile. Religion obviously made her uncomfortable. He'd have to remember that.

"And the light?"

He gave her a blank stare.

"Don't worry, you're not in trouble. I just was curious where the light came from."

He shook his head. *Is she crazy?* He just sat in the pitch black for hours.

"You should know, there isn't a place you can go where there isn't a camera. I could see you, and I clearly witnessed a light. What was it?"

He stared at her, unsure what game she was playing. He was afraid to answer. If he said there wasn't a light, she might get angry and throw him back in. *But how do I lie?* He didn't have a clue. "I don't know what you saw, Agent Black, but from my point of view, it was pitch black."

She bit her bottom lip, her eyes focused on his. Obviously, she was assessing his lying capabilities. "Fine. We have training to do. Let's go."

They entered the warehouse and she hit a red button on the wall. A siren sounded.

Myers covered his ears. "Do you mind if I use the facility before we get started?"

"You have two minutes."

He ran for the restroom, so grateful to be back with the group. He wouldn't let them down again.

****

Bryce pulled on a clean black shirt and met Laura by the door. Several times, he'd caught odd looks from her. It was like she was sizing him up. Maybe it was because she wanted to make sure he wouldn't impede her authority. After all, they were obviously close in age.

She had good reason to doubt him. He'd been tossed out of the military for bucking their orders.

Orders to kill an innocent person. He refused. The Army shot the man anyway, then blamed it on Bryce. Now he would be trained to be an assassin. Something he couldn't possibly do. He wasn't a murderer. Why he thought he could be an Army ranger was absurd. He just wanted to serve his country, not kill anyone. His unit called him a Boy Scout. Maybe he was. But he couldn't help it. He was a God-fearing man who deemed each life valuable. *Some soldier.*

"You sustained an injury?" Laura touched next to a small wound on his bicep.

A chill swept up his arm. He cleared his throat and pulled his sleeve lower. "It's nothing, ma'am. Just a scratch."

"One thing we won't tolerate is someone falling behind because they haven't attended to themselves. If you get injured, you report it and see the nurse. Understand?"

He met her gaze. "Yes, ma'am."

"Good."

Their eyes locked for a moment and a strange chemistry encompassed them. She was gorgeous. He glanced away; happy to see Myers approach.

"You made it back." He held out a fist and Myers knocked it.

"Yeah, thankfully."

Charlie, Eri, and Denise walked up.

"I'm so glad you're okay," Charlie said to Myers. "Don't do that again."

"I didn't know you cared." Myers smirked.

"Okay, let's go. In the future, you need to be ready faster." Laura opened the door and they stepped outside.

The sun's position indicated it was about six in the morning. They walked in silence down a dirt path to a firing range. Green plastic targets lay scattered at different intervals. This part would be easy. If there was one thing Bryce was good at, it was shooting. Well, as long as it wasn't a flesh and blood target.

"Are you kidding me?" Charlie rubbed his hands together. "We get to shoot. That's so cool."

"You've never fired a real gun, have you?" Denise asked.

"No, not really. But I'm totally the best. Hours of playing video games, I'll beat you all."

Laura held up her hand. "Your mission is simple. Knock down all the targets in your lane in the allotted time given, and you can leave to eat breakfast. Don't, and you'll have to wait for lunch."

"Allotted time?" Eri asked.

"Sixty seconds, ten targets." Agent Harding walked up and handed Laura a suitcase. She snapped it open on a wood table and held up a gun. "This is 45-caliber, single-action, high-capacity, semi-automatic pistol. Your weapon for the day."

Bryce had this.

"Oh, and if you get some crazy idea about shooting me and running for your freedom, think again. You are surrounded by over fifty-eight cameras, two electric gates, over thirty armed guards, and miles of dense jungle filled with all sorts of vicious wildlife. You're not going anywhere, so keep your guns on the target." She handed Bryce a weapon. "Also, remember the shot we gave you when you first came? It is a tracker. You go anywhere, and we'll find you."

Bryce stared at the pistol in his hand. Someday,

they'd want him to kill something besides a plastic silhouette.

He dreaded that day.

Because it would probably be his last.

Chapter Eleven

Eri's hand trembled as she reached for a gun. Her uncle's words rang in her mind, "We do not seek to kill anyone. Martial arts are for your protection only." Though he could kill a man with his bare hands, he never would have approved of this barbaric weapon.

"Are you okay?" Charlie whispered.

She shook her head.

"I thought you were like a tough Kung Fu girl?"

"I've never shot a gun." She glared at him with a pinched smile. "I've only worked with swords."

"You know how you visualize the next move your opponent will make?"

She nodded.

"Just imagine this is the same. When the target pops up, fire like you would strike your sword against an opponent."

She stared at Charlie. His appearance might lend one to assume he didn't have a care in the world. His hair hung slightly shaggy past his ears and he always wore a beanie. He reminded her of the grunge band member who lived in the apartment above her. But he had nice green eyes. Her uncle always said to judge a man by the window in his eyes, not his appearance.

Laura stood at the end of the range and held up one arm. "Get on the ground and in the prone position."

The five of them dropped down and aimed.

"Ready."

They inhaled almost in unison.

"Fire."

Green targets popped up in front of her. Eli removed her safety and slowly squeezed the trigger. The gun shot back, almost hitting her in the face. Gunpowder burned her nose. But the target remained upright.

To her left, she could see Charlie's targets fall one after the other.

She aimed again, but feared firing. She positioned her head from behind her hand, dug her elbows in the dirt, and shot. Dust clouded the still standing target.

Tears welled in her eyes. She pointed the gun again and pulled.

The green silhouette remained upright.

Her vision blurred. *I can't do this*.

"You'll never hit anything that way," Laura said at her side.

"I know." She sniffed.

The agent lay in the prone position next to her and took the gun. "Watch. Breathing is a big part of this." She dug her elbows in, held her hands next to her nose, took a deep breath, and fired. The target plummeted down. "Now you try."

Eri wiped her sweaty hands on her legs and then retrieved the gun. Her hands shook and she had to grasp the handle firmly to keep from dropping it. She glanced to her right. All four of her team members were done, waiting, ready to go eat.

"Don't look at them. They can't help you." Laura nodded to the target. "Keep your focus on your mission—always."

Eri stared at the green enemy and repositioned the gun. "Please, Lord, let me do this," she whispered.

Laura gave her a strange look, but said nothing.

It was as if someone else took hold of the pistol.

Eri fired.

The target dropped to the ground. She pointed to the next one and exhaled with the shot. Down it went. Three. Four. Five. Finally, all the targets ate dirt.

Charlie hooted.

The team clapped.

Even Agent Black seemed a little surprised, and possibly impressed. "Fine job. Let's find you some breakfast."

****

Laura sat at the conference table and studied each of the team's files. It was her job to find their weaknesses. In order for them to do well as an agent, she needed to strengthen them to a cohesive unit. Charlie couldn't swim. Myers was afraid of the dark. Bryce was afraid to shoot another human being. Denise couldn't trust another human being. And Eri couldn't shoot. All of these things needed to be fixed.

Harding slid into a chair next to her and lifted Charlie's file. "Studying how to break them?"

"Actually, I'm figuring out how to make them stronger."

"Hmm?" He flipped the file open and read down the page. "I guess a black hat doesn't really need to know how to swim."

"No, but an agent does."

Harding laughed. "You know he's never leaving this building again. He's a computer dork. His time will be spent analyzing data, not field work."

Her partner was probably right, but who really knew. Greenstone could surprise them. Odder things had happened at S.I.U. "I just think they need to be ready for anything. If for some reason Charlie gets thrown into a situation where he has to swim, he'll die."

"You ever think maybe Greenstone would want it that way?" He closed the file and slid it back to her.

"What do you mean?"

"We all have our weaknesses, Black. If he wants us dead, then he'll use them against us." Harding glanced around the room and frowned. "When it is time for Charlie to die, he'll be sent to some place surrounded by water."

Unbelievable. "And that's okay with you?"

He shrugged. "It's the way it is."

Laura couldn't live with that. "Well, this is my team. Greenstone gave them to me, and I plan to prepare them any way I can."

"Suit yourself." Harding rose from the chair. "But you can't protect them from everything. They're not your children to protect. You're supposed to train them and move on."

"I know."

He touched her shoulder. "Then be careful, Black."

"I will." She squeezed his hand. "See you in the bay in half-an-hour."

"Sounds good." He walked away.

Laura glanced around the room, her eyes falling on a camera ten feet away. She prayed Greenstone hadn't seen the exchange. Her care and concern was written like a novel on her forehead. She couldn't help it. No matter what Harding said, she would mold these five kids into strong individuals. Maybe they could last longer than the team she trained with years ago.

****

Laura walked out the locker room door, to the pool edge and gasped. Bryce stood a few feet away in black swimming trunks. His abs were tan, hard, and cut. He turned away from his conversation with Myers and smiled.

Afraid of blushing, Laura looked down at the clipboard in her hand. "Okay, today, we're going to work on swimming. You never know when you'll have to come out of the ocean or cross a raging river."

"I know how to swim," Myers said. "I used to be on a team in junior high."

Laura offered a fake smile. "Marvelous. Then you can keep an eye on Charlie."

Charlie's face looked ashen. He stared at the black bottom pool like it was a lake of lava.

"Are you okay?" Eri asked.

"Not sure," he said.

Myers came behind him and wrapped his arm around Charlie's shoulder. "I've got you man. You'll be fine. If you start to drown, I'll be there."

Charlie nodded, but his expression didn't indicate he was any less afraid.

"Okay, everyone. We'll be running drills. There are ten items hidden in the pool. As you can see, this isn't a traditional pool. It's a bit harder to see down there than if the sides were turquoise."

"Charlie, you can stay in the shallow end and concentrate on staying afloat, while the rest of you, bring me those ten items." Laura stepped back and blew a whistle. The four youth jumped in the pool, while

Charlie stared. "Come with me, I'll help you," Laura said.

"I can't swim at all."

"I know." Laura led him to the end. "It's only three feet here, Charlie. If at any point you're scared, just stand up. The water goes to your waist. Okay?"

"No tricks?"

Inside, she laughed. Of course, there were trust issues built between her and the team. Almost everything they did had some test attached to it. "No, no tricks. My only goal today is to get you water ready."

"Promise."

Wow. "Yes, Charlie, I promise." She walked down the steps and into the water. "Now get in the pool."

Slowly, he inched into the water and to her side. "Thank you."

That surprised her. "For what?"

"I'm just thanking you ahead of time for not drowning me." He smiled, nervously. "That way if you do, you'll feel awful."

Laura laughed, despite herself. "Okay, first lesson—"

Bryce popped out of the water, water droplets shining on his bronzed muscles. He swam to her side and handed out the metal envelopes from the bottom of the pool.

She coughed nervously. "You have all ten?"

He laughed. "Yeah, even out smarted Myers."

Right now, she'd never been more attracted to another human being. Yeah, he was gorgeous. She couldn't deny his body was a distraction, but his ability to complete this task with 100 percent accuracy, made her want to kiss him.

"Agent Black?" Charlie said behind her.

"Um, how would you like to help Charlie learn to swim?" she asked.

Bryce peered over Laura's shoulder and nodded.

"Great. I'm going to get out and prepare for this evening. Greenstone would like you to do drills way into the night." *Why am I telling him?* "Um…when the rest of the team comes up for air, let them know to get dressed."

"Yes, ma'am," Bryce said.

Laura stared at him a moment, an electrical current drawing her to him. She bit her lip and turned to Charlie. "Bryce is going to help you."

Charlie looked at Bryce and said, "Thank you for not drowning me."

"What?" Bryce said.

Laura laughed and walked out of the pool. Her heart still fluttered and it unnerved her. What was it about Bryce? Thousands of new soldiers, all ages, many of them gorgeous, had made their way through here over the years. Why did he make her feel this way? She glanced back and he caught her eye. Whatever it was, she had to get it under control. And now.

****

Bryce stood at parade rest with the rest of the team, while Laura outlined what they would be doing throughout the night. He'd worked hard on the swimming drill and the four-mile run they'd done just before breakfast. He was tired. Little sleep and small portions of food, it felt like basic training all over again. He wondered why he didn't get some kind of pass. After all, being an Army ranger, he'd been through this "breaking" ceremony a few times.

The one thing that made up for it was seeing Laura Black. Yeah, sure, she was his superior, and he shouldn't like her at all—most of the team hated her. But he couldn't help it. Something about her made him pause. There were times he wanted to punch her, but most of the time, he wanted to kiss her. What a dilemma. The coolest part—there were also times he thought she might feel the same.

Laura walked to his side and handed him a shovel. "I'm sure you know how to dig a fox hole? It should be six by three. Bryce, you show them how. I want two people to a hole and I suggest you have them ready by sundown if you want to survive."

Eri's eyes went wide. "What does that mean?"

"There are buckets behind that tree." Laura pointed to a palm tree about fifteen yards away. "They are filled with paint pellets. Next to them, your weapons for the evening. I won't kid you. It will be war. If you get shot near an organ or in your head, you spend the next two nights in solitary confinement as if you were dead. If you get captured, you will be treated as a PoW."

"And how do we win?" Myers asked.

"You take out the enemy, of course." Laura picked up another shovel and tossed it at Myers. "Okay, good luck."

"That's it?" Myers peered around at the team. "You give us a shovel and tell us where some paintball guns are, and that's it."

Laura laughed. "I should think this would be fun for you, Myers."

A slow smile crept on his face. "Actually, yeah, I think it will be."

"You should do good." Laura looked at Bryce. A chill swept over him. "Your only weak link is Eri, but if you can help her shoot, I think the night should be fun." Laura broke their stare and glanced around at each of them. "I'm on the other team. Take me, and you get steak for dinner tomorrow."

Bryce's heart leapt. This would be more fun that he thought. *Let the games begin.*

Chapter Twelve

Laura opened her studio door, flopped to the futon, and pulled off her boots. Twenty-four hours without sleep still hurt after eight years. But she knew her mind wouldn't shut down that easily. She glanced around at the room. The light gray textured walls always seemed gloomy. She'd tried to brighten them up with red and black Asian prints and a few plants. It didn't matter. The small place was depressing all by itself. A small kitchenette sat just left of the front door, a bed folded into the wall to her right, which she had no energy to pull down right now, and a bathroom in the middle of both. *Home sweet home*.

If she ever did find a way to escape this place, she'd want an enormous house just so she could spend a different night in each room. Being closed up in this closet for her entire adolescence was enough to drive anyone crazy.

She grabbed the remote from the shelf that doubled as a headboard and pressed the red button. A TV folded out of the wall next to the bed. Polar bears wrestled in the middle of an artic body of water. She changed the channel, but as always, the cable was modified. Nothing from the outside world made it through.

She shut it off, exhaled dramatically, and flopped to her back. Her "kids" formed in her mind. She felt sorry for them. It was too late for them to escape, but it wasn't too late for her to help them survive. That mission alone would get her up in the morning.

But that wasn't it, was it? *Bryce.* A smile formed on her lips. When he captured her last night, she almost kissed him. She closed her eyes and sighed. Her pulse increased at the thought of him. That boy would likely get her in trouble. *What is it about him anyway?*

****

Bryce cut into his steak, smiling at the reason that had brought this slab of meat to his plate. When he captured Laura, he wanted to pull her into his foxhole and keep her to himself. Of course, that was a dumb notion. She'd probably have him executed just for thinking that. But he couldn't help enjoying holding her tightly until Myers was able to tie her up.

"Do you think it's true?" Denise said.

Bryce blinked. "I'm sorry, what?"

"Do you think it's true about what Black said about us having trackers in our body?" she repeated.

"I've seen the cameras, the fences, the guards. She wasn't exaggerating about them. I'm sure she's telling the truth about the rest."

Myers set his fork down. "This whole situation is bunk. We're smart kids. There has to be a way out."

Bryce glanced at the camera over Myer's head.

Denise seemed to follow his stare. "There is no way we're getting out of here alive."

"I refuse to go there," Myers said.

"I would think you out of all people would have a clear idea about this place." Charlie pushed his empty plate to the side and leaned forward on his elbows. "After what you've been through."

His eyes glazed over a moment, then he said, "I survived something I shouldn't have survived. I did that when I started praying." He nodded to Eri. "She prayed, and look, she hit the targets."

"It's just a coincidence. Don't get religious freak on me," Charlie said.

"Myers is right." Bryce tossed the napkin on the tray and folded his hands under his chin. "There is something innately evil here. I think we could all use a little God in this place if we want to survive."

"Good evening." Laura walked into the dining room. Her face looked rested, and her wet hair indicated she recently showered.

Bryce couldn't help but notice how pretty she was. Silently, he scolded himself. Liking the enemy was stupid.

"I trust you're all fed and ready for night exercises."

They all shifted in their chairs to face her.

"Thanks for the steak," Eri said.

Laura glanced at Bryce. "Thank him."

Bryce licked his lips and set his eyes on Laura.

"We will be learning some hand-to-hand combat skills for the first two hours and then we'll set you free to use them." She waved. "Let's go."

"I may pretend to everyone in the world that I'm a tough chick, but inside, I hit like a girl," Denise whispered to Eri loud enough for Bryce to hear.

Eri giggled. "You are a girl."

"You know what I mean. You're going to have to help me here."

"Sure. No problem," Eri said.

"Cool. Thanks."

They walked outside and entered a downward tunnel. Laura punched a code and led them inside a hall lit only by dim green lights. They passed through several more doors, before ending in a sparing room with padded walls.

"Pair up," Laura said.

Denise spun around, probably intending to join Eri, but found herself face-to-face with Myers.

"Hey." He smiled.

"Um...hey." Denise peered over his shoulder. Eri had teamed with Charlie. She looked back at Myers, and said sarcastically, "Do you know what you're doing?"

"I took Karate for three years," Myers said. "I've got this."

"I thought you were a swimmer?"

"Yeah, that too."

"Really?" She raised an eyebrow. "Okay. What belt?"

"Does it matter?"

She shrugged. "Well, yeah. It will tell me if you know what you're doing."

"More than you, obviously."

"Just tell me."

"Brown, happy?"

"Ecstatic."

Bryce smiled, and then realized he didn't have a partner.

Laura stepped in the center of a sparing circle and waved her arms out. "In here, you will train in ways that will save your life. If you hold back, you won't learn enough to survive. And your life will be over all too quickly."

She pointed to Bryce and then beckoned him with her finger to join her.

Bryce glanced around and stepped forward. His stomach knotted. Not because he was scared, but because she made him nervous.

"Grab me."

"What?" He laughed uncomfortably.

"Do it. Grab me."

He didn't move.

She rolled her eyes. "You had no problem grabbing me last night."

"There was steak involved," Myers said, laughing.

"True," Bryce laughed nervously.

"Just grab me," Laura said, a bit irritated.

Bryce reached for her shoulders, but before his hands touched her, he lay flat on his back. The exchanged happened so fast he wasn't even sure what Laura did to put him there.

"Every second counts." Laura put out her hand to him. Bryce hesitated, but took it. He didn't know if he was angry or embarrassed. Maybe both. She pulled him to a stand.

"Now, to start, pick one person to be the assailant, and one to defend." She flicked her hand in the air. "Go."

Laura met Bryce's eyes. "Ready to grab me again."

Adrenaline pumped through his veins. He felt like a school-aged boy with a crush on a girl. He couldn't speak.

"Get ready." Her hand reached out and grabbed his arms.

He didn't respond quick enough, and once again, landed on his back. Her face inches from his.

"You have to be ready. Your attacker will use everything in them to bring you down. If you don't fight back, you'll lose." She stood up and held out her hand. "Attack me, Chappelle."

Butterflies swam in his belly. *Gladly.* He knew how to do hand-to-hand combat. It was part of his ranger training. He just had to stop thinking about his hormones and get in the game. This time, he kicked at her legs. She blocked, but he countered with a flip of her wrist. He almost succeeded.

"Better," she said. "Again."

For the next two hours, Laura led them through drills. Places to grab and hit, the best places to strike, and how to free oneself from any situation.

"Okay, good." Laura grabbed a towel from a bench on the side of the mat and dabbed at her forehead. "You all have two hours to reach the front gate." She clicked her watch. "Go."

Eri and Denise jogged out in front of Bryce.

"Sorry about that," Eri said.

"Myers turned out to be okay." Denise pushed her sleeves to her elbows. "He didn't hit me hard, but he didn't hold back completely either. Maybe I had him pegged wrong."

Bryce glanced back at Laura; her eyes were on him. She didn't break their stare. Maybe he had her pegged wrong, too. Only time would tell.

****

Myers had learned his lesson, now a team player, he held the door for everyone to exit, then ran behind them.

They jogged out into the night without any gear. The warm air didn't feel that great after sweating in the dojo, so he was kind of glad he didn't have the extra layers of a vest and helmet.

"How far could the front gate be?" Denise yelled. "There has to be more to it."

They jogged under a tree line and the moonlight disappeared. Only the tromping of their boots and labored breathing could be heard. Little seen.

Eri screamed.

Myers peered around in the darkness, unable to figure out what was happening. Someone grabbed his shoulder. On instinct, he spun around and thrust his fist out.

An agent tossed him to the ground.

Myers's head hit hard. He tried to stand, but the man kicked him in the side. Myers gasped for air.

Eri came out of nowhere and kicked his attacker, sending the villain a few feet away. She put her hand out and helped him up. "Come on, we have to keep moving."

Someone touched his shoulder. "Name?" He sounded like Bryce.

"Myers Luther."

A second later, "Charlie Smyth." Then, "Denise Kruger." And also, "Eri Lee."

"All present and accounted for. Come on," Bryce said. They ran out of the thicket and into a clearing. The moon shined high above. "Anyone hurt?"

Myers touched his side. "I'm cool."

Everyone else echoed his or her "fines."

"They're going to attack us again. We need a plan," Bryce said.

The group halted in the middle of the field.

"Like what?" Charlie asked. "It's not like we know

when they're coming."

Myers coughed and clutched his side. Maybe he wasn't cool. It really hurt. "I think I might have a broken rib."

"Can you make it?" Bryce said.

"Yeah, I think so."

Eri raised her hand. "I have an idea."

Bryce nodded.

"Remember in the ring when Agent Black had us stand back-to-back, then came at us one-by-one?"

"Yeah?"

"We could walk in a similar formation."

Charlie laughed. "Yeah, because the military formation you had us in just gave them a chance to pluck us off one at a time."

Bryce grunted. "Fine, let's do it."

They each turned in a different direction, some having to walk slightly backward and started for the next tree line. Myers felt a strange anticipation as adrenaline coursed through his body. Almost like a kid playing capture the flag. They could win this game.

They walked through the trees, but to his surprise, no one attacked them. "That was weird," Myers said. "That would have been the ideal place to get us."

They stepped out of formation and started through a patch of long grass. Suddenly, Charlie fell out of sight. Followed by Denise, who screamed.

Anxiety pumped through Myers chest. "Denise!"

Bryce stood next to him; the whites of his eyes were wide. Not a good sign. "They pulled them underground. Get on your belly," he said.

Eri, Myers, and Bryce dropped to the dirt.

Myers started to crawl forward, but Bryce grabbed

his hand. "Wait. There are wires. They open the traps. Look." A fishing wire glowed in the moonlight. "You hit that, you're going down."

"What do we do?"

"We find our fallen men and get them out of there." Bryce shifted to his side and glanced around on the ground. "Look for a stick."

He peered around in the dark, trying not to move too much.

"Here." Eri handed him a branch.

"Scoot back."

Myers and Eri obeyed.

Bryce followed and then touched the twig to the wire. The ground opened up like a trash chute.

"Help, we're in here!" Charlie yelled.

"We know." Bryce shuffled forward, trying to get a better look inside. "How far down are you? Can you reach the top?"

"If you could reach down without falling in, we could probably get out," Charlie said.

Myers touched his belt. "I have an idea." He pulled his belt out from his loops and fed the leather down the hole. "Can you grab it?"

"Denise, step on my hands like Bryce did at the wall," Charlie said.

Myers waited and then there was tension.

Bryce grabbed hold of it too and together they pulled. After struggling for a few minutes, both Denise and Charlie were free.

Charlie adjusted his beanie and rolled his shoulders back. "How many other traps do you suppose they have out here?"

"You okay?" Myers asked Denise. He wasn't sure

why, but he cared. Lately, they'd been getting along.

"Yeah, I'm good."

"From now on, you stick with me. I'll keep you safe."

She giggled and tilted her head away.

"I think I may know where the entrance is," Bryce whispered.

"Really?" Charlie said. "Because that would be amazing."

"I'm going to go on ahead and see. No use anyone else falling into a trap. You all stay here. If I'm not back in ten minutes, come find me."

Myers nodded. "Good luck, man."

Bryce ran on ahead.

Denise folded to the ground and started plucking at the grass.

Myers joined her. Suddenly, he felt nervous. He wanted to talk to her. Get to know her. But in some ways, she intimidated him. She was bolder than most of the girls back home. "So, you're from Arizona?"

She shook her head. "Not really. I mean, that's where I was when they picked me up, but I'm not from there originally."

"Can I ask where home is?"

She seemed to hesitate.

"Sorry, I didn't mean to pry." He dropped his head back and stared at the sky, so many stars.

"No, I'm just not used to opening up and trusting people. Every time I do, I get burned."

Myers met her eyes. "Same here. But guessing our situation, there isn't a whole lot I can do to hurt you."

"I suppose." She twisted a piece of grass between two fingers, brought it to her lips, and blew. A whistle came from the air that slid across the blade.

"Well, I was born in the O.C."

She smiled. "Really?"

"Yep. Newport Beach. This is the first time I've ever left. Too bad I have no idea where I am."

"I grew up in Reno, Nevada. Lived there most of my life, until—"

He scooted closer. "Until?"

She bit her lip and sighed. "Until my dad remarried and my step-monster started beating me. I hitched a ride and ended up in Phoenix. Never planned to stay there forever."

Their eyes locked and he couldn't help feeling drawn to her. He might just like her. "Thanks."

She wrinkled her brow. "For what?"

"For trusting me."

Charlie walked by their sides. "Should we just be sitting here? Maybe we should span out, in case Bryce can't find it."

Myers stood and helped Denise to her feet. "Let's give him a few more minutes, then we'll continue our search."

****

Laura stared at the monitor, a slight smile curved on her lips. From her vantage point, she knew they were less than ten feet from the main gate, but like every class, they would go in circles, never finding it. It always amused her. Probably because when she found out the truth, she felt so stupid.

The front gate was a false wall, not unlike one found on the lot at a movie studio. It looked like a big boulder, covered in trees. Not once had someone tried to climb it. The point was to disorient them into

94

thinking that leaving was impossible. That they were lost in a dense jungle and the idea of trying to escape would be pointless.

"How are they doing?" Greenstone said behind her.

Laura straightened. "Same as usual, sir. They haven't found it."

"Keep them out there all night then. No need to bring them back in."

She frowned.

He eyed her. "Do you have a problem with that, Agent Black?"

"No, sir. I just think they're tired after last night. I don't know if that will enable them to be ready for tomorrow."

He shook his head. "I don't care. This isn't summer camp."

She knew. How she knew. *Fun isn't allowed. Laughing prohibited. Forbid that anyone should actually enjoy the training process.* "Should I go join them?"

"You may, but don't interfere."

She nodded. "Of course, Sir."

He peered over her shoulder at the screen once more and then disappeared out the door.

Jerk. She rolled her eyes and then pulled on a black leather vest over her tank top and zipped it up. Then strapped on a web-belt, complete with canteen, flashlight, and knife, before exiting the compound. It wouldn't take her long to find them. Though they probably felt they'd been walking for miles, they'd really only gone about fifty yards.

She shot the flashlight beam side-to-side on the ground, searching for wires. She didn't want to accidentally trip one. Then she'd be interfering, because they'd have to rescue her.

"Hey, someone's coming," Charlie yelled.

"Get in formation," Bryce said as he ran up to the group.

Laura smiled. He really was something.

"I come in peace," Laura said, hands high.

"It's Agent Black," Eri said.

The group ran to her all talking at once.

"One at a time, please."

"Are we done?" Myers asked.

She shook her head. "I'm afraid not. Greenstone has ordered you to stay out here until dawn if you can't find the entrance."

"But we have." Bryce stepped into the beam from the flashlight. "It's over there."

She followed his finger. It was aimed at the false rock. Her heart skipped. *Remain calm, play this off. Not interfering, just playing devil's advocate.* "I don't see anything."

"We've been walking in circles all night." Bryce removed his black cap and rubbed his shaved head. "I'm an Army ranger. You didn't seriously think that wall would fool me?"

She wrinkled her brow. "I'm sorry, what wall?"

"That one!" He shot his arm out to his side, obviously exasperated.

She stepped closer to him, her expression stern. "Take me to it."

He held her gaze for a moment then nodded. "Fine."

"You guys stay here," Laura ordered. She aimed her light at the ground and they stepped around the wires to a dirt path. She hoped he'd stayed to the trail. It would lead him back here. But he didn't. He veered off into the grass again, his point of direction straight for the entrance.

"See these tire marks. They're fresh." Bryce kneeled to the ground. "You tried to cover them with leaves, but you failed."

Again, why did Greenstone think recruiting a man with the mind of a sleuth was a good idea? She narrowed her eyes as if to say, "You're crazy, but I'm listening." Out loud she said, "Okay, but where is the gate?"

He grabbed her hand.

Her eyes went wide. She thought to yank it away, but knew it would probably cause more of an issue than ignoring it. He led her forward, and she worked to block out his warm fingers and the chill that tingled up her spine.

He pushed past the few fake trees and slapped the painted wall. He had indeed found it, in the dark, without any signs.

"You can't tell the others."

He dropped her hand. "What?"

"You can't show the others. They have to find it for themselves."

He looked back past the trees where the group waited in the grass. "They know where we came, and they heard me say it. They're not stupid."

Laura inched close to him and lowered her voice to a barely audible whisper. "If you value their life at all, you will not show them this gate. You will pretend you were wrong."

He stepped back, studying her features. "I don't

understand."

How did she tell him without telling him? Why'd he have to be so smart? So amazing? *So cute.* "Look, there are rules and you've just done something that upsets those. No one has ever found this wall, and there is a reason for that."

"You don't want anyone to leave."

"Among other things, yeah."

"But they're going to find out sooner or later."

She diverted her gaze to a patch of grass at her feet. "Later is always better in this place."

"You seem scared."

She met his eyes. "You should be, too."

Chapter Thirteen

Denise stared at Myers across the room cleaning his weapon. Every once in a while she'd catch him glance around his hair, meet her stare, and smile.

Laura must have seen the exchange. "Denise, come with me."

Great. Denise laid the barrel down on the sheep cloth and walked out the door. Her nerves swam in her stomach. Whenever Laura called someone out, they ended up in the pit or stumbling in the dark.

Laura stopped at the back of the building and leaned against the wall, arms crossed, expression austere. "I see what you're doing, Miss Kruger, and it needs to stop."

She shifted from one foot to the other. "I don't know what you're talking about."

"Really?"

Denise thought she knew, but in case not, she didn't want to offer up anything. "Really."

"You like Mr. Luther, am I right?"

Denise shrugged. "He's a nice guy."

Laura dropped her arms and stepped closer to her. "Nice guy, huh? You're not here to make friends. Trust me."

That's just stupid. "Why not? This place is bad enough, but without friends, we'll go crazy." Denise noticed something in Laura's eyes. Was it genuine concern? Fear?

The agent glanced at a camera a few yards away, then swung around so her back faced it. She lowered her voice. "I'm trying to do you a favor here. Getting close to people in this place is a mistake."

"Why, because you lost some guy once?" She shook her head. "With all due respect, ma'am…"

Laura held up her hand. "I didn't lose a guy once." Her ominous tone made Denise listen. "I've lost everyone I trained with. Everyone I've ever cared about in this place. Sooner or later, so will you."

Denise stared at her, not sure how to respond, or even if she was supposed to. It wasn't in her to be scared easily. Living on the streets had taught her to survive. Acting gave her an outlet to be whoever she wanted to be. It also greased her pocketbook. This new world of captivity was a foreign concept. She needed to be in control. "Can I go now?"

Laura studied her for a moment and then nodded.

Denise swung open the door and stomped back to her station.

Myers stared at her, obviously wondering what had happened.

"Are you okay?" he whispered.

She barely looked up. "Fine." A lone tear threatened to fall. She swiped at it and concentrated on her gun. Though she played it low-key, she'd like to toss it at that Laura chick. Constantly trying to scare them. Everything out of the woman's mouth held doom and gloom. If they tried to escape, they'd die. If they made it through training, they'd die on a mission. What was the point? They were obviously all destined to die in this place.

Eri slid in the seat next to her. "Just remember, they may take every physical thing we own, but they can't take our soul."

Denise blinked.

Eri smiled, patted her arm, and went back to her spot.

Was she here on earth to be an assassin? No. But she probably wasn't supposed to be a con artist either. *I'm not giving into this fear.*

****

Bryce stepped in the sparring cage and faced their fearless leader.

"Pair up," Laura said.

Eri joined Denise. Myers with Charlie. That left Bryce with Laura again. He moved to her side and cracked his knuckles. This time, he was ready to do some damage. For weeks, she'd been trying to break him and his friends. Today? Payback.

"Ready?" She glanced around. "Go."

Bryce balanced, his feet shoulder-width apart, knees slightly bended. He'd wait for her to attack. He wasn't disappointed.

She swung, hard.

He ducked.

She flipped around and kicked at his chest.

He grabbed her ankle and tossed her to the mat.

She jumped up and swung. Her knee cracked against his jaw.

He fell, but recovered quickly.

The two of them danced around in a circle, both focused on the other.

How he hated her. How he liked her. The two

conflicting emotions annoyed him. One without the other had a consequence—a determined outcome. The two swam together like an oil spill in Alaska.

"Come on, Chappelle. You can do better than this," she taunted him.

He swung again.

She flipped out of the way.

He kicked at her instep.

She tripped him, but her leg got caught on his on the way down. They both fell, him on top. He lifted his head, only inches from hers. A great desire to kiss her overcame him.

She pushed back, looking flustered. "Better."

"You're holding back."

"So are you. Don't." She swung again.

He blocked.

She punched again, this time nailing him in the face.

He grabbed her wrist and tossed her to the mat. She kicked at his leg, dropping him next to her. She rolled over and leapt up, then kicked again. He rolled, just missing contact with her heel.

He found himself finding ways to touch her. Most people flirted with subtle words, gestures, or looks. They seemed to have mastered a different kind of foreplay.

She punched.

He grabbed her wrist.

She hit with the other hand and he blocked, then bound both her arms to her chest and pulled her close. She seethed, her breathing hard.

His heart beat wildly in his chest.

Her eyes locked onto his.

"Agent Black," Denise said.

She pushed back and smoothed her hair. "Yes, Ms. Kruger?"

"Can you show me how you did that move a second ago?" Her expression seemed odd. Like she knew something had just happened.

But it hadn't, right? It had to be in his imagination. Bryce needed to dismiss any feelings for this woman. Something told him liking her would eventually be his demise.

"Yes, of course," Laura said. "Switch partners."

****

Laura jogged around the compound to the one place she knew was dark, without cameras. She needed to think. *What is with this group?* For almost nine years, she'd managed to block out almost all emotion. Okay, at least eight of the years. Her time in training hadn't been so easy, but she'd learned quickly. Feelings were a deadly distraction. She'd felt very little and what she did feel, she impeded.

Then this team had arrived; she'd been unable to shut emotions off. She felt pity, sadness, anger, and remorse. And worse, passion—the precursor to love. She had to get these emotions under control. She knew the outcome of all of them. Either she'd get these kids killed or herself.

She rested on a rock and allowed herself to remember the team she trained with at S.I.U. She loved them all. Especially, her best friend, Anne Grainer and her boyfriend, Rex Wilson.

Greenstone had learned of their affair and sent both Anne and Rex on a suicide mission. When Laura questioned it, he made it very clear love was a defect. It would put an entire team in danger and put the objective second. He equated falling in love to a flawed machine coming out of a factory, the only solution— termination. Once a person crossed the romantic line, there was no going back.

Laura boldly asked why he couldn't send them to another unit. Separate them instead of killing them. His response, "They would always pine for one another, it would never work."

Unable to block out the emotions anymore, Laura crumbled to the ground and folded her knees to her chest. More and more, she began to question everything. A very dangerous place to be.

I've got to get it together. Only two more weeks and they'll be ready for a mission and out of my hands. Buck up, Laura.

She wiped at her eyes, rolled her shoulders, and stood. *Two more weeks. Piece of cake.*

Chapter Fourteen

Bryce watched Laura as she led the group into an open bay with a small stage set up at the end. A row of metal chairs faced the blocks.

"Take a seat. Your instructor will be here shortly," Laura said.

"What's on the agenda today?" Myers asked, flipping one of the chairs around and straddling it.

"You'll see," was all she said as she left.

"That always makes me nervous," Eri said.

"Ditto." Myers' gaze darted around the room.

Bryce followed suit. He hated these tests. Everywhere they went someone or something was jumping out at them. This room seemed open enough. Not too many places a combatant could hide.

The metal door at the back banged open.

The group seemed to jump in unison.

"Well, hello, everyone." A middle-aged woman, with wide hips and a plastic smile, sauntered to the front. Her hair lay in big red curls; she wore a bright-blue sweater and a long, flowered skirt. Her lipstick was orange, clashing with her fire-red hair. Reaching the front, her hands swung wide, as if to encompass the room. "We are going to have so much fun. I promise."

Myers met Bryce's stare with wide eyes.

"My name's Selma Ward. I'm to be your acting

coach."

"Acting?" Denise stood. "This is some kind of joke, right?"

"You must be Denise Kruger."

"How'd you know?"

"Lucky guess." She smiled, revealing more lipstick on her teeth than on her lips. "And I would assume, out of everyone here, this would be the most enjoyable class for you yet. You're a natural, am I right?"

Denise sucked her bottom lip in and cocked her head to the side. Her posture indicating she was ready for a trap. After all, everything in this place was a trap.

"Good. I will let you start." Selma waved her hand toward the stage. "Entre' vous."

Denise glanced around, her expression unsure.

"Don't be shy. I know you're not."

Charlie raised his hand.

"Yes, Charlie?"

Apparently, the woman had done her research.

"I was wondering why we need acting school? Aren't we being trained to be killers," he said with disdain.

A melodic chortle flowed from Selma's lips. "I prefer the word spy. And a good spy must know how to penetrate any situation. You have to become whatever the target needs you to be. Just putting on a wig and hoisting a gun won't get you the end result. You need acting classes, proper etiquette training, and even lessons in hygiene." She tugged Charlie's beanie off and his blond hair stuck up in disarray. "When I'm finished with you, you'll be completely new men and women."

Bryce stared at her. In some ways, this appeared

absurd. But in a way, he was just relieved he wasn't going to be fighting for his life today. Acting lessons gave him and the team a much-needed break. "Cool. Let's do it."

"Ah, Bryce Chappelle. You seem awfully eager."

He rubbed his hands together and nodded. "Sure. Why not?"

Another enormous smile broke across her face. "Wonderful. Then join Miss Kruger on the stage, would you?"

Good deal. Just had to open your mouth, huh, dummy? He forced a smile and walked to the stage.

"Okay, Denise, I want you to imagine you're a Swedish woman at a bank. Your objective is to get the teller to leave long enough to swipe something off his desk."

"Yah." She curtsied, then giggled.

"Bryce, you're a gruff teller. Don't make it easy on her." Selma nodded and backed off the stage.

Denise quickly braided her hair into two braids.

"Can I help you?" Bryce said.

"Jes. I wondered if you can 'elp me." Her accent was hilarious. She began swaying back and forth, while twirling her hair. Her eyes were wide and innocent. It made Bryce want to laugh, but he remained composed.

"What can I do for you, miss?"

Bryce and Denise both jumped into their roles, and for a moment, he was actually having fun. It almost made him forget reality, like a kid on the playground pretending to be someone else.

When she stopped them, he was disappointed.

"Good. Now, let's talk about what you did wrong," Selma said.

Just as they were finishing that discussion, Laura entered. Just the sight of her made Bryce's heart accelerate. How she unnerved him.

"I assume you're all doing well," Laura said. "Show me."

"Agent Black. Marvelous!" Selma clapped her hands together and crossed to Laura's side. "It's been years since I've had the pleasure of working with you. You, my dear, were one of the best."

"Hello, Selma."

"Shall I set up a situation? Let them see how a pro does it?"

A smile tugged at the corner of Laura's mouth. She nodded.

"Wonderful." Selma flipped around, spanning her arm out toward the blocks. "Take the stage, my thespian friend."

Laura walked up the stairs and faced them.

"Okay, Mr. Chappelle, please join her."

Bryce swallowed. *Why me*? He didn't move.

"Mr. Chappelle?"

He glanced at Selma. "Yes?"

"Take the stage. Hop, hop. We don't have all day."

He stood reluctantly. *God, if this is your way of a joke, I beg you to stop being so funny.* He climbed the steps with his hands in his pockets, not meeting Laura's gaze.

"Okay, this is probably the hardest con, but one of the most necessary," Selma said. "Girls, pay attention, because you'll be forced to use this more than you'll want to."

Bryce dreaded what that meant.

"Agent Black, you know where this is going."

Selma walked to the edge of the stage and handed him a bag of chocolate-covered cashews. Bryce loved cashews. How could she know? "I am certain you'd love to eat those, am I right?"

After all the bland food they'd been eating, his mouth salivated at the idea. He nodded.

"Well, the only way you're going to get to eat them is if you can last ten minutes with Agent Black not getting them." Selma laughed and hit a stopwatch. "Good luck."

Bryce glanced down at the bag in his hand, not daring to look up.

"Don't worry, this is a dumb exercise. I won't hurt you." Laura stepped closer to him and whispered, "I know you don't trust me, and I'm sorry. It's all an act, you know?"

He looked up. "What is?"

"How mean I am? I do it in order to keep Greenstone happy."

"Really?"

She smiled. "The truth is…I think I'm falling for you."

Bryce swallowed.

Her finger slid down his arm, landing at his free hand. "I know this sounds dumb, but I care about you. I'm hoping that after this is over, we can be more than friends."

Denise audibly cleared her throat.

Bryce glanced out at the audience and back to Laura. "Should you be saying this here?" he whispered. "I thought caring about someone in here could get you killed?"

Her expression appeared serious. Laura brought her

mouth to his ear, her breath hot on his neck. "Yes, that's true. But I can't deny how I feel any longer."

Adrenaline coursed through him.

Her lips slid across his jaw-line, nearing his mouth. Hungrily, he wanted to kiss her.

Suddenly, she backed away.

He blinked.

"Very well done," Selma said.

Laura held the cashews high in the air.

Confused, Bryce stared down at his now empty hand. He'd been tricked and didn't even know it. Heat rose throughout his body.

"Don't feel bad." Selma laughed. "Ms. Black is our very best. No man could ever win against her wiles. At least, not that I've seen thus far."

Laura met his gaze, her expression revealing nothing.

He hated her. She took his candy and his heart.

****

Laura kept her shoulders erect until she was clear of the warehouse door. Outside, she fell against the metal building and breathed deep. She closed her eyes and imagined her mouth just inches from Bryce's. How she wanted to kiss him. But hadn't she already crossed a line? She had the candy. That was the task. Anything more would be suicide. And now, he was clearly angry with her.

This wasn't the first time Selma had used her for this demonstration. Laura never lost. But usually, when the man stared back at her with piercing eyes, she shrugged it off with a smug pat on her back. Not today. She felt awful.

How can I win Bryce's trust back?

Her eyes flew open, her heart raced. *Why do I want to?*

The conflicting emotions were going to eat her up. She needed the next evening off. It was too much. She desired to take a mission and clear her head.

She stood, wiped her pants off, and started for Greenstone's office. It was time to get back in the field.

****

The following evening, the team finished setting up makeshift tents and sat around a campfire. Laura was not with them, and for the first time, Bryce felt they were truly alone. Of course, there had to be cameras somewhere. This campout wasn't for fun. Surely, there would be some sort of training involved. Always was.

"What do you think happens when we graduate?" Eri asked.

Charlie shrugged. "We go on missions."

She shook her head. "I mean…do we get to leave campus and live in a house. Go to the mall. Live a normal life."

Bryce pursed his lips and sighed. "No, we get to live underground like Black and the rest of the agents. This *is* our life. Home sweet home."

Charlie frowned. "I can't do it, man. They're training me to work in tech ops. I won't even get out of here to go on missions. I'll be underground on a computer for the rest of my life."

"At least you'll be safe," Denise said. "They're training me to take on aliases, pretending to be someone I'm not, so I can get close to the enemy."

"Didn't you do that before?" Myers said.

Denise smirked. "I assessed the situation. If it was dangerous, I didn't do it."

"Well, maybe you shouldn't have done so well in our acting class," Myers said.

She elbowed him playfully.

Charlie pulled his beanie off and twisted it in his hands. "I'm serious. We can't live like this."

"Living isn't the point, is it?" Eri said, then eyed Bryce.

He looked away, because she was right. What did Laura say the life expectancy was anyway? Her former class now all lay under the ground as worm food. Would that be their end as well?

"I'm with Charlie." Myers crossed his legs and leaned back. "I'm not dying in this place."

"And, I'm not killing for them," Bryce said. "God made life. It is up to Him to take it away." He wouldn't murder for anyone. All eyes swung to Bryce. It was obvious they all thought he was the one person who would fit in here. After all, wasn't he supposed to be G.I. Joe?

"What, you think I want this?" He tossed a stick in the fire and sparks flew into the air. "I've never killed anyone in my life. It's the whole reason the Army cut me loose. When it came down to it, I couldn't pull the trigger."

"You're screwed." Charlie laughed a nervous chuckle.

"I don't understand," Myers said, sitting forward, "If they knew that about you, why risk bringing you here? To what? Terminate you anyway?"

Bryce shrugged. He had wondered the same thing. Laura had hinted at his "detective skills," whatever that meant. "Basically, Charlie is right."

A tear slid down Denise's cheek. "How do we get

out of here?"

Charlie and Eri glanced around; obviously praying no one heard that.

"We don't," Myers said.

Denise shook her head. "I refuse to accept that. There has to be a way." Her eyes pleaded with Bryce. "Please tell me they're wrong. You have a plan, right?"

Being the eldest must have made him some kind of leader to these kids. But did he have any more answers than they did? He held up his hands, head shaking. "Why are you all looking at me? I'm no leader."

"Maybe..." Charlie laughed. "But you have the boss lady's number. Am I right?"

His pulse quickened. "What are you talking about?"

"Dude, she's totally into you." Charlie slapped Bryce's back. "It's so obvious. You just need to play that card."

"Play that card?" Bryce laughed. "Ha! She played me."

"Oh, don't get all self-righteous about yesterday. It was an act, yeah, but anyone watching could sense the chemistry," Myers said. "It was real."

Denise shook her head. "I don't think she'd go for it."

"She lectured you about it, right?" Eri smiled. "Just use that against her."

"Why'd she lecture you?" Myers asked.

A red glow burned Denise's cheeks; she glanced away.

"Look, what are our gifts?" Charlie sat forward, resting his elbows on his knees and rubbed his hands together. "How will our talents work in our favor? We need a plan."

"What about the tracking chip?" Myers pointed to his neck. "It's not like we're free."

Bryce scratched his face. He wondered about the chip, too. This almost felt like an unbeatable challenge, one he wasn't sure he was up for yet.

"Look, let the computer geek worry about our chips. That's my gift." Charlie tapped his chest and then pointed to Myers. "You're the genius, dude. Think."

Myers rubbed his goatee. "Yeah, okay. Give me a few days. I'll think of something."

"It will take all of us," Charlie said.

"What are you asking me to do, exactly?" Bryce asked. He feared their answer.

"Payback." Charlie winked.

"Payback?"

Charlie grabbed Bryce's shoulder and squeezed. "You need to woo her, like she did you. Only this time, not for cashews, but freedom."

Bryce sighed. "Okay."

"Are we all in?" Charlie peered around at everyone.

In unison, they agreed. They wouldn't die in here or take another life. Not without a fight.

Chapter Fifteen

Laura relaxed on her bed, with a novel one of her colleagues recommended, hating Sundays. Down time. Not something she did well. It wasn't like Greenstone allowed her to go shopping or see a movie. A day off was spent in her room or walking the grounds. The only time she saw the outside world was on a mission, but then the feeling of freedom was replaced with the disquieted spirit that comes with the reality she might die.

She tossed the book across the room, pulled on her black sweats and tennis shoes, and started for the yard. Maybe a run would cool her cabin fever and calm any anxiety.

She stepped in the hall.

Wilson and Taylor, two recent graduates, smiled at her. They'd always been nice, but she refused to make friends. She nodded, donned a black beanie, and walked to the exit.

The midday temperature remained warm, despite the overcast conditions. She stretched her legs, arms, and neck, then began to jog.

"Hello, Agent Black."

Laura looked, startled.

Bryce ran beside her and grinned.

She resisted the urge to smile back. "What are you

doing out here?"

"We were given the afternoon off."

Her eyebrow rose. "Really?"

"Well," he glanced back to the barracks and smiled sheepishly, "Two hours anyways."

"And you're jogging?"

He shrugged. "Not much else to do."

"Yeah." She knew.

"Besides, I saw you."

Her heart quickened, as did her pace. Every inch of her body felt him next to her. She didn't know what to say, almost didn't know how to run. Suddenly, she felt winded and slowed. "You know, it isn't a great idea for you to be hanging around me."

He turned around and jogged backward. "Why?"

"Isn't it obvious?"

The corner of his mouth turned up. "Yeah, I like you too."

Her eyes grew wide. "What, um, no, I meant…"

He flipped around and ran ahead of her.

She matched his pace, not sure how to respond. When was the last time anyone made her flustered? *Never*. "Look, don't get a boyhood crush on me. It isn't smart."

He laughed. "One, I'm not a boy. I turn twenty-five in a week and you're what, a few years my senior?"

She pursed her lips and stared at the ground. "I'm twenty-six."

"See."

"You said one, what is two?"

He shook his head, looking confused.

"A second ago, you said number one, what is your second reason?"

116

"Oh. Two, it's not a crush."

She blinked. "It's not?"

He stopped and faced her. "I care about you."

Her eyes darted to all the possible cameras. She shook her head and backed up. "Follow me."

She ran ahead, leading him to the only blind spot she had ever known of, where "big brother" couldn't see them. Hopefully, that was still true. When she felt they were safe, she faced him. "You realize that any feelings in here are a death sentence. Let's not forget I'm your superior and that…"

He grabbed the back of her head and led her lips to his mouth. Hungrily, he kissed her. His lips soft, warm, moist. She drank them in, afraid to let go, afraid not to. Never had she felt this way. Nor should she. She pushed back and stared him in the eye, horrified. Her voice cracked as she spoke. "You'll get us killed."

"I don't care." He kissed her again.

She pulled back and paced a few steps away, wiping at her wet eyes. "Don't you get it? This place is about washing you of all emotion. If you fall in love, they send you on a suicide mission. It's a death sentence."

He stepped close to her, his eyes searching. "Then I'm in trouble, because I've liked you since the moment we met."

Her throat constricted. How could she admit she'd felt that way from the day she saw his mug shot? Or that she watched him sleep? Or read his file more than a dozen times? She cared about him deeply, but she wasn't willing to risk his life to have him. "Please," her voice wavered.

He lined her jaw with his finger. "Can I trust you?"

"If you only knew how much I protect you daily, you wouldn't have to ask."

"If we had a plan to get out of here, would you come with us?" He brushed his lips to hers. "With me?"

Panic seized her chest. "It can't be done." She backed up, her body trembling. "They'll kill you all. Please don't try."

He reached for her hand. "Laura, listen."

Hearing her name uttered for the first time in eight years, she almost broke down in sobs.

"Before you judge the final outcome, are you willing to hear our plan?" He caressed her fingers, soothing her nerves. "If you hear it and decide it's too dangerous, we'll toss it."

She studied his eyes. So green and brilliant, they still held light. "Why would you want me to go? I'm filled with darkness. I don't have a soul anymore."

He smiled. "Because every living soul can be saved. Damnation only comes with death."

She fell into his arms and cried into his shoulder. For the first time, she didn't see him as her pupil, but rather a man she could love. A man she may already love. For over four months, she'd denied her feelings. Now she couldn't any longer. She brought her lips to his, then whispered, "Okay."

****

Bryce waited until it was time for showers to tell the guys about Laura's involvement.

Myers cranked some Reggae music. They each turned on one of the showerheads and then met in the middle wearing towels.

Laura had told Bryce there weren't any cameras in the restrooms, but there were microphones near the mirrors. The key was to stay by the water and blast music. Music that she supplied due to "good behavior."

"So, we're good to go," Bryce said. "She agreed to hear us out."

"Are you sure she won't run back to the boss man with all the details?" Myers asked.

Charlie smirked. "No, because he got lip...didn't you, buddy?"

Bryce bit his smile.

Charlie snapped him with a free towel. "You stud. I knew you could do it."

This isn't accomplishing anything. He cleared his throat. "Look, we have to focus here. We only have ten minutes before that Harding guy comes to check on us."

Charlie tilted his head. "How do you know that?"

"Standard procedure. I've got their schedule now."

"You *are* good," Myers said.

Bryce glanced at the door, then back to them. "We meet with her tonight when she's on duty."

"But where? Doesn't Greenstone watch us, too?"

Bryce nodded. "Yeah, but she's going to plan a surprise drill for us. It's within her parameters to do that."

Myers nodded. "Cool, go on."

"Charlie, you'll stay back. After we're all gone, you'll sneak into the control room and disrupt the cameras at 1600 exactly."

He shook his head. "Are you nuts? There are cameras all over that control room. I've seen them."

"Laura said she'd take care of that."

"Laura, huh?" Charlie winked.

Bryce rolled his eyes. "You guys aren't going to let up on that, are you?"

"Not on your life." Charlie elbowed him. "So, she'll make a window for me to get in the booth, and I'll make a window for you to talk. Where at? I mean, what location?"

Something moved by the door. Bryce flinched. He stared for a moment, waiting. Nothing.

"You okay, man?" Myers asked, following his gaze. "You seem jumpy."

"Just thought I saw something." He waved it off. "You'll block out the area where we had our campfire. The sound isn't that great out there anyway."

"Why not just go to the blind spot like before?" Charlie asked.

"Because when the cameras come back up, we need to be somewhere visible or Greenstone will get suspicious." Bryce looked at the door again. "Just give us a two minute window. It takes Greenstone that long to get down here from his building."

"Word." Charlie held up a fist.

Bryce knocked his knuckles.

"Harding." Myers nodded at the door.

Bryce dropped his towel and jumped under the warm water.

The guys followed suit.

Harding stood in the doorway with hands on hips, eyes narrowed. "You're wasting water, and we have an exercise after chow. Turn it off."

Myers pointed to the radio. "The music?"

Harding waved his finger around the room. "The music, the water, all of it. Let's go."

Myers turned and winked at Bryce.

It was on.

Chapter Sixteen

Charlie waited until the group had cleared the compound before sneaking down the corridor to the control room. His heart raced like a jackrabbit on sugar. He hoped he could pull this off. Of course, it wasn't the technical part that scared him. That he could do without a hitch. It was the not getting caught and shot part that made him nervous.

The narrow white hallway felt endless. Door after gray door, each numbered at the top in red numbers. Laura said to look for door twenty-nine. In front of him lay a set of stairs. *I guess I'm going up.*

He walked up the five steps and turned to his right. Room twenty-nine. Odd. It was the only door on this level. He punched in the code Laura gave him. The door clicked open. He peered down the steps, and then entered.

A long counter covered in monitors, topped by a wall with more monitors, lay to his right. A swivel chair was in the middle of the room. He shut the door and glanced to the screens. There were his teammates. Laura had them rolling on the ground with their weapons, some silly exercise to appease the big honcho.

Charlie cracked his knuckles and sat at a computer at the end of the counter. Laura also provided him with the access code so it wouldn't take long to complete his mission, but he had to wait for the right time. He took a deep breath and stared at the clock on the wall.

A minute never took so long. Sweat beaded on his forehead and top lip. He glanced at the monitor near Greenstone's office. Obviously, his room was camera dark, but if he came out, Charlie would know.

The red hand clicked over. It was time. He punched in the code and the monitor buzzed with snow. Instantly, a phone started to ring. His eyes shot to the red button on the wall and the receiver next to it. No guessing who called on the other end. He just hoped their two-minute meeting went well.

****

"It's time," Laura said. She glanced over at Bryce and pinched her lips together to keep from smiling. "Okay, let me hear it."

"Charlie has found a way to bug our bugs, so to speak." Bryce rubbed his hands together and leaned forward. "He can make us invisible once we get over the walls."

"Yes, and that's the trick, isn't it?" Laura sighed. "You've not been beyond them. You don't know what's there."

"Do you?" Denise asked.

Laura nodded. "Yes, for the most part. There are guards all along the wall and through the brush on the ground. Where they aren't, there are mines and electric fences. Getting out of here is harder than East Germany. And once you're free, you're not really. You're still surrounded by miles of jungle and its natives."

"Where are we exactly?" Bryce asked.

She hesitated to answer. Once they knew, it

changed everything. "Escondido Mona—an island just off the coast of the Puerto Rico."

"Escondido? As in hidden?" Bryce said.

Laura nodded.

"Why don't we escape on our first mission?" Myers said. "Think about it. They'd assume they could track us and we'd let them until we were ready to go."

Laura stared around the circle at each face, afraid. She'd seen people try. They always died. "Without a concrete plan, I can't in good conscious back this. I don't want to see you all end up in a black bag."

Bryce crossed through the group and stood next to her. His very presence made her dizzy. "You get us the specs to our first mission, and we'll get you a plan."

She shook her head. "They're kept confidential until right before they're implemented. Likely for this very reason."

"Somebody must know them."

"Yes, they're logged into the computer, but even then, it's only a few hours before they're passed to the agents."

Bryce grazed her arm with the back of his hand.

She closed her eyes. How she wanted to help him. What she wouldn't give to feel his lips on hers again. To walk free with him, to call him hers. But it didn't seem realistic. Death was more likely.

"You tell Charlie how to get those, and we'll do it. I promise."

Something in Bryce's eyes made her believe him.

Laura's watch beeped. She touched the side button. "Drop!"

The group's eyes went wide and they complied.

"Mr. Luther, you'd better pick up the pace or we'll

be out here all night," Laura said, with mock anger. How long could she put on this charade before Greenstone became suspicious? One of his gifts was reading people. She hoped he stayed blind to her.

****

Greenstone marched out of the door, looking very angry.

Charlie replaced the chair and ran for the door. He hoped he had enough time to reach the group before Greenstone made it to him.

He skipped down the steps, ran down the hall, and slid into the barracks room. He was about to head to the main hall, when the outside door opened.

Charlie panicked, dove into his bed, and covered himself. This was not going to be good.

He heard footsteps come into the room and stop.

Charlie worked to even his breathing.

The footsteps approached his bed.

He squeezed his eyes shut.

The blanket flew to his waist.

Charlie flipped over slowly and looked up groggily into the eyes of Mr. Greenstone. The man's curt expression frightened him. One order from him, and Charlie was as good as bantha fodder.

"What are you doing here, Mr. Smyth?"

Charlie pretended to shiver. "I was sick. Agent Black thought I should rest."

"Have you been to the nurse?"

Charlie shook his head, keeping his eyes at half-mast.

"When they get back from their drills, have Mr. Chappelle take you, understood?"

Charlie nodded.

"Good." Mr. Greenstone stormed down the hall, toward the control room, out of sight.

Charlie exhaled. Now he'd have to convince the nurse he was sick or be in big trouble.

****

Laura rolled her shoulders back and entered Greenstone's office. He sat behind the large silver desk staring at a large monitor on the wall.

"Sir?"

"Sit down."

Laura came around to a stuffed black chair, sat, and crossed her legs.

"We have a problem."

Inside, her stomach twisted in nerves and her heart thumped madly; outwardly, she remained still and composed. "We do?"

Greenstone held up a remote to the monitor. Technical "snow" played on the screen. "For three minutes, this is all I could see in the yard yesterday."

Two actually. "What went wrong?"

"That's what I want you to investigate." He ejected the CD and passed it to her. "I'd start with Smyth. He was in the building while the rest of you were on drills."

"He was sick. I told him to stay back."

"I asked the nurse about his condition and she said he may be exhausted, but beyond that, he seemed fine to her."

Think, think. What could she say? "I'm surprised. He threw up right after lunch. Almost got my boots. I was the one to suggest he stay in. Maybe he had food poisoning."

"No one else got sick?"

"Miss Kruger said she felt nauseous later that afternoon, but never got sick, no."

Greenstone stared at her. "Check into it."

"Of course, sir."

He waved. "Dismissed."

She stood and walked out of his office. The floor below buzzed with agents supporting or preparing for missions. Kids, as young as ten, wore body armor that held guns and grenades. How long had she blocked out her feelings to the morality of the organization. It was easier to just go along with it. But Bryce and her team were handing her a reality check. They didn't want to kill or be killed. They just wanted to live normal lives. And they deserved that. *She* deserved that.

Laura stepped in the elevator and selected ground level. Her head throbbed. All the tension of what Greenstone might say or find out was getting to her. She needed a break. But she was on duty for the next five hours. Her only consolation, Bryce would be there. And then that brought about its own issues. To be so close and so far away. To desire to touch and not be able to. Many kinds of torture had been implemented on her since she'd arrived, but this had to be the worst.

She walked in the barracks, mulling over more than her brain could process.

When she arrived, the group sat up at her presence. Their eyes filled with worry and expectation.

"Mr. Smyth, I need to see you in my office."

Charlie glanced around at the others, then stood and followed her out.

How could she pull this off? It had to be real, but she hoped Charlie acted accordingly. His answers could either blow it for the team or destroy him. She prayed for neither.

She pointed to the chair by her desk and then sat across from him. "You stayed here while we were in the field yesterday?"

"Yeah, you told me I could."

She nodded, then peered at the camera briefly. "Why did you stay?"

"I was sick."

Good boy. "What did you do while we were gone?"

He ran a hand through his hair, his expression not revealing if he knew this was an act or not. "I slept."

"With your boots on?"

His eyes darted to the camera.

Laura's heart sped. *Just answer the question, Charlie. You look guilty.*

"I didn't know I had my boots on. I was having trouble focusing."

She folded her hands on the desk and leaned forward. "The nurse said you were fine."

He shrugged. "By the time I went, I was feeling much better. I think it was something I ate."

"The same lunch all of us ate."

Charlie scratched his head and leaned forward. "Actually, no."

She raised an eyebrow. "Oh?"

"I did something bad, Agent Black." He shifted in his chair. "I found a turkey sandwich in the trash and ate it. I was just so hungry."

Laura could have kissed him. She covered her smile with the back of her hand. "I see."

He faced away from the camera and winked.

"Okay, you may go. But stick to the mess hall food

from now on, understood?"

"Yes, ma'am." He stood, shoved his hands in his pockets, and started for the door.

"Mr. Smyth?"

He faced back.

"What would cause static on a camera?"

He shrugged. "Could be a number of things. Satellite disruption, downed power lines, broken equipment, you name it. Why?"

"Thank you, Mr. Smyth."

"Sure." He smiled and left.

Since this agent thing isn't working out, maybe acting would better suit him. He did marvelous. She dialed Greenstone's line.

"I saw it," he said before she had a chance to speak. "Investigate the whole team. If you find anything, let me know."

"Yes, Sir."

"I want to see you in the morning."

"Yes, Sir."

The phone went dead.

It was evident she had to hurry and get this group ready. The sooner she had them field certified, the quicker they could taste freedom. Besides, if Greenstone or any other agent sniffed out any wrongdoing, they'd all be dead.

She walked into the bay and stopped.

The group sat in the middle holding hands, eyes closed. Bryce mumbled something she couldn't hear.

The group said, "Amen" in unison, and then dropped hands. Their eyes fell to her.

Laura didn't know how to react. Never had she seen this. She knew Greenstone wouldn't approve.

"What's going on?" she asked.

"We were praying," Eri said.

Laura crossed her arms, legs shoulder-width apart. "I can see that, what I mean is, why?"

Bryce walked next to her. "We've all discovered something since coming here."

"What's that?"

"We are not alone."

Laura laughed. "You just now figured that out. I told you. Big brother is watching you at all times. You are never alone."

Bryce shook his head. "That's not what I meant."

Myers stepped forward. "I grew up in a church that talked about spiritual warfare. About demons and angels fighting for our souls."

"What…the little angel on one shoulder and demon with the pitch fork on the other?" Laura sneered.

Bryce's jaw clenched, his eyes revealing hurt.

"He's not joking Agent Black." Denise glanced around to each member of the group. "We all believe it. Since our stay began, we've all seen evil and yet miracles at work. There is light in the darkness."

Laura pursed her lips, not feeling good about the direction of this conversation. Her training said to run them until midnight doing drills or drop them in the pit, but something else she couldn't explain held her steady. "For example?"

"Myers in the pit," Charlie said. "It was like Daniel in the Lions' Den."

"He never went to the floor," Laura said.

"Trust me, they were close enough to grab me if they wanted," Myer said. "But someone is totally looking out for me."

"And how about Eri and the targets?"

"I helped coach her."

Eri shook her head. "God is watching us."

Laura's stomach soured. She didn't want to hear anymore. There was no God here. This place was Hell. If only these kids knew what she'd done since coming here. "Enough!"

"Laura," Bryce whispered.

"Agent Black!"

His eyes went wide, and then he nodded and moved away from her.

I'm a jerk. But she had to be this way, didn't she? If Greenstone witnessed this interchange, he'd be furious. No, she had to stand firm and stop this nonsense.

"Suit up for drills. We leave in ten minutes." She hurried out the door and into the early evening air, gasping. She was an atheist. No beliefs. It was that fact which made it possible to live this life. If her team took that from her, and the plan to escape didn't work, what then? She squeezed her eyes shut and breathed deep. But no matter how much she tried to block out the conversation, she couldn't seem to shake it.

Chapter Seventeen

Bryce stared at his boots as Laura distributed orders. In no way could he meet her eyes. How could he love and hate someone so much, at the same moment? Maybe he'd been wrong about her. His spirit grieved almost daily in this place. He pushed Laura, because he wanted them to be equal in all things. But she had rejected not only his beliefs, but had embarrassed him in the process.

"Is that clear, Mr. Chappelle?"

He looked past her. "Yes, ma'am."

"Good. Then move out. You have one hour."

Bryce exchanged looks with the group and then led them out. It was going to be a long night.

****

Laura stared at Bryce as he left. She never felt this helpless. But she'd never allowed herself to care for anyone before now. Maybe she should have remembered why. She tightened her belt and walked out the door.

Once they had cleared the building, Laura brushed past Charlie, dropping a note in his hand. He started to look at her, but she gave a quick nod for him to act normal.

"There are five stations. Go!"

The group sprinted down the hill. Laura waited

until they were out of sight, before walking back to the control station. She hoped Charlie understood.

Her stomach rumbled. She'd spent the whole afternoon thinking and forgot to eat. She glanced around the room and then in the desk drawer. Nothing.

The kids had to have something in their bags. She always did when she was in training. She stepped out of the room and walked down the stairs to the barracks. She rustled through Myers things, then Charlie's. What kind of teens were these? No contraband. She peered at Bryce's duffel and sighed. Did she dare? The nauseous feeling of an empty stomach told her to swallow her pride and invade the man's stuff.

She flipped her legs over his bunk and zipped open the bag. Instantly, she spotted a candy bar. She'd repay him later. Not hesitating, she snatched it out, ready to tear into it, when a letter floated to the floor.

She picked it up and opened it.

Dearest Bryce,

I'm so sorry all of this has happened. First you were off to war and now to prison. I don't think I'll ever get used to not having you here in my arms. I know you're a hero no matter what they say. My dad is a little upset, but don't worry, he'll get over it. I love you so much and I will wait for you. For the day we'll have our dream wedding like we always talked about.

With all my love, your fiancée,

Shawna

Laura choked back the tears. She needed to get off camera now. She stuffed the letter back in his bag, zipped it up, and shoved it back where it had been before. Holding the candy tight in her hand, she ran back down the hall and up the steps to the control room.

She started to enter, but stopped short of the nearest camera, and collapsed to the ground. She had allowed herself to fall for a man who was promised to another woman. A woman who actually believed she'd see her man again. And the only one helping him do that was her. And her only reason for doing it was to be with him. Despite it being empty, her stomach heaved.

Laura covered her mouth with her palm to keep from crying out loud. This wasn't happening. She had allowed herself to be sucked in by these criminals. After all the years she'd played others this way, shouldn't she have seen the signs? Wasn't she the master of romantic manipulation? How was she so easily fooled?

Her watched beeped. They would be on their way back.

Laura pushed herself with the use of the wall, wiped her face. What would she do with Charlie? He would be here soon to help her loop the signal. It's over. She wasn't helping them escape. But then, she needed a chance to tell Bryce off. And in order to get that, she needed the looped tape. Maybe she'd even need it to torture him while he slept. The evil thought plagued her. Jealous or not, her revenge would come. No one used her. No one! His time at the "Hilton" was over. He was about to do hard time. They all were.

****

Charlie read the note again. He couldn't believe he might pull this off. He stuffed the note in Bryce's hand. Bryce met his eyes, but didn't say anything.

They entered the barracks and Charlie did as the note said. He slid to the floor on the far left wall, closest to the hall to the control room. According to Laura, the

133

camera could only see a portion of him in this position—his legs. Two mock legs leaned against the wall. He shifted one out, then the other. Once they were in position, he glanced at Bryce. "Bryce, why don't you tell Myers that story you were telling me this morning."

His friend had a blank stare for a second, and then the light went on. "Right."

Charlie edged against the wall and followed the diagram on the sheet. It indicated all the "dark" spots down the corridor. He reached the stairs and looked up. The camera revolved to the other side and he jumped over the rail and into the control room.

Laura turned around with a finger at her lips.

He nodded.

She pointed to the computer and stepped back. He noticed something hung over the camera in the corner. He hoped that didn't raise any flags like the snow.

Laura pointed to his beanie and sweatshirt.

He handed them out.

She put both on and left him in the room.

Charlie watched the screen. The "legs" slowly moved back and Laura, dressed as him, came into the shot. But she didn't stop. She pulled the sweatshirt up, as if to remove it, just long enough to block her face as she climbed into bed. *Man, she's good.*

The guys followed suit.

Charlie glanced at the girls' room. They too climbed in bed. He waited until they were completely still to start.

He produced loops for all of the living areas, the path to the front, and the gate beyond. Each one looped for five minutes, but took him almost an hour to do. He hoped the guys were okay. He glanced at the monitor.

No one stirred.

Charlie set the loop on the barracks so he could openly talk to Laura when he returned.

****

Laura hid under the covers, but she sensed Bryce staring at her. *Who cares?* She hated him. To think she trusted him. That she might have given her life to save him. And what was she doing now? Still putting her life on the line, for what purpose? These recruits weren't escaping. They would be here a few more weeks and then be assigned to a mission. Fifty-percent would probably die then, and then most likely, the rest not too long after. Only ten percent of the recruits brought in every year made it to their twentieth birthday. Nobody worried if they lived or died. To the outside world, they were forgotten. Dead already.

Charlie walked back in the room and everyone tossed off the covers.

Laura's eyes shot to the camera.

Charlie held up a hand. "It's looped. We can talk freely."

Laura sighed. She pulled off his beanie and tossed her hair. "You all should get some rest. We have a big day tomorrow."

Charlie shook his head. "Shouldn't we talk about our next move?"

Laura glanced at Bryce. "There isn't going to be one."

Bryce's eyes met hers.

Myers jumped up and over the bed. "What are you talking about, lady?"

She held back the desire to correct him. He was obviously angry. Provoking him wouldn't help diffuse

135

the situation. "Look, I thought about it and I just can't go through with it." She glanced at Bryce again. "My reasons for going are now gone."

Bryce tilted his head to the side, obviously confused.

Myers punched his hand. "Your reasons? What about our reasons? I can't die in this place."

Laura looked back at him. "You will."

He visibly seethed, fists pumping, and for a second, she thought he might swing at her. No matter, she'd take him.

"I'm sorry."

Eri and Denise appeared in the doorway.

"What did we miss?" Eri asked.

Myers shook his head, angry. "Oh, only that Agent Black is reneging."

"What?" Denise walked to her. "Tell me you're not backing out. Please."

Laura held up her hands. "It just won't work."

Bryce's jaw tightened. He licked his lips and stepped forward. "Can I see you for a second in the hall, alone."

She stared at him a moment and nodded. "Fine."

She heard the mumbling behind her as she exited. The morale lost. Respect, gone.

Once they'd cleared the door, Bryce cornered her against the wall, arms crossed, face stern. "What is your deal? For some reason, you're angry with me. I got that the other day when you snapped at me, but to take it out on the group. That isn't right."

"You think I was mad at you then? I was acting. Learn the difference."

"You were acting?"

"Yes, for the cameras after Greenstone and I had an interesting conversation. I wanted to make sure there were no suspicions."

"Oh, then we're okay?"

Her eyes narrowed. "There is no *we*."

"So you are mad?"

She bit the inner part of her bottom lip and stared at the white speckled tile. "Yes, now that I know the truth."

"What truth?"

Anger boiled inside her again, the desire to slap him great. "That you used me."

He crossed his arms and stepped back. "How so?"

Laura shook her head as she met his gaze. "You can stop the act. You're caught. You're not escaping. That's final." She turned for the stairs, but he caught her arm and drew her back. She landed inches from his face. No matter how angry she was, she still couldn't deny the crazy speed of her heartbeat or the fact he was gorgeous and stirred intense emotions she couldn't control.

"What are you talking about? What do you think I've done?"

"How long after we were outside these walls did you plan to tell me about Shawna?"

He blinked.

Caught you. Laura pursed her lips, nodded once, and stormed away to the control room.

Chapter Eighteen

Bryce lay in the dark clutching Shawna's letter to his chest. For many nights, it had helped him sleep. He needed to know there was a reason to make it out alive, and there was someone who believed in him. But the truth went deeper.

He closed his eyes and thought back to the day he left for Iraq. Shawn cried so hard, and yet, he felt nothing. Leaving her didn't hurt like he thought it would. She loved him and begged him to stay. He proposed in some vain effort to soften his departure. When he got to Iraq, he felt bad about that at first, but after many lonely nights, he was thankful for her weekly letters. He began to appreciate what she meant to him. Maybe he used her love to help him cope at first, but eventually, he began to imagine a life with her. Friendship could evolve into love over time. He just knew it.

Well, he did. Then he met Laura Black. The most exasperating and wonderful woman he'd ever met. The feelings he had for her surpassed any torch he'd ever felt for Shawna at any point in their two-year relationship. But how did he explain that to Laura. It broke his heart to see her face. When she confronted him, he was too shocked to respond. And how could he without sounding like a jerk. Of course, it looked like he used Laura to escape. Wasn't that what the guys asked him to do originally? How could he convince her it wasn't an act? That he really did care for her. Maybe even loved her. His stomach twisted. A familiar feeling as of late. He imagined his father telling him to stop worrying before he developed an ulcer.

He pinched his eyes closed, praying for an answer.

I care about this woman. This whole situation is screwed up. He opened his eyes. Should he use the word screw in a prayer? He closed his eyes again. *Sorry about that. I need you now. I need a miracle.*

Myers groaned and turned over in the bed next to him.

I won't kill anyone. I can't. I promise.

Something exploded inside him. He jumped out of bed and ran down the hall toward the stairs to the control tower. He knew she could see him. Hopefully, she'd turn on the loop.

He skipped two steps at a time and threw open the door. His heart stopped. "Agent Harding?"

The agent held a gun on him. "What are you doing here, Mr. Chappelle?"

"I came to ask for a sleep aid. I can't seem to fall asleep."

Harding walked forward, with a cutting stare that caused Bryce to retreat into the hall. "You need something, this isn't how you get it. You know that. Why are you really here?"

Sweat rolled down his back. His throat tightened. He needed a better excuse, but none came. "I know. I shouldn't be here. I just wanted an aspirin." He held up his hands in surrender. "I promise."

Harding studied him for a moment and then flailed

the gun in the direction of the barracks. "Go back to bed. I'll inform the nurse."

Bryce nodded, backed down the steps, and ran back to his bunk. His heart boomed in his chest. That was close. Too close.

Where is Laura? It was normally her shift. He pulled the covers tight around his jaw and inhaled deep, then let it out. He needed that miracle.

****

"Sir, I think it would be best for all of us." Laura sifted from one foot to the other. "I need a day in the field and they need a kick in the pants. They've gotten to used to me. I think it is time for the final drill."

Greenstone rubbed his chin. "You think they're ready?"

She nodded.

"And you realize when you return, they'll be set to go on missions?"

"Yes, Sir."

"Fine, I'll allow it." He slipped a file out among the ones on his desk and handed it to her. "You assist Echo Twelve tonight. You roll out in two hours."

"Thank you, Sir." She couldn't help but ask; she had to know. "Who will you send in my stead?"

A sardonic smile crossed his lips. "Agent Tyrone."

Instantly, a chill swept over her. As angry as she was with the group for using her to escape, she wouldn't wish that animal on anyone. Six-foot-five, three hundred pounds; the bald, black man could kill any one with his bare hands. Not to mention, he specialized in torture. When someone wouldn't talk, they sent in Tyrone. The victim either spoke or succumbed to death. There was no other alternative.

Laura dressed for her assignment, hoping she was doing the right thing. The image of Bryce's letter flashed through her mind and she pushed her concerns aside. Maybe they deserved Tyrone. As weak and wishful as they were, they couldn't go into the field. Their minds were too set on escaping and not enough on surviving. The fact was they would be agents by the end of the week. Tyrone would make sure they were ready.

The siren sounded in the hall. It was time. She tightened her black vest and stepped out of her room. Her handler stood ready at the door and gave her a pouch filled with weapons.

"Reece. Long time no see." She jammed two pistols in her belt, followed by a couple of knives and a smaller gun into her ankle holster.

"I thought you moved to babysitting."

She rolled her eyes. "I'm still the best agent there is, and you know it."

"No doubt." He slapped her back. "Load up. I'll meet you in the bay."

She walked down the hall to a black SUV. Two other agents stared at handheld electronic devices in their laps, most likely studying the mission. She recognized both of them from an assignment in China last winter. The Hispanic guy was called Diego—a real sharp shooter with an attitude to match. He didn't talk much, but when he did, it was usually harsh. The other agent was a female named Marta. How she made it this far was probably the biggest miracle in the agency. The girl was dense and almost always made the wrong choices. About the only thing going for her was quick reflexes.

Laura snapped open her device and examined the map as the car pulled out. They were flying to London to assassinate a sleeper named Bered Alhrain. The information scrolled on her screen. She glanced at Reece sitting next to her. "I don't understand. There is no exit strategy."

He didn't answer.

No! She'd been sent on a suicide mission. Had Greenstone found out about her plan? Did he know about her and Bryce? Her blood ran cold and she shivered. Now her team made sense. They wanted to dispose of Marta for her incompetence. Diego had an attitude. And Laura was a traitor.

****

Bryce's lungs heaved, gasping for air. This new agent didn't let up. For nine hours, they'd been running drills. Though Bryce couldn't be sure, it had to be two or three in the morning.

"Looks like Agent Black raised a bunch of pansies." Tyrone taunted as they ran by. "You will not sleep tonight. You will not eat. If you're good, you just might get some water."

Myers shot Bryce a look that clearly said, "Help."

As if Bryce had the power to do anything. He'd lost his edge all because Laura felt betrayed. With her, this all seemed bearable—to a point—now, if a mission didn't kill him, Tyrone might. Ahead lay a large hill. Every muscle in his body ached. It was apparent no mercy was in sight.

"I want Black back," Denise whispered to Bryce as the ground started to incline. "Whatever you did to peeve her off, fix it…please. I'm begging you."

"I can't."

"Why not?" Denise reached to a nearby tree to steady herself.

"Because I overheard Greenstone talking to Tyrone. Apparently, Laura returned to field duty. She's not here."

Myers ran alongside him. "You mean…she might never return."

Bryce nodded. He couldn't think about that now. It hurt his heart, worse than her angry stare. Her last words had been filled with so much anger. *God, keep her safe. Give me a chance to fix this.* He wanted the opportunity to make things right. To explain. To tell her the truth. To tell her—he loved her.

****

Laura crept along the basement wall, her eyes darting left, then right, searching for unfriendlies, as well as a way out. They'd completed their mission, but were officially trapped. The way they came in was completely blocked off.

Reece buzzed in her ear. "Black, two enemies approaching from the northeast."

"Get me out of here, and I'll shine your boots for a month."

Bullets ricocheted against a tattered bookshelf to her right. She dropped behind a trashcan. The smell of sewer permeated strong, making her stomach turn.

A man dressed in black stepped out from behind a wall.

Laura fired three times.

He fell, but not before firing a few rounds.

Marta screamed.

Laura searched the room, her eyes falling on the injured woman. Laura hunched down and maneuvered to her body.

Another man fired.

She shot back.

He dropped.

"Are you okay?"

Marta didn't respond.

Laura checked her pulse. A sticky substance adhered to her finger. She pulled it back. Blood. She'd been shot in the neck. "Marta's gone."

"Black, concentrate and look around. Do you see a steel grate above you?" Reece asked.

Her eyes searched the overhead space. "Yeah."

"That's your exit. Take it."

"It must be new. It wasn't in the specs."

Reece cleared his throat, his message clear. He was only now given permission to tell her the truth. There had been an exit all along. Marta was the obvious target. The chances of Laura and Diego surviving were much higher.

Diego ran beside her.

"Did you get the new Intel?"

He nodded and then made a cup with his hand.

She placed her boot in the makeshift stepping stool and pushed up to the grate. It popped open. She pulled herself up and then put her hand out for Diego.

A gun fired.

Blood seeped down Diego's face from a hole in his temple.

Laura didn't wait. She closed the grate and crawled forward. Though she never got used to seeing someone die, she'd learned to block the emotion. Lots of training helped. If she didn't, she'd end up in a mental ward. Some agents did.

"They got Diego." Her line buzzed in her ear. "Reece?"

Nothing.

She tried several more times. No response.

She found the exit and dropped to the ground. The van was gone. She pulled her stocking cap from her head and peered around the forest. Something shiny caught her eye. She crossed and lifted it. Reflector tape attached to a small note lay on the ground.

"Agent Black caught fraternizing. Terminate."

Her stomach turned. She wasn't supposed to live. Reece had helped her, but it must have been off com. He left this for her to find.

For the first time in almost a decade, she felt lost. She missed Bryce.

Oh no, Bryce. Her heart lurched. If they came after her, he would be next. She had to get back and somehow save him.

Chapter Nineteen

"Bryce!"

Bryce spun around, gun extended, and then exhaled. It was Charlie.

"Yeah, man?"

"Do you get the feeling Agent Tyrone is actually trying to kill us? We've barely slept in more than forty-eight hours, and now, they're jumping us for real."

Bryce wiped sweat out of his eyes. The exercise drills had stopped, now he hid to stay alive. Twice, he'd been attacked, but managed to escape. Unfortunately, the team had scattered. It was every man for himself, which didn't make the ranger in him feel confident. The Army stuck together.

"I don't know what this is. It isn't like the drills Black had us run. These men aren't holding back. They could kill us."

"Yeah I know." Bryce sighed. "They stabbed Myers in the thigh, and now he's in medical."

Charlie held out his wrist, exposing several cuts. "They're playing for keeps and we're losing."

Bryce imagined his own cuts were bad by the stinging beneath his clothes. He'd attend to them later. His training had taught him to keep going, despite personal injury.

A gunshot rang by Bryce's head. His left ear

burned and then everything blurred.

Charlie yelled at him in muffled tones.

His body slumped; everything fell black.

****

Laura had somehow maneuvered around several checkpoints, through the jungle, around hidden wires, and now crept toward the side gate of the compound she had called home for so many years. She knew their routine. They had agents guarding twenty-three hours a day. The hour lost was split up over the entire day of breaks. She waited for her window of two minutes.

The guard disappeared. She didn't hesitate. She darted around the rock wall and into the compound.

A fist slammed into at her face. She fell back and hit the dirt. She reached for the gun in her ankle holster and cocked it, then stopped. "Eri?"

The girl paused mid-punch. "Agent Black?"

"Yeah. Nice hit."

"Sorry." Eri put out her hand and helped her up. "Are you back?"

Laura shook her head. "No. Actually, they tried to kill me. I came to get you guys out."

Fear showed in her eyes. "They've been trying to hurt us all night."

"It's called final drills. They do it to all new recruits before they are officially made into agents." Laura thought she heard something a few feet away. She crept forward, gun poised in front of her. "If you survive, you graduate."

"And if we don't?"

"Six-feet-under."

Eri audibly gulped.

"Come on. We have to find the others."

They ran through the forest, avoiding several agents. She knew their hot spots. *So predictable.* The reason she was one of the best was because she had learned to mix up her routine. Most of the others didn't.

"Someone is laying on the ground." Eri pointed to a patch of grass ahead.

Laura's heart quickened. She rushed forward and fell to her knees. It was Bryce. "Oh, no." She touched his neck and detected only a faint pulse. Blood seeped from his shoulder. "He's been shot."

Eri gasped. "Is he…?"

Laura shook her head. "Not yet. We have to move him. We'll come back for the others later. Come on, help me." They wrapped his arms around their necks and drug him toward the entrance. An agent jumped out, ready to shoot. Laura fired, dropping the man to the ground. If there was any question of her returning to S.I.U., it was now gone.

"Wait!" someone yelled behind her.

Laura spun around, almost dropping Bryce.

Charlie approached, hands high. "Where are you going?"

"We have to get Bryce out of here or he'll die." Laura continued shuffling forward.

Charlie grabbed her arm. "But the others. Myers and Denise are in medical."

"You can come or stay, but rescuing them will have to happen another day."

The guard lay ahead, positioned on the wall. He stood with his back to them.

Laura checked her watch. Twenty minutes until the next change. *Shoot!* They couldn't wait that long. They still had a half hour hike to her vehicle and maybe another hour before they could find help. No, twenty minutes could be the difference between Bryce living or dying.

Charlie came into her peripheral vision.

"You coming with us?" Laura asked.

"If you promise to return, yeah, I'm in."

She nodded. "Then I need your help. Eri and I will take out the guards. Charlie, you get Bryce to safety. Can you do that?"

He looked to the top of the tower, breathed deep, and then agreed with a bob of his head.

"Good." She handed off Bryce then motioned for Eri to follow her. "Don't hesitate, Charlie. You may only get one shot at this." They ran forward toward the rock wall.

"How do we get up there?" Eri asked.

"We climb." The stairs were locked by a code, one that was changed daily. Up and over was their only option. Laura jumped for the boulder and pulled herself up.

Her companion did the same a second later.

Laura glanced to the ground.

Charlie was gone. *Good boy.*

She wedged her boot into the wall and began her climb to the top. She waited until the guard looked east before approaching him. She dropped in the booth, grabbed him by the neck, and twisted. His spine snapped and he dropped at her feet. They had one more guard and Eri was on top of him. She bashed her pistol against the side of his head. He collapsed, unconscious.

Laura nodded her approval, and they started their descent to the other side.

Charlie met them a few yards into the jungle.

"What about all the wires and stuff you told us about?" Eri asked, staring at the dark ground.

"Use your laser on your gun as you take a step. It reflects on the wires." Laura pointed hers to the ground to show her. "Charlie, you walk in our shadow and you'll be safe. Be careful not to drag Bryce too far away from your body. His foot could trigger something."

"Okay."

They inched forward. The night air lay sticky and warm. Mosquitoes nipped at their arms, and the sounds of frogs and parrots set the music for their hike. The moon provided only a sliver of light as they waded through knee-high leaves in search of a trail.

"Stop!" Eri held up her fist. "Agent Black, there are wires."

Laura aimed her pistol to the ground. The red beam bounced off thin, silver strands. "Good work. They will be every two feet, so take small steps."

"How far out?"

"I'm not sure, but be careful."

Charlie cleared his throat. "How am I supposed to get Bryce through with only two feet?"

Laura walked to his side. "We'll carry him together."

Charlie nodded and balanced his torso.

Laura grabbed his legs. "Eri, you'll be our guide. Just tell us what to expect."

The girl's voice wavered. "Okay."

They stepped forward. Eri stopped them every few feet. For what seemed like a mile, they crept forward in search of free land. Finally, it came in the form of asphalt placed here for the agency.

"My car is only a few feet farther. Come on."

They found it buried under a makeshift bush and climbed in. Laura turned on the engine, but not the lights. "Inside the glove compartment are some night vision goggles and a first aid kit. Hand me the goggles and Charlie the kit."

Eri complied.

"Charlie, I need you to try and stop the bleeding. There is some superglue in the box. Pull the skin close and seal it. From the amount of blood, and the two holes, I'm thinking the bullet went all the way through so seal both sides."

Laura flipped on her goggles and the road appeared in a green hue. She pulled out and drove fast. The nearest city was quite some distance, but she had one contact closer—an old man who had befriended her once on a mission. He had told her to look him up if she ever needed a hand. Now would be that time. She only hoped his loyalties didn't now lie with S.I.U.

After a few miles, the car hit dirt, and the path turned bumpy.

"Great. I just got glue all over the seat," Charlie complained.

"Sorry. The road is going to be rough from here on out."

"What are we going to do?" Eri glanced back at Bryce and Charlie. "Aren't we on an island?"

Laura didn't answer. Did she have an answer? Never had it occur to her to be worried. She had taught herself to block out emotion to cope. Now a twinge of concern threatened to invade. It started with Bryce. He was destroying all reason, including returning to the compound in the first place. Greenstone was right.

Caring about someone in this business could get him or her killed.

And why care? The man had used her, yet loved another.

A sign lay ahead that read, "Nalga De Maca." Perfect. They could use the campgrounds in case her friend didn't help. She turned the vehicle onto the road. Ahead stood the familiar bamboo shack. She cut the engine and let it roll into the dirt lot.

"Where are we?" Charlie asked, looking out the window.

"Possibly a friend's." She opened the door. "Stay here and be ready for anything." Slowly, she crept up the driveway, gun extended between both hands. The sound of a TV came from inside. She took a deep breath, wrapped the gun behind her back, and knocked on the screen door.

The TV volume decreased. "Who is it?"

"Laura Black. I'm looking for Julio Peron."

The door flung open and the obese man encompassed her in a bear hug. Not something she'd experienced in over a decade. "Laura, how have you been?"

She stepped free of his grasp and sighed. "Not good, actually."

"Come in, come in."

"I have an injured man in the car. Can you help him?"

Julio peered past her and scratched his hairy chin. "Should I be concerned?"

"I'll explain everything inside. Can you help him?"

He nodded and turned for the door. "Bring him to the living room."

Laura ran back to the car. "Quickly. We have to get him inside."

Charlie stepped out and pulled Bryce over his shoulder.

Eri followed them.

Julio led them through the small house to a room in back. He pointed to an Army cot in the corner. "Lay him down."

Laura pointed over her shoulder. "Eri, go in the kitchen, find some towels, and wet them with hot water. Also..." She looked at Julio. "Where do you keep your liquor?"

"I didn't think you drank," Julio said.

She gave him perturbed look.

He half-smiled and pointed Charlie to a cabinet behind him.

Julio dropped to his knees by Bryce and began ripping his T-shirt off. It was hard to tell where the wound was from all the blood. "Do I dare ask who shot him?"

"It's better that you don't know."

He nodded. "And you can't take him to the compound?"

"We've just come from there."

Julio met her eyes with fear. "They'll kill me for helping you."

"Only if they know."

He seemed to consider that a moment. "You owe me, Black."

"Yeah, wouldn't be the first time."

"No, it wouldn't." He started swearing in Spanish, but didn't appear to be ready to send them away. He turned on a light so he could see better.

Charlie handed out a bottle filled with an amber liquid, most likely Tequila.

Julio unscrewed the lid and poured it over Bryce's shoulder.

Bryce screamed and flailed.

Julio and Charlie worked to hold him down.

Eri placed the towels by Julio's side and stepped back. Her face pallid, her eyes filled with horror.

"Good job on the glue. Looks like you stopped the bleeding," Julio said. "Not sure how much he lost, but you can't move him right now. He needs to rest."

"In a perfect world, yes, but you know as well as I do, we can't stay here long."

"I'll do what I can. Why don't you guys get something to eat from the fridge? You look horrible."

Laura kissed the top of his head and motioned for them to follow her. They walked into the square kitchen and she pointed to two stools. "Sit."

"How do you know him?" Charlie asked as he straddled one of the wooden stools.

Laura opened the icebox and studied the contents. "We were on a mission not too far from here years ago. He got in the way and the agency threatened to kill him. I talked them into using him instead."

"So he's part of S.I.U.?" Eri's voice cracked.

"Not exactly." Laura placed a block of goat cheese, corn tortillas, and horchata on the counter. "He's a lookout. Whenever there are planes, foreign cars, or suspicious people nearby, it is Julio's job to let them know. But he isn't on the regular payroll, if you know what I mean."

"He's not an agent," Charlie said simply.

"Precisely." Laura located a knife and cut some

cheese onto the tortillas and handed them out. The group devoured an entire dozen before calling it quits.

Julio entered. "He's resting comfortably. If you can wait until tomorrow, he should fare better."

"And what if they come looking?"

He sighed. "You can stay in the bunker."

Laura raised an eyebrow.

"You think I'm loco." He laughed. "As soon as I knew about the agency, I built a safe place to hide."

"I always knew you were smart." She hugged him. "Thanks, Julio."

He smiled. "Anytime, chica."

****

Bryce opened his eyes slowly. They burned. His vision was blurred. He blinked several times to clear it. *Where am I?* A cement ceiling lay above his head, the light dull, and the space smelled of mildew. He pivoted his head to the right. Cans of food and guns were stacked against the wall. He looked the other way and smiled. *Laura.*

"You're awake," she whispered.

"Where am I?" he rasped.

"It's a long story, but we rescued you from the compound. You're in a friend's bunker."

"You have friends?" He laughed and then winced. His shoulder throbbed all the way down his arm and side.

"Funny." She stood and offered him a bottle of water. "Try not to make yourself laugh. You've been through quite an ordeal."

"What happened? It's all kind of fuzzy."

"One of the agents shot you during the final test."

"So, I failed."

She pinched her lips together and nodded. "Yes, I'm afraid you'll never be a S.I.U. agent."

His eyes locked with hers.

Then they both chuckled.

Pain shot down his arm again. "Okay, you have to stop making me laugh."

"Sorry."

His mood grew serious. "Did we get the others out?"

Charlie and Eri came into view.

"We weren't able to get Myers and Denise." Laura sighed. "But we'll go back for them when we can. Right now, we just have to find a place to hide for a while."

Bryce frowned. He imagined the torture his friends would endure. After all, the company shot him. He was lucky to be alive. They had to go back. "We can't wait. What if they kill Myers and Denise?"

"They won't."

"How do you know for sure?"

Laura ran a hand through her hair. "If you survive the final drill, you graduate."

"Which means what?" Charlie asked.

"It means that, in the morning, they will be considered agents, and by night fall, they will go on their first mission."

Eri began to pace. "But Myers was stabbed and who knows what happened to Denise. How can they put them in the field so soon?"

A great question; one that didn't have the best answer. "If they are mobile, they'll send them. There is no break, no vacation. In all the years I've been with S.I.U., I can't remember one team who didn't go out the next day. It's like the final test."

"So, they'll be on a mission tomorrow for sure?" Bryce said.

Laura nodded.

"Couldn't that work to our advantage?" Bryce tried to sit up, but winced and fell back.

Charlie looked at him and grinned. "Right. Smart, dude. We get them while they're out."

"What about the chip?" Eri rubbed the base of her skull.

Laura crossed her arms, a smug look on her face. "There is no chip."

"What?" they all said in unison.

"Yeah, we just tell you that. The shot we gave you when you first came was a truth serum. It helps us ask you questions so there are no surprises."

Bryce stared at her a moment. He wasn't fully ready to trust her. Not yet. She had let them down before. Could this be a set up? "So you're saying they have no way to trace us…that you know of? How is that possible? Surely, when you're in the field, they want to keep track of their men."

Eri cleared her throat.

Bryce grinned. "And women."

"Thank you," Eri said.

"Honestly, I don't have the answer to that. I was told the chip thing was bogus years ago, but then I'm sure you're right. Maybe it was in the equipment, or our badges, or who knows what." She took a sip from her canteen. "I know they tracked us by satellite, but I don't know how."

"Well, you better hope the whole blowing our heads off thing is fake." Charlie pulled his beanie tight.

"Because I kind of like mine where it is."

Eri nodded, her eyes filled with tears.

Laura peered around to each of them. "Yeah, well, you guys like to pray. I suggest you start with that."

Chapter Twenty

Myers had just finished dressing when Mr. Greenstone walked in the medical bay.

"Agent Luther. Looks like today is your lucky day."

He stared at the older man, not exactly sure how to respond. Greenstone seriously frightened him. "How's that, Sir?"

"You're still alive. Therefore, you've graduated and are officially an agent." He handed him a badge.

Myers took it and stared at the plastic card. It was his picture, but not his name or birthday. As a matter of fact, nothing on the ID was real, including the agency listed. It said C.I.A. He met Greenstone's eyes with a curious stare.

"We can't have anyone knowing who you really are. Myers Luther is dead." He nodded to another agent at the door. "Agent Gunner will escort you to your new home. I'll expect to see you in my office at 1700 this evening."

"Yes, Sir."

Greenstone left to probably torment someone else. Possibly the rest of his team. Hopefully, they all had made it. Maybe they would catch up to one another later and plot their escape.

"This way," Gunner said. The man had a crew cut

and looked like he could bench press a car. If this was his new handler, Myers feared he was in trouble.

They walked down a narrow, gray hallway. Steel doors lined both sides about every five feet, dozens of them, all the way down. About the thirtieth one or so, Gunner stopped. "Let me see your badge."

Myers handed it to him.

Gunner swiped it over a small red light on the side of the handle and it clicked. He pushed it open and motioned for Luther to enter, then handed back his card.

Myers' bags sat in the center of the room.

"This is your studio. The mess hall is down the hall to your left. Chow's at 0700, 1300, and 1900. Miss a meal, and you don't eat." He handed a piece of paper to him. "This shows you how to get to Greenstone's office later and the tech room where you'll be working. You're not allowed on any floors above this one. Understand?"

Myers nodded.

"Good." Gunner turned to go.

"Wait, do you know where the rest of my team is staying?"

Gunner looked him in the eye, but didn't answer, then closed the door behind him.

Myers slumped down to the charcoal carpet. For the first time in weeks, he felt isolated. His leg throbbed and his stomach churned from the meds he took earlier. He glanced around his new digs.

A modern metal desk and chair sat to his left and that was it. *Where is the bed?* He stood and crossed to an opening and looked around the wall. A bathroom.

He twisted his mouth side to side. Did he sleep on

the floor? He crossed to the desk. A remote control lay on top. His eyes darted around the room. He pushed a button and a TV almost hit him coming out of the wall.

"Whoa!" He stared at it for a moment. "Cool."

He pushed another button. A bed dropped down. A big grin spread across his face. "Now this is what I'm talking about." He flopped on the bed with the remote and punched another selection. Music began playing. Another button. The TV snapped on. "I could get used to this."

He checked his watch. Several hours until he needed to be anywhere. He turned off the TV and closed his eyes. Maybe the nightmare was almost over. This was surely better than jail. He exhaled and allowed himself to relax for the first time in months.

****

Bryce's eyelids felt like bricks as he tried to open them.

"How are you feeling?" Laura asked.

He squinted, her image appearing in a foggy outline. "I think I'm going to say 'no to drugs.' Let me endure the pain without the killers, okay?"

"You were thrashing too much last night. We had to sedate you." She touched a wet cloth to his face. "You're still running a fever, but we gave you a shot of antibiotics. I'm hoping you aren't looking at an infection."

"Did you give me the shot?"

A smirk appeared on her face and she gave him a quick nod.

"Bet that was fun for you."

"Yeah, maybe." She glanced to where Eri and Charlie slept against the wall in sleeping bags. "I don't know why I'm helping you."

His mind still reeled. He wasn't sure if he could make coherent sense, but he had to try. "So I kept an old letter to get me through some tough days, but I'm not going back to her. I promise."

"You used me."

"Yeah, maybe at first."

She bit the inside of her bottom lip, her expression hard to read. But then it usually was. He sensed she hadn't been able to feel anything for a long time. It was no wonder she treaded lightly with him.

"This discussion can wait." She laid a wet cloth on his head. "You should get some more rest. We have a long journey this evening."

He stared at her a moment, then closed his eyes. The bed seemed to sway underneath him. It made his stomach uneasy. He opened his eyes.

She still stared at him.

"I may love you, Laura Black." He closed his lids again and within minutes, dreams of another time overtook him.

****

Laura stared at him, dumbfounded. *It's the drugs talking. I can't let myself be sucked into this.* Emotions would only make the task that much harder. Look what they'd done to her already. They were in this predicament because she couldn't hold her feelings in check.

Julio rushed in the room, a gun at his side. "Helicopter!"

Charlie and Eri jumped up, eyes wide.

Laura didn't know if she should wake Bryce yet. He wouldn't be much good to them in his current state.

"How far?"

"About twenty yards to the west. Hovering with search lights."

"Are we safe here?" Eri asked.

He shook his head. "Not for long."

"Where should we go?" Laura glanced at Bryce again. "If we leave, we're sitting ducks."

Julio tossed some keys at her.

She caught them. "What do these go to?"

"If you can get to the airport, you can use my plane."

Laura nodded. She knew where it was. It wouldn't take long to get there if they could get their patient up and moving. "Charlie, lend me a hand. Bryce is out on pain killers and he's going to be dead weight for a few more hours."

Charlie walked to the bed and Laura helped position him over Charlie's shoulder. Bryce was not light, and it was evident Charlie might struggle under the soldier's mass.

"We don't have to go far." Laura kissed Julio's cheek. "Bless you, my friend. I owe you big time."

"Yes, amiga, when the time is right." He opened a back door that led to a riverbed. "Keep your heads low. About ten feet from here, you'll enter a tunnel. It will keep you hidden from the bird."

"Thanks." Laura motioned for Eri to step out, then Charlie with Bryce, and she followed.

Quietly, they maneuvered along the rocky ground. The familiar sound of a helicopter buzzed to their right. *God, if you are real, get us out of this.*

She couldn't believe she had prayed. But suddenly, she found comfort in the idea of prayer. Maybe it would help, maybe not. But for now, she was glad to try.

****

Myers woke to pounding on his door. He opened it.

"You have your first assignment. Suit up and meet me at technical," Gunner said, then walked down the hall.

Adrenaline pumped through Myers' system. This was it. The real deal. He prayed he lived to tell Denise about it. With shaking hands, he donned his black uniform, web-vest, combat boots, and a baseball hat. He didn't know if he should be psyched or scared. Maybe he'd wait to see what the others felt. They'd help him gauge the situation. He was brilliant, but sometimes the simplest of things threw him.

He walked to technical and stood amazed. The room was bright and silver. About one dozen or so monitors were attached high around the circular area, glowing with information. A group of people sat at stations, some on headsets, others online. It reminded him of something out of a science fiction movie—like a spaceship.

Gunner waved him over to one of the monitors.

Denise stood behind him.

Meyers could have kissed her. Instead, he winked.

She offered a polite grin, but fear lingered in her eyes. Did she know something he didn't?

"We have a situation." Gunner clicked a remote and pictures of their teammates appeared on the screen. "Four trainees have gone rogue. We need you to find them and terminate."

Myers and Denise exchanged glances. They weren't expecting Denise and him to kill their friends, were they?

Gunner must have assumed what Myers was thinking. "The agency is very aware you have history with these people, but you have two choices: You can either follow through with your assignment, be commended, and live. Or you can fail and die with them."

Myers swallowed. No way could he kill any of them. He'd made his choice. Not that he would voice it here.

"Your weapons can be collected over there." Gunner pointed to a station next to a big metal door. "Once you're ready, you'll be given instructions from Greenstone. Any questions?"

Denise and Myers shook their heads.

"Good luck." Gunner walked to another group of agents.

Denise opened her mouth to speak, but Myers shook his head. "It's not safe," he whispered. "Later."

****

Bryce held his shoulder, willing himself not to pass out. Twice, he'd thrown up. Beads of sweat covered his body, and yet he was freezing.

Charlie placed his boot on a barbed wire fence and helped Bryce and the girls over.

They entered the dark tunnel, and Laura turned on a flashlight. A stream of water ran past their feet, making the ground slippery. The air smelled of day-old garbage and Bryce's stomach convulsed again. He swallowed against the bile in his throat. Perspiration seeped into his eyes and his heart hammered in his ears. Silently, he prayed.

"Up ahead," Laura whispered.

A shaft of light lay in front of them. Bryce hoped it

would lead somewhere safe. With each painful step, he cursed the day he enlisted into the military. How did he ever think he would make it? He couldn't kill anyone. What did he think he would do? Not one of his brighter choices. He just wanted money for college. Money he would never see and a future he would never have.

Laura held up her fist.

The group stopped and knelt down.

She inched forward and peered out the opening, left, then right. "Clear," she whispered, as she crawled out and motioned for them to do the same.

Charlie helped Bryce over the small mound and then joined him.

"Where do we go now?" Eri asked.

The blank expression on Laura's face said it all. She had no idea.

"We just need a place to hide out," Bryce said. "We can't leave the island. We still have to rescue our friends."

A gunshot echoed in the jungle. A bullet whizzed by Bryce's head, plummeting into a tree. He dropped, falling on his wounded shoulder. He cried out in pain.

Laura practically tackled him to cover his mouth. "Sshh…"

The rest fell next to him, looking around for the shooter.

"There!" Charlie aimed his gun, ready to shoot, then pulled back. "No way. You're not going to believe who it is."

Chapter Twenty-One

Myers crept close to Denise. Two other agents were on their heels. He fired his gun as a warning shot to Bryce. *How do I let them know I am on their side?* That when the moment allowed, he would take out his new "team."

At the same time, he had to convince the agents with him that he was following through. If not, surely they'd kill both him and Denise.

"You missed, rookie," a dark-skinned man said to his right.

"I'm nervous." Myers wasn't lying.

"No excuses. Miss again and the next bullet will be in your head." The agent ran forward.

Denise sent Myers a panicked look.

He nodded. *Yeah, I know. If they reached the team first... Wait!* Myers waited until they were both out of earshot and leaned to Denise. He covered the com with his hand and motioned for her to do the same. "We have them pinned. You get the redhead, I'll get the other one."

Her eyes went wide. "You want me to shoot him?"

"Yes."

She bit her bottom lip.

"Denise, we're trained to do this. This shouldn't be a problem."

"I've never killed anyone before."

"It's them, or us and our friends. You choose."

That did it. A determined looked crossed her face. She nodded and looked forward.

They jogged to where the two of them hid behind a tree. Myers held up his gun as if to shoot beyond them. "I see one."

The dark-skinned man peered around the tree.

Myers fired.

The man fell to the ground.

The red head spun to shoot Myers.

Denise shot.

His body crumpled.

Nausea swept over Myers. He prayed he never had to do that again.

****

Laura peered over her shoulder.

"Did you hear that?" Eri asked.

"Shh…" Laura held up her hand and stopped. Yeah, she heard it and it wasn't directed at them. The forest behind them didn't move. All seemed serene. She glanced around, looking for the shooter.

"Agent Black!" someone shouted from the trees.

"Did you hear *that*?" Eri said. "It sounded like Myers."

"There." Bryce pointed to two people running their way. "It looks like Myers and Denise."

"Can we trust them?" Charlie asked.

Laura didn't know. She knew how the agency was—choose between life and loyalty of friends. "Assume nothing."

Myers approached first.

Laura aimed a gun at Myers' head. "Let me see

your hands."

He looked confused.

"Hands, Agent Luther!"

He threw them in the air.

Denise followed and did the same. "We just killed the guys we were with." Her voice wavered. "You're safe now."

"Give me your weapons."

"Laura, maybe we shouldn't assume..." Bryce started to say.

She cocked her gun. "You don't understand. The agency would have them turn on everyone. Pretend to be our friends and then shoot us all."

Myers nodded, handing out his weapon. "Yeah, that's exactly what they wanted us to do. But we killed the two agents following you. If you don't believe me, go look."

Laura examined and sniffed the barrel of his gun. It had recently been fired. "If you betray any of us, I will not hesitate to shoot you. Understand?"

"Yeah, of course," Myers said.

Denise nodded her head like a bobble head doll. The fear in her eyes assured Laura. No way could Denise betray them. The girl looked ready to pass out.

She handed the gun back to him.

The group visibly relaxed.

Charlie slapped Myers on the back. "Nice to have you back, man."

"Yeah..."

Eri and Denise hugged.

"Hey, Denise?" Myers said.

She spun around to face him.

Myers grabbed the back of her head and kissed her

passionately on the mouth.

Eri giggled.

"Whoa," Charlie said.

"We need to keep moving." Laura didn't revel in this reunion. She knew the danger had only begun.

****

Bryce found an indentation in the side of a mountain and pointed it out to Laura. "I need to rest."

She peeked inside the man-made cave and nodded. "Okay, but we'll guard the opening in shifts."

The group trudged in, each face haggard and dirty.

With Myer's help, Bryce was able to get a fire burning deep within the cave. He thought about collecting bugs to eat, but determined that most wouldn't eat them anyway.

He glanced at Laura. Her eyes seemed to glaze over as she stared at the fire.

He scooted next to her. "Are you okay?"

"We have to go back."

"What?"

She slowly shifted her gaze to him. "We need to go back and take them out."

His stomach tightened. "No. We'll end up hurting innocent people."

Laura looked from one team member to the other. "Better a few casualties of war than never knowing freedom, always looking over our shoulders. Is that what you want?"

"I just want to go home and see my little sister," Denise said. "I never treated her right, and I left her with that evil step-witch. I owe her."

Laura shook her head. "You don't get it, do you? You can never return home. Never go anywhere familiar again."

Denise stood. "Why not?"

"Because they will kill everyone you know. Then they'll terminate you," Laura said.

Silence fell like a hot blanket around the space as the reality of their situation became clear.

"What can we do?" Eri whispered, her voice hoarse.

Bryce sat straighter. He refused to hurt anyone. "We can fight the twenty-first century way."

Laura raised an eyebrow. "Explain."

"Expose them?"

"That's suicide."

"And breaking in the compound isn't?"

She stared at him, her emotions hidden behind her "mask."

"Laura?" He touched her arm. "We have to get to the plane."

She sighed and nodded. "We'll figure it out in the morning. Get some rest."

Chapter Twenty-Two

Something snapped and Laura shot awake. Her eyes darted around the dark space. Bryce wasn't there. She grabbed a rifle, cocked it, and crept to the opening. The sun had just begun to peek over the horizon. The morning birds chirped their happy song, having no idea the pyre that surrounded them.

In the new-morning twilight, something moved in the undergrowth below. She peered through the scope on the gun. Several agents scoured the area.

"Where can we…" Charlie said.

"Shh!" Laura hissed with a finger over his lips, then pointed to her eyes, then down to the ground.

Charlie cussed.

"Charlie!" Eri said.

Laura flipped around and glared. "Everyone shut up! We have company."

That did it. Everyone readied his or her weapons.

Bryce came alongside her, peering through his own scope. "How many?"

"Where you been?"

"Sorry, mother nature."

"Four agents that I can see. Plus a local tracker."

"Anyone you know?"

"Yeah. They're all good."

Bryce shifted beside her and groaned.

She glanced at him. His face had more color, but he was still obviously in a bad way. "You okay?"

"I'll live."

"I hope so."

He sighed. "So, what do we do?"

"If we stay here, we're cornered." She glanced back over her shoulder. "You all ready to move?"

They nodded, but their wide-eyed expressions said they would rather curl up into the fetal position than leave this cave.

"Stay low. No unnecessary movement."

"They've got this, Laura," Bryce said. "They were trained by the best."

She met Bryce's stare and offered a tight grin. "Then let's go."

Slowly, they slipped out the cave to the right, staying hunched as they walked. Laura led them up an embankment, not sure where to go next. *Oh no.* Ahead lay a field without any cover.

"This isn't good," Bryce whispered.

"I know." She peered around the jungle, looking for an answer.

"Agent Black," Denise said behind her. "Look."

She followed Denise's pointing finger to a storm drain about ten feet from their position. This area didn't have regular sewers, but they had several drains to keep it from flooding.

Laura nodded.

Everyone ran for the metal tube.

"Están en el dren," the tracker yelled.

"Hurry." Laura pushed them forward, running backward, ready to fire.

Several shots rang overhead, pelting the tree next

to her head. She fired back, then ducked into the drain, and ran. Both sporting injuries, Bryce and Myers struggled to keep pace.

"Charlie and Denise, you keep them going. No one gets left behind." The ground sloshed under Laura's feet. The sound of a waterfall lay up ahead. That was good news. "Get ready to swim."

The panic on Charlie's face was instant. "I can't…"

"I've got you," Eri said. "I used to help my cousins swim."

He nodded and took a deep breath.

One by one, they jumped from the end of the pipe to a river below. Laura was last. She fired a few rounds down the drain to be sure, and then jumped, holding her gun above her head, hoping to preserve it.

The water was cold, dirty, and flowing rapidly. It carried them down too fast to grasp onto anything.

"Charlie!" Eri screamed, panicked. "Oh no! I lost Charlie."

Laura glanced around, fear pitting her stomach. "Charlie!"

Everyone began to sing his name. How could she be so stupid? She knew he couldn't swim. "Charlie!"

"I'm okay." He coughed, clutching onto a nearby rock.

Laura sighed, then swam to him, and clutched onto the rock, too. The rest of them managed to swim to shore and climb out.

Out of the corner of Laura's eye, she spotted four figures dropping into the water behind them.

"They're coming. We have to move." Bryce ripped off his belt and tossed the end to her. Laura wrapped her arm under Charlie's shoulder and helped him paddle to the bank. Bryce helped them ashore with his good arm.

"Thanks." Laura wiped the water from her eyes and pushed her hair back. Her clothing was soaked, and she doubted her gun would fire.

"Ahead!" Denise nodded to an airport just ahead.

Relief washed over Laura. They might make it. "Let's go."

The team took off full speed for the airfield. Laura prayed they could reach it before the agency did. It would be standard procedure to come here and ground all outgoing flights.

Laura dug in her pocket and pulled out the key. The tag read, "Ala-D." Wing D. Where would that be? "We're looking for D."

Bryce saw it first.

They sprinted for the white hangar, purposely ignoring the gang of Hispanic men watching them from Wing A. Hopefully, they wouldn't bother them. But the team must have looked a sight. Wounded, wet uniforms, guns dripping.

The team ran inside to a red Cessna. "Everyone in."

"Can you fly this thing?" Bryce said.

Laura nodded. Though she wasn't about to share that she'd only had one solo mission, and that was over a year ago.

They shut the door and she started the engine. The plane rolled out the open bay door. The sunlight beamed down on the cockpit window, making it hard to see if the road was clear. Laura only hoped the agents weren't on their tail.

She accelerated just in time to spot the men come out of the jungle and lift their guns.

Laura floored it.

Only one shot fired. *Their guns must be water logged, too.*

The plane lifted and they were airborne, but not before taking that one crucial shot. The engine sputtered.

"They hit us." Denise yelled.

"I know. But we're in the air." Laura hit a few gauges. It was the gas tank. "Look, we're putting distance between us. Even if we crash a few miles down the road, we've escaped." She hoped that was true.

"Crash! What?" Myers shook his head. "We can't crash. We'll die."

"Have a little faith." Eri closed her eyes.

The longer they were in the air, the better.

Ahead, the ocean came into view. Suddenly, Laura was grateful for Eri's prayers. A strip of land lay just before the beach. If they missed the strip, they would at least have the water. She started descending. Everyone grabbed onto something, obviously scared.

Charlie started praying, "Our Father, who art in heaven, hallowed be thy name…"

Everyone mirrored his action, finishing The Lord's Prayer.

Laura's heart raced. She hoped she could do this.

Bryce came alongside her. "Live or die, Laura Black, I really do care about you. Maybe even love you."

Tears filled her eyes. "Stop! Not now. I can't concentrate."

"Right." Bryce climbed in the seat next to her and strapped in. "Anything I can do?"

"Hold on." The engine shut out, taking the control out of Laura's hands. They were officially hang-gliding. Laura inhaled deep and prepared herself for an abrupt landing. She aimed for the strip, but knew they probably wouldn't make it. A clump of trees stood in their way. And at the rate of decent, that was more likely their target drop.

The rudder shook in her hand. She held on, trying desperately to steer. Adrenaline coursed through her system. She blinked to focus. The wing smashed against a branch. The plane catapulted against another. Dropping. Slamming against the cluster. Laura's head hit the window. Glass shattered. Everyone screamed. Nose first, it rammed into the ground.

Chapter Twenty-Three

Shade from the trees and squashed windows made it hard to assess the damage. The air smelled of burning fuel. Bryce pushed the dash from his lap and unsnapped his seatbelt. His head spun and his arm throbbed, but he seemed to be okay.

"Laura?"

She didn't answer.

"Is everyone okay?" Eri said.

"I'm okay," Charlie said. "Just a few scratches here and there."

Myers pushed some rubble off his lap, revealing black hair. "Oh no, Denise."

"Laura?" Bryce said again.

Still no answer. He couldn't see her. A small amount of light in the back of the plane made it possible to see the silhouette of the other passengers, but not her. "Laura, honey, come on."

"Denise is hurt bad," Eri said.

Myers held Denise against his chest, crying. "No, please, God."

Bryce knew he should attend to Denise, but not before he knew what happened to Laura. He saw her seat a few feet from where it should be. He leapt at it. She lay unconscious. He touched her face, then her neck for a pulse. It wasn't strong, but it was there.

"Laura." He jiggled her. "Come on, Black, wake up."

She moaned.

Bryce smiled. "That's it. Come on."

"What happened?"

"You crashed." Bryce laughed with relief.

Laura touched her head and winced. "Ow."

Bryce pulled a bandana from his pocket and handed it to her. "I think you bumped your head."

She took it and placed it to her temple. "Is everyone else okay?"

Bryce peered over her shoulder. "No, I think Denise is hurt pretty bad."

Laura pushed up.

"Easy."

"I'm fine. Nothing an aspirin won't cure." Laura crawled through the rubble to where Myers and Eri leaned over Denise. "What's happened?"

Myers tried to answer, but his voice cracked.

"Something sliced a hole in her stomach." Eri lifted her shirt to show Laura the large cut.

She exhaled through her mouth. "We need some material. Anyone have extra clothes on?"

Myers pulled off his t-shirt, leaving him bare-chested. "Here."

"Thanks." Laura balled it up and pushed it on the open wound. "Myers, you keep this pressed firmly on her at all times."

He nodded.

"What do we do now?" Charlie asked.

"Not sure." Laura crept out of the plane and Bryce followed.

They'd landed in a thicket of trees just shy of the

beach.

"We have to get her to a hospital. She won't make it," Bryce said.

"You made it." Laura glanced at him, her expression unreadable.

"I wasn't losing that much blood."

"You lost a lot." Laura faced the water, obviously in deep thought.

What is she thinking? Probably about the incredible odds against them. That she wished she'd never met this team. He didn't blame her if she bolted. Left them for dead.

"We could use some glue on the opening, but we can't move her," Laura said.

"She'll die."

"I'm sorry," Laura choked.

Bryce placed a hand on her shoulder, not sure what to say. They stood there for a while, staring at the breaking waves, without a word.

Myers ducked out of the plane. "We have to do something."

Laura nodded. "Yes, you need to find a doctor. There's a hotel just south of here down the beach. There must be at least one tourist who is a doctor." She offered him gun. "Be persuasive if you have to."

The new agent stared at the gun, not taking it. "Are you sure that's the right—"

"Only as a last resort." She looked at Eri. "You stay with her. Charlie, you're with us."

"What are we going to do?" Bryce asked.

Laura glanced at him. "Follow your plan. We're going to fight S.I.U. with modern day technology. We're going to alert the media."

****

Denise shivered. She couldn't get warm. Her side ached and her head whirled, making her nauseous. Several times she'd vomited. Not that she had anything in her stomach to push out.

"How you doing?" Eri placed a wet bandana on her head.

"I think I'd take jail over this moment any day." She laughed and then cringed at the pain.

"Yeah."

Denise felt herself drifting to sleep.

Eri shook her awake. "Don't you dare give up on me, Kruger."

"No way," Denise mumbled. "Did you see that kiss he gave me?"

"Yes, and Myers would be devastated if you gave up. So no falling asleep." Eri shifted to face her. "That's an order."

"I've never been that great at following orders." Denise coughed and blood splattered on her chin.

Eri jumped up and repositioned the cloth from Denise's forehead, wiping her mouth. "Well, this is one I intend to make you keep."

A branch cracked outside.

Eri scooped up a gun, crept forward, and peeked out.

"Who is it?" Denise whispered.

"Shh!" Eri held up her free hand.

The wait seemed an eternity. Denise strained to hear something, anything that would indicate who approached.

"Freeze!" Eri yelled and stepped out of the plane.

There was a muffled interchange and then Myers,

followed by a man dressed in a Hawaiian shirt, crawled into the body of the plane.

"Denise, this is Doctor Wilson."

"Hi," she said through clenched teeth.

"Hello, Denise. I'm going to take a look now, okay?"

She nodded.

He pulled the shirt away from the wound. The air stung and she grimaced.

"Sorry." He positioned a black bag by her ear and pulled out a needle. "Just relax."

Denise felt a prick, then darkness.

****

Laura crouched low behind a banana tree and waved for her two companions to do the same.

"What is this place?" Bryce asked.

"The only news station I'm aware of." They stared up a two store metal building, topped with several satellite dishes and antennas. "Come on."

He grabbed her arm and yanked her back. "Are you sure about this? What if the media has been bought off to keep the S.I.U. secret."

Laura thought for a moment. "We kidnap one of them. Make them cover the story, and then we ship the tapes back to the U.S."

"We're not kidnapping anyone. That sends the wrong message. Then we'll be running for a different reason."

Laura shrugged. "I suppose."

"Wait." Charlie shifted next to her. "You forget you have me. If we can get a camera out of there, I can make sure the people on the mainland get the full blown tale of the illustrious S.I.U."

That sounded good. Laura nodded.

"Is this enough?" Bryce asked.

"What?"

"Just telling the story. Will they stop?" Suddenly, he looked nervous.

Laura faced him with a furrowed brow. "This was your idea. Remember?"

"I know, it's just..." He blew through his lips, exasperated probably more at himself than the plan. "They could do a major cover up if all we do is expose them."

"True, but you didn't want to fight them. What do you propose?"

The soldier ran a hand over his dirt-covered face, smearing it. His eyes appeared tired, but still beautiful. Laura had the sudden urge to kiss him. Not that this was the appropriate moment to do that. Charlie sat less than a foot away, and they were running for their lives.

"What if we bring a witness from Washington?" Charlie asked.

"Who?"

Charlie shrugged. "I have a great uncle who is a senator. We could try him, maybe?"

"I say we get the camera, and we'll go from there," Laura said. "Sound good?"

Bryce tucked a strand of her hair behind her ear. "If it means we are one step closer to being free from S.I.U. forever, then I'm your man."

She liked the sound of that. "Then let's go."

Chapter Twenty-Four

The studio was fairly empty. Security lights led the way. Bryce tucked a satellite phone in his vest pocket and crept down the dimly-lit hallway. All he needed was a camera and he was out. An employee stood in one of the doorways. Bryce ducked in one of the rooms and behind a metal shelf. He would have to wait for the man to leave.

"No, I'm telling you, Ricardo." The man now stood in the doorway, feet from Bryce's location. "It won't work." He finished his conversation in Spanish.

Bryce inched back behind a shelf filled with black binders, praying the man stayed out. He really didn't want to fight anyone. He just wanted to get the equipment and get out.

"Fine, Ricardo. Bye." The man snapped his cell phone closed and entered. He turned on the light and looked right at Bryce. "What are you doing in here?"

Adrenaline coursed through Bryce, and without thinking, he jumped up and aimed a gun at the man's head. "Taking you prisoner. Where are your cameras?"

****

Myers paced along the ocean shore, staring at the rocky sand. How much longer would the doctor be? When the portly man emerged from the wreckage, Myers ran to his side.

"How is she?"

"She has lost too much blood, young man," Doctor Wilson said. "I really think you should get her to a hospital. I can take her myself."

Myers shook his head. He feared for his friend's life, but he knew that wasn't an option either. They would be looking for all of them there. "Doctor, I really appreciate your help. But we can't risk it."

"I know I didn't ask who you were, but I can tell you kids are in some sort of trouble." He snapped his bag closed. "Why don't you let me help you?"

Eri sighed. "We couldn't risk your life, sir. It's just too dangerous."

The man laughed. "My life? That's a little dramatic, don't you think?"

Myers pulled back his coat and revealed a gun tucked in his waistband. "You have no idea what we're up against."

He lifted his hands, shaking his head. "Young man, you need to toss that gun away and let me help you."

"Tell him," Eri said.

Myers met her stare. "He won't believe us."

She shrugged. "Doesn't matter now."

He glanced back to the doctor and sighed. "Fine. About five months ago, we were kidnapped by an agency to be trained as assassins. Yesterday morning, we escaped and now we're on the run. If they catch us, we'll die."

The man looked from Eri to Myers, obviously trying to figure out if they were full of it or not. "I see."

"Told you he wouldn't believe us." Myers closed his coat, hiding his gun again.

The doctor backed up a few feet. "It's not that I

don't believe you."

"But?" Eri matched his steps.

"But…" The doctor reached in his bag and pulled out a derringer pistol. "I'm afraid you kids were right."

"What?" Myers heart skipped. He peered back at Denise, more for her life than his own. "You're with them?"

"I work in the S.I.U. infirmity. You don't remember me?"

Eri visibly swallowed.

Myers couldn't breathe. This man would shoot them and that would be it. But more than fear, he felt anger. How could a man who swore to save lives, end them so easily. "What's your problem, man? Don't you value life at all? You're a physician. Don't you take an oath or something to save lives?"

Doctor Wilson chuckled. "I was ten when they took me from an orphanage. My science skills were off the charts, so they trained me to be a doctor rather than an assassin. The only oath I ever took was to be a loyal solider to the agency."

"But I found you on vacation at the hotel." Eri took a small step toward him. "I thought they don't allow you to ever leave."

"When you get to my age, they know where your loyalties lie." He rubbed his sweating forehead with the back of his hand holding the gun. "Notice I didn't vacation in the Bahamas. I was still on their island. That will never change."

Myers exhaled aloud. "Doesn't that bother you? Don't you want a better life?"

The doctor faced him, eyes narrowed, face crimson. "This is a great life. They put me through medical school. I ask for nothing, they give me everything. They are the only family I can remember."

"You lost your parents." It was statement, not a question. Eri frowned. "I'm sorry."

"Yes. And I hated living in the foster system. The people allowed to care for me were barbaric. Greenstone saved me from all that. Gave me a purpose. A reason to live on this god-forsaken world."

"I'm an orphan, too, but I did not wish this life for myself. I wasn't given that option." A small tear made it down Eri's face, cutting through the dirt on her cheeks. She didn't bother to wipe it away. "I wanted that option. I *want* that option now."

"But here you have a higher purpose. You're serving your country." The doctor shook his head. "Don't you understand that?"

"By killing people." Myers face burned. Anger he hadn't felt for a while surfaced, boiling, ready to ignite. He thought of Denise, the girl he may love, barely holding onto life and the organization that refused to let them live. Something snapped inside. He charged the doctor with all that was in him, yelling as he did.

The whole thing played out in slow motion.

The doctor fired.

Myers dodged it and tackled the man to the ground. They wrestled for the gun. The doctor got it first and aimed at Myers's head. The piercing sound of a gun vibrated in the jungle. Doctor Wilson fell back, blood pouring from a hole above his eye.

Myers stared in shock. He patted his own body. No holes. He pushed the man off him and scrambled to stand. He peered to his side.

Eri remained frozen with her arms out, smoke

seeping from the gun's barrel in her hand.

"Good shot," Myers said.

"I prayed."

"Thank you." Myers smiled, and then looked up with folded hands. "And thank you."

"You're welcome." She finally lowered her arms. "And I'm sure He would say the same thing."

Myers laughed. He grabbed the doctor's gun and tucked it in the waistband of his pants. Most likely, there was only one more bullet. The size of the derringer didn't promise much more. "We need to get out of here in case he informed them somehow."

"Leave?" Eri glanced back to the plane. "But how can we move Denise?"

"We'll make a stretcher from a part of the airplane."

Eri nodded and they went to work.

****

Laura took a drink from her canteen and then almost choked on it. Coughing, she tried to understand why Bryce walked their way with a gun held to a Hispanic man's head.

Bryce led him to the place where they hid and ordered the man down.

The man trembled as he fell to his knees. He began begging in Spanish.

"What are you doing?" Laura asked, glaring at Bryce.

"He saw me. I had to think fast." Bryce sighed. "What else could I do?"

Nothing. Laura knew. "Fine. Maybe he can help us."

"What is this?" The man rubbed his arm, looking

188

from Charlie, to Bryce, to Laura, back to Bryce. "You're just a bunch of kids."

"I'm not a kid." Laura popped out the magazine on her gun, checked it for rounds then shoved it back in its slot. "We have a situation, sir, and we need your help. What is your name, please?"

"You don't know me?"

"Should I?"

The man laughed. "I'm the local weatherman. My name is Leo Gomez."

"Sorry, I haven't been allowed to watch the news for almost nine years." Laura perused the trees and ground, searching for something to bind the man's hands. "See I was kidnapped by a bad company and brought here to be a killer. This is the first time since then that I've been on my own. You're going to help me keep it that way."

He didn't respond.

Bryce crossed his arms and squatted in front of the man. "Aren't you a little curious what she means, Leo?"

He pursed his lips together and stared Bryce in the eye. "I assume you're talking about S.I.U."

Laura's heart skipped. She glanced at Bryce. *How does he know that? Is he one of them?* After all, they hadn't left the island yet, and anything was possible. Years of service taught her that.

Bryce's expression soured. He aimed the gun at Leo's ear and cocked it. "How do you know that name?"

It took a minute for the weatherman to respond— either shaken by the gun or maybe wondering if he should say anything. Laura would have hesitated too.

Telling the truth never offered peace. Leo focused on the dirt as he spoke. "My father worked for S.I.U. my entire life. It's how we got to the island. But he was never *one of them*."

"And he told you. Does that sound right to you?"

Leo's eyes locked with Laura's. "When I was about thirteen, my father quit. Said something about having a bad back and needed to change professions. They threatened him with his life and told him he could change jobs, but he could not leave the island. We stayed, but they were always watching us."

Laura bit the side of her cheek, willing herself not to cry. The sudden influx of emotion annoyed her. She didn't like that she could feel anything. Blocking emotion made it easier to function in these circumstances. "So, you've been a prisoner your entire life, so to speak?"

"They killed my father five years ago when he tried to attend my grandmother's funeral in Oaxaca."

Laura couldn't hold back. She turned away. Not sadness, but rage made her want to cry.

A hand touched her shoulder. It was Bryce. She didn't like him to see her so weak. Why did Leo's story hurt her so much? She wiped at her tears, angrily. Proof once again existed that S.I.U. destroyed lives. They had to be stopped.

She looked at Bryce. Her expression felt hard. "They will pay."

Chapter Twenty-Five

Myers' back and arms ached from hours of carrying Denise. But he wouldn't stop. She meant too much to him.

"You want me to take her for a while?" Eri asked.

He shook his head. There was no way Eri's four-foot-eight, ninety-pound waif body could lug this airplane door and Denise. He didn't want to imply she couldn't, but he knew Eri would do it just to prove him wrong. This was his burden to bear. He would do it.

"Look." Eri pointed to a small tin shack with a picture of a dog and cat drawn on the side and the words, Clínica Veterinaria. "Maybe we can get medical supplies."

"For dogs?"

She laughed. "I promise…there will be something we can use."

"Okay, but let's wait until we have some cover. The sun should set pretty soon." Myers shifted the makeshift gurney around and pushed it behind a boulder.

Denise moaned.

"Sorry, babe." He folded to the ground next to her and pulled out his canteen. She looked frail and possibly close to death. It hurt his heart. He unscrewed the lid, lifted her head gently, and placed it to her lips.

"You need to drink some water."

The clear liquid poured out into her mouth. Some of it went down her throat, but most of it dribbled on her chin.

"You're too good to me," she wheezed.

He touched her lips. They were still warm. "Shh. Save your strength."

"I may not have much time left. I need to say this."

He shook his head. No goodbyes. He refused to believe she might not make it. He needed her.

"I think I love you," she whispered.

His eyes bore into hers and it choked him up. *God, please don't let her die. I really need her.* "Me, too."

A partial smile flittered across her face.

He leaned and kissed her lightly on the mouth. "Now, save your strength. We're almost to help."

The sky grew dark, and Myers decided it was time. He instructed Eri to guard their approach while he drug Denise to safety.

His partner ran ahead and scouted the area, then waved for him to follow. He couldn't move too fast, because the scraping of the metal on dirt echoed in the street. When he cleared the road, Eri broke through a window and opened the door.

Dogs barked and rammed their cages down the hall. Most likely the owners lived on the premises. Myers prayed the noise wouldn't bring them back. "Find some tranquilizers. Enough for Denise and all those dogs. Hurry."

"You're going to give Denise a tranquilizer?"

"I need to sew her up. I want her relaxed and unaware."

Eri nodded, then opened and closed glass

cupboards, rummaging through bottles. "They're all in Spanish. What would it be called?"

"Something that looks like Diazepam or Lidocain."

Eri glanced at him. "Do I want to know why you know the names of drugs for dogs?"

He laughed. "Lots of the guys break into Vet Hospitals back home to steal them. It's a free high."

Her eyebrows rose.

"Not me."

"Of course."

He spotted two clear bottles that read, "Lidocaína."

"Score!" He handed them out to Eri. "Now we need some needles."

"Let me guess…they also shot up and you only witnessed how to do it."

He rolled his eyes and started rummaging through the drawers. "For your information, one of my foster brothers had diabetes. I helped him a few times."

"Sure." She smiled.

A few needles were in a drawer; he loaded them up and handed one to Eri. "So, you want the dogs or her."

"Dogs."

It was Myers's turn to be surprised. "Really?"

"I can stick a dog. I hate them. Not my friend."

He nodded and handed her a few more.

Eri grabbed them and walked down the hall.

Myers leaned over Denise. Her breathing was shallow, her skin searing. Time was running short. He pushed up her sleeve and poked the needle into her arm.

She flinched, but continued to sleep.

He lifted her shirt above the wound. It looked bad, but the blood had started to clot some. During his search for medicine, he'd found towels, surgical thread, and a semicircular needle. Due to being a skateboarder, he'd watched lots of doctors giving him stitches over the years. He was pretty sure he could do this.

He wet the towels with hot water and alcohol, and then cleaned the area around the wound.

Eri returned and helped him clean the area above her bra line.

He faced away, his arms crossed. "Any trouble with the dogs?"

"Not really." She held out her arm. A red scratch ran from her wrist to her elbow. "One got me, but I repaid him good."

Myers laughed.

"Why don't I remove her shirt?"

Myers pressed his lips together, not turning around. "I have to sew her and that would make my hand shake."

She laughed. "Fine. Over there are some scrubs." She pointed behind the door. "I'll put this on her after we're finished, and in the meantime, I'll cover her with the towels."

He agreed and Eri made it happen.

Once he'd finished sewing her up, he covered the cut with iodine and a bandage. "I think she's lost a lot of blood. I really hope she'll be okay."

"We'll have to pray she will be." Eri patted his shoulder before tossing the bloody rags in a hamper. "Did you find any antibiotics?"

The door banged open and they both jumped.

"¿Cuál es usted cabritos que hacen adentro aquí?" A woman in a white robe stood poised in the doorway with a shotgun cradled in her arms.

Myers and Eri threw their hands in the air.

"What did she say?" Eri whispered.

"Wants to know why we're in here." Myers forced a fake smile. *How can I grab the gun tucked in the back of my pants?*

"My amiga…" Eri pointed to where Denise lay on several towels on the floor. "Is, uh…"

"Mi amigo está lastimado y necesitamos ayuda," Myers said.

"What does that mean?" Eri asked.

"My friend is hurt and we needed help."

The woman glanced to Denise, but kept her gun trained on Myers. "Al hospital, no aquí."

"You're right. It's not a hospital. We'll go." Myers reached down to scoop Denise up, making sure Eri could see the gun when he bent over. "Usted tiene razón. Iremos."

"Stay!" the woman said in a thick accent, bobbing the rifle back and forth between the two of them. "No move."

Myers felt a slight tug at the back of his pants. Eri had confiscated the gun.

"We didn't mean to bother you." She nudged him forward.

The woman stepped back and leveled the gun. "No move. Policía here."

Myers shot a panicked look to Eri. They couldn't have the police coming here. That was a death sentence. Who knew how much S.I.U. paid them to do their bidding. "Eri, do something," he hissed under his breath.

"Step to your left," she whispered back.

Myers moved.

Eri leapt forward, tossed the gun to Myers, then

kicked the rifle out of the woman's hands, and ended with it aimed at her face. The woman, startled, fell to the ground, hands up, trembling. "Por favor. Por favor."

"We're not going to hurt you. We just want to go." Eri nodded to Myers to pass her and the woman.

"Tie her up or something," he said.

Eri nodded and pulled her inside.

"And for the record, Eri, that was awesome."

She smiled. "Thanks."

Myers rushed out the door with Denise cradled in his arms, to find cover in the jungle and their friends.

****

Laura held her fist in the air and the group stopped. "We'll camp here."

Bryce poked his head over her shoulder.

A chill swept through her as his breath warmed the side of her neck. She closed her eyes for a second to will away the way he made her feel.

"But that's the enemy," Bryce whispered. A group of men dressed in black uniforms guarded a gate less than a hundred yards from their position. "Are you sure it's safe? We're awfully close."

"Exactly. They'd never suspect we'd camp here." She motioned for everyone to sit behind a broken brick wall. "We just have to be quiet and no fires." Laura put her back against the rough surface and dug in her pack. Her eyes burned. *When was the last time I slept?*

Bryce smiled and sat next to her.

What would she do with this man? She knew she loved him, but should they survive this crazy mission, he had another woman waiting for him back home. Sure he said Shawna didn't matter, but if the situations were reversed, Laura would lie, too. He needed her to escape.

"How are we going to plan our attack if we can't talk?" he whispered.

She faced him. Her mouth was only millimeters from his. "I, um…" Her heart pounded so hard, she hoped he couldn't hear it.

"Yes?"

She licked her lips.

"Agent Black?" Charlie said.

Laura turned her head away to face Charlie. "What's up?" her voice cracked.

He knelt next to her. "What are we going to do next?"

Laura glanced at Bryce, then to Leo and back to Charlie. Motioning, she waved them all close, ready to explain her plan.

****

Myers, Eri, and Denise walked for a good hour without talking. Finally, Myers held up his hand to rest. His arms were numb from carrying Denise. He set her against a log and tucked his jacket under her head.

Eri sat with her back to them, probably to protect the perimeter.

"How do we know where to go?" Denise rasped.

Myers sat next to her and offered his canteen. "We don't, but we know approximately what direction the compound is. That's where Laura will eventually go."

"I thought she wouldn't kill them."

Myers and Eri exchanged glances.

"I don't think that's the plan. They are taking in TV cameras." He wiped a strand of hair from her forehead. "How are you feeling?"

"Like someone stuffed something in my stomach." She laughed, but immediately cringed.

"Careful." He pulled her head into his lap and stared at her. Sweat beaded on her forehead, her pale face lay almost green, her eyes purple and sunken, and yet, he still found her attractive. Never had he felt so much for a person. He'd do whatever it took to keep her safe. Alive. "I love you."

Tears filled her eyes.

"Oh, I'm sorry. I didn't mean to make you cry."

She shook her head, smiling. "No, I'm not crying for that. I just—"

He kissed her cheek.

"I love you, too."

He moved his lips to her mouth. They were cool, but soft.

A twig snapped in the jungle to their left.

Eri must have heard it too. She crept to his side and leveled her weapon to the sound.

Myers pulled his gun out and cocked the trigger. "Do you see anything?" he whispered.

She lifted two fingers, then pointed with one ahead.

"I need to set you down." Myers positioned Denise behind him and handed her the derringer the doctor had carried. "Just in case they get past me."

She nodded.

Two men dressed in khaki shorts and T-shirts walked their way speaking in Spanish. From what Myers could translate, they were college guys discussing cute girls. Neither appeared to be armed. Myers prayed they didn't see their position. He'd hate to involve them.

Myers hunched closer to the ground.

Eri suddenly jumped up and ran to where they stood.

"No!" Myers hissed, but she ignored him. *What is she doing?*

"Excuse me."

The men turned and smiled, flirtatious.

"Hola, chica," the smaller of the two said.

One of the guys was skinny and probably spent more time in a library than in sports, but the bigger of the two looked more menacing. He had cropped black hair and a scar by his left eye. Muscles bulged from his white T-shirt. He would be harder to take.

"I wondered if you could tell me where the road is?"

"No habla Ingles," the smaller one said.

"You're American?" the bigger one said in a thick accent. "I'm Antonio. This Miquel."

"Nice to meet you." She smiled. "So, do you know where the road is?"

The two men looked at each other, then back to her. Antonio stepped toward her.

Eri giggled nervously. "Do you understand my question?"

Both men moved inside her personal bubble.

Myers prepared his weapon.

"Look," Eri backed up. "I guess you can't understand me, so I'm just going to go." She started backing to Myers's position. Antonio touched her butt.

Myers jumped up, ready to shoot.

Eri stepped on Antonio's foot, grabbed his wrist, flung him like a sack of potatoes to the ground, and slammed her fist into his temple. His body fell limp.

Myers fell back to his position, hoping Miquel didn't see him.

She glanced at Miquel. "You want a turn?"

Miquel held up his hands and backed away. When he stood at least ten feet away, he spun on his heel and ran away.

Antonio moaned.

Eri kicked him the face.

He passed out.

She ran back to Myers. "Let's go."

Myers stared at her, dumbfounded. She really was built for this line of work. When she'd first come to S.I.U., he thought she was the weakest link. He now realized, she may be the strongest. She reminded him of Laura.

"That was amazing."

Eri offered a closed-mouth smile. "Yeah, well, he had it coming."

"I can see why you don't really need a gun. You're kind of like your own weapon."

She grinned, shyly.

Myers scooped Denise back up and they began walking again in the direction of danger.

Chapter Twenty-Six

Bryce stared at Laura as she slept. Never had she looked that peaceful. Every day for the past decade, she must have lived with the stress of staying alive. He couldn't imagine the horror she'd experienced. But something inside her had obviously been locked away. In order to function, she must have buried compassion—and the ability to love. He saw it today when she started to cry. She was like ice cream on a hot day. He was her sun and she was beginning to melt. *Wow, that was cheesy.* He smiled.

"Bryce?"

He blinked. "Yeah?"

"Why are you staring at me?"

Caught. Great. Did he lie? "Um, I guess I'd never seen you so peaceful."

She rubbed her eyes and sat up. "You're weird, you know that?"

"I do now." He diverted his gaze to the jungle. A flicker of light caught his eye. He grabbed her shoulder.

"What is it?"

"I don't know."

The others were sleeping.

"Do we wake them?" Bryce pointed to Charlie.

Laura shook her head and grabbed her gun.

Bryce quietly flipped the safety from his weapon

and crept beside her behind a boulder. A loud crack of thunder boomed overhead, and rain instantly fell in sheets. Great, now they wouldn't have a clear view of the target. He pulled his cap tighter over his face and squinted.

"They are wearing S.I.U. uniforms." Laura readied her weapon.

He wiped the water from his eyes. Something told him not to shoot. "Can we fire a warning shot?"

"Not if they are company guards. That will alert everyone, and then we'll all be dead."

He could barely hear her over the rain. "So what do we do?"

"Wake up, Charlie. We're going to surround them and take them out one-by-one without gun fire."

His kind of idea. No killing.

Bryce slipped to Charlie's side, put a hand over his mouth, and shook him.

Charlie leapt up, eyes wide.

Bryce put a finger to his lips and held up his gun, then motioned with his head to the jungle.

His friend nodded and grabbed his weapon.

"We need to try and take them out without our guns," Bryce whispered in his ear. "The noise will alert the guards at the gate."

"I wish we had Eri. She's better at martial arts than even Agent Black." Charlie slung his rifle over his shoulder and crouched next to Laura. "So, what's the plan?"

"We'll go in different directions and take them out."

Bryce ran to the left. The ground sloshed underneath his feet, making it hard to walk. He crawled forward and positioned himself behind a tree.

A woman approached.

He jumped out and grabbed her.

An elbow hit his jaw, sending him back a few feet. But not before he yanked her ankle, sending her with him. She somersaulted up to a standing position. He jumped up, ready to swing.

"Bryce?" the woman said.

He wiped his eyes. "Eri?"

She ran into his arms and gave him a wet hug. "I'm so glad we found you."

He pulled back. "How's Denise?"

She pointed to where Laura stood with Myers, who held Denise in his arms.

Bryce walked to their sides. "How is she?"

"I'll live, I think," Denise said. Her face was bit paler than usual, but she looked better than the last time he saw her.

"Let's get you out of the rain," Laura said. "We have a makeshift tent just ahead."

They crawled to the brick wall, where Bryce had made cover out of banana tree leaves—something he'd learned in his special forces training.

Laura held out a canteen. "Fill these, Charlie. The rain is our friend."

He nodded and gathered everyone's taffy-colored container.

"So, what's the plan?" Myers asked, once Denise was situated.

"We wait until dark, then we sneak Leo here into the camp with the camera. We shoot footage of everything. Our objective is to keep Leo alive long enough to tape every square foot of the place." Laura wiped her gun with a piece of cloth. "Eri, you'll be the scout. You deal with anyone who can be taken out without a gun."

Eri nodded.

"Myers and Bryce, you are with me. We will protect the perimeter. Keep the guards off Leo. Charlie, you're the cameraman."

Charlie smiled. That was obviously a relief. Bryce wished he had the same assignment. Then he wouldn't have to risk killing anyone. But then, he knew Laura was right. He had the most field experience, the most training. His injury could be an issue; but he knew how to block out the pain. Whether he liked it or not, he was her best man.

"Are you okay?" she whispered in his ear.

He closed his eyes and nodded.

"I know you don't want to shoot anyone, but if you don't, then someone you care about might get hurt."

Bryce faced her. "I know."

"Do you?" She exhaled. "I'm not just talking about us. I'm talking about Shawna, too."

Bryce cringed. Not because he feared for Shawna's life, but because Laura brought it up. "Laura, I don't want Shaw…"

She touched her finger to his lips. "I just want you to understand the importance of your decision in the field. If you can't pull the trigger, then I need you to stay here."

"I won't let you down." He held her gaze, hoping she could see he loved *her*.

She nodded and turned to the group. "Ready?"

"What about Denise?" Myers asked.

Laura hadn't thought about her. She wasn't used to

caring for fallen soldiers. In S.I.U., they left them to their fate. "Hide her. She should be okay if the enemy can't find her. Leave her water and a gun. We shouldn't be gone more than a few hours."

Myers looked unsure.

"It's okay, Myers," Denise said. "I'll be fine."

He knelt by her side and kissed her slow.

Bryce glanced at Laura. He could tell she saw the exchange as well. How was he going to convince her she was the woman he wanted? Shawna was no longer his concern. The girl he'd once cared about had already mourned his death. That chapter was now closed.

"You with us?" Laura asked.

Bryce nodded. "Let's do it."

****

The group fanned out in different directions like players at a football game, leaving Charlie and Leo to run the field goal. Charlie held the camera in one hand and a pistol in the other. His pulse quickened the closer they got.

Ahead, he saw the silhouettes of men dropping to the ground. Then one strobe from Laura's flashlight meant it all was clear. "Let's go."

Leo visibly swallowed, his eyes as big as moons.

"You okay?" Charlie whispered to him.

"I grew up hearing stories about this place, you know?" Leo clutched a gun to his chest, his knuckles white, his hand shaking. "I know what they do to traitors."

Charlie gave a tight smile. "Not just to traitors, man. To everyone."

They walked to the entrance and glanced around. Everything appeared clear. No longer could he see his team, but that was likely a good thing. If he didn't see them, then most likely neither did the enemy. Just ahead was the main compound. How they would get in there to shoot footage was a mystery. Laura said they were to get in and get out, and the team would have their backs. The plan didn't seem possible. None of it did.

It was clear Bryce didn't want to kill anyone. But that decision could cost all of them their lives.

Charlie propped the camera on his shoulder and nodded to Leo.

Leo swung around and held the mic to his mouth. "I'm Leo Gomez live at the Secret Intelligence compound on an island that many think is deserted, the Island of Escondido Mona. What you're about to see is quite disturbing and highly classified. The grounds here have been inhabited for decades by a private agency set up to train kids as young as ten to be assassins."

A gun fired behind them and Leo jumped.

Charlie rotated his finger in circles, indicated he should continue.

"It may be hard to believe, but I promise you, this is very real. My life is in danger just for being here." Leo pulled the mic to his chest. "Follow me, and I will show you this horror for yourself."

The two of them hunched over and started for the compound. Charlie kept the camera rolling and Leo narrated.

"This is the main compound where the soldiers live and plan missions," Charlie whispered, and Leo repeated it into the mike.

Charlie punched in the code; they slipped around a metal door and into an elevator. Laura stood over a fallen guard. She caught Charlie's eye and nodded.

When the door opened, Bryce and Eri fought a pair of guards. Charlie pulled Leo through them. They walked down a dark corridor to another door. Beyond it was the main control room.

"We should wait here for our team."

Leo didn't object. His face was mint green. Charlie hoped he didn't puke or pass out. He patted his shoulder. "You're doing great."

Laura ran down the hall and stopped to look through a small glass window. "There aren't a lot of guards in this room, but it's filled with agents doing their work. One push of the button and 100 guards could be in this room in seconds."

That did it. Leo turned to the side and expelled his dinner on the floor.

Charlie cringed. "So what do we do now?"

Eri ran up behind them.

Where was Myers?

As if she read his thoughts, Eri said, "Myers is in the control room."

Laura glanced at her watch. "In about thirty seconds, this entire place is going to go pitch dark. Charlie, I need you to hand Bryce the camera so you can disable the alarms."

All too happy to do something that used his skills, Charlie handed off the camera. "Where do I go?"

"There's a room just off the main floor to the left. Look for a door with a yellow circle on it. That's the control room."

"Everyone put your night vision goggles on. Bryce, flip the camera to night vision."

"How do I do that?" he asked.

Leo shifted next to him and hit a switch.

"You film like there's no tomorrow. Our window will be small." Laura faced Eri. "You and I will take out as many as we can before the lights pop back on."

"Won't that be bad publicity on the film?" Leo asked. "I mean...you want people to see this place for what it is. If you are taking them out, what are they seeing?"

Laura seemed to ponder that a moment.

"Can't we go in, take the footage, and get out, without them ever knowing we were here?" Bryce asked.

"We can try." She locked eyes with Eri. "We'll hold back, but if you see any danger to our team..."

"I'll take them. Got it."

Black out.

The people in the room started panicking, some screamed.

Charlie turned his goggles on and the room appeared green. How he was supposed to find a yellow circle was beyond him. He pushed past his group in search of the control room. He hoped he could find it and turn off the switch in time.

A room lay ahead. He ran for it, tripping over something. He squatted down. A body lay on the floor. His heart raced. *Forget the body and keep running.* He shot for a door with a big circle on it and shut himself in. A computer monitor and several control panels lay against the far wall. Suddenly, he realized the dumbest thing; without power, he couldn't do this job.

****

Bryce hoped Charlie was able to disconnect the alarms, because when the lights popped back on, he and

Leo would be exposed.

The green hue probably didn't do the room justice on camera, but Leo whispered commentary in the camera as they moved around the room. He hoped the world would see this place for what it was, but he doubted it would.

Laura came alongside Bryce. "Let's go. We'll finish up in the barracks."

They hurried for the exit.

Lights flashed on and blinded Bryce. He yanked off his goggles and swung around. A room full of teenagers glared at him. He lowered the camera.

Laura bit her lip, obviously assessing the situation.

The alarm sounded and red lights flashed around the room.

"Run!" Laura yelled.

He didn't have to be told twice.

The team took off down the hall they'd entered through. The sound of thumping feet echoed down the hall. The "100 soldiers" were on their way. Bryce tossed the camera into Leo's arms and cocked his weapon. "God, get us out of this and I promise I go into ministry or something."

Eri giggled in front of him.

"What?"

"I can just see your resume."

He grunted.

Bullets whizzed down the hall, hitting off the metal walls. Bryce pulled Leo to the ground and hid behind a pillar. "How many?"

"About ten or so," Laura said. "But they'll be behind us soon."

Bryce locked and loaded his weapon.

Laura and Eri fired several rounds.

The enemy fired back.

Bryce took a deep breath. This was it. Live targets. He swung his weapon around and fired. A person dropped. Bryce physically felt ill. *But this is self-defense.* He continued to coach himself as he fired again.

Bullets started flying from the other direction. They were officially surrounded. "Laura?"

"Leo, get that camera on!" Laura yelled.

Sparks hit by Bryce's head. He flipped to the other side of the pillar and fired again. His gun jammed. He quickly removed the magazine, hit it on the ground, and shoved it back in his weapon.

The gunfire in the hall was almost deafening. His ears rang. He shot again, this time successfully.

"Come on," Laura said. "They only have a few left in front of us. Run when you can and don't stop firing."

Laura didn't wait. She dashed ahead, firing like Rambo. Bryce couldn't help but be amazed by this woman. In seconds, she dropped all four of the guards who were left.

The team leapt from their hiding places and rushed toward her. Suddenly, the camera toppled to Bryce's side. Confused, he picked it up and glanced back. *Oh no!* Leo lay on the ground, covered in blood.

Bullets continued to ricochet off the walls.

Bryce tucked his gun in his waistband, grabbed Leo by the back of his shirt, and dragged him toward the exit. When he reached Laura, he handed her the camera.

"We can't take him. He'll slow us down," she said.

Bryce shook his head, disgusted. "You don't leave

a fallen man behind."

"This isn't the Army, Bryce. Things are different here."

"Maybe for you, but not for me." He slung Leo over his shoulder and ran for the trees. Maybe if he hid the body for now, he could grab him later.

The sound of gunfire echoed behind him. Bryce laid Leo down behind a bush.

The man's eyes squinted at half-mast. "Thank you."

"For what?"

"For letting me help avenge my father."

Emotion clutched Bryce's throat. He nodded. "I'm sorry we couldn't get you home unscathed."

"I knew it would end like this the minute you kidnapped me."

A pang of guilt shot through Bryce's stomach. *How could he bring this innocent man to this place?* "I'm sorry."

"Don't be. I'll be seeing my father soon." Leo smiled, and then his body fell limp.

Bryce wiped at his tears, closed the man's eyes, and stood. In the distance, the war continued. He refused to see another man from his team die today. He ran ahead; ready to win.

****

Laura saw Charlie enter. She thrust the camera in his hands. "Shoot. We have to get out of here. This was a stupid idea."

Charlie swung the camera around and began filming.

"How'd you find us?" Eri asked Myers when he ran in.

"I followed the sound of bullets."

They filmed the barracks and then followed Laura down to a secret tunnel. "They know about this place, too, so you can bet we're not in the clear."

The dark passageway smelled of mold and decay. Creatures rushed passed their feet. She glanced back to Myers, hoping he didn't notice. "Put your night goggles on, but keep your eyes straight ahead."

The team obeyed.

"How long before they storm the barracks?" Bryce asked.

"Minutes, if they haven't already." Laura ran down the long, narrow corridor to a metal-rung ladder. She quickly climbed up and punched in a code. It didn't budge. She tried again. Nothing.

"Oh no!"

"What?" Bryce came next to her and looked at the pad. "They change the code?"

"Yes." *What do we do now? I've led them to a dead-end.*

"I'm on it," Charlie said.

Myers laughed. "No way. I'm way better at this than you."

"Says who?" Charlie spat.

"My I.Q. scores."

Laura let out an exasperated sigh. "Work together! Those men will not care who's the bigger genius. You all die the same way."

"Point taken," Myers said.

Charlie made room for Myers.

A metal door creaked open down the passageway. Laura peered over her shoulder at the two guys. "They're coming. Hurry."

Eri, Bryce, and Laura readied their guns.

"I got it," Charlie said.

"We got it." Myers touched Laura's shoulder. "Let's go."

They piled out the hole. They would have cover for about ten feet, and then they'd be exposed again.

Charlie swung the hatch closed and Laura shot the pad. That would hopefully keep the guards from following.

Searchlights soared across the ground. Furious dogs barked next to running feet. Soldiers surrounded the perimeter on all sides.

"We're trapped!" Charlie said, the panic evident in his voice. "We'll die for nothing."

Another emotion begged to seize Laura—fear. She pursed her lips, not allowing it to take hold. She'd been in worst skirmishes over the years. "Our mission hasn't changed. We have to get that camera out of here."

"We should get to Leo's body," Bryce said.

Laura laughed. "Are you serious?"

"No, he's right." Charlie held up the camera. "Leo is a big reporter here. If we show that these people killed him, it could go a long way. We should shoot his body."

Bryce grimaced.

"I meant, film his body. Sorry. Bad word choice."

What to do? He was right. But running back to where they had come from was suicide. Troops littered the area. "Not everyone. Charlie, you and Bryce will go. The rest of us will make a path for you to leave. Aim for the outside wall."

Bryce touched her elbow. "Thank you."

A passionate shock ran up her arm. She offered a

tight smile. "Sure."

Once the area appeared open, the team split up. Eri, Myers, and Laura sprinted to the stone barrier. Two men fired. One just missed Laura's shoulder. She fired back. One fell. Myers rushed the second one. The two plummeted to the ground. Myers swung. Bones snapped in the man's jaw. The soldier withdrew a knife. Myers grabbed his wrist. The man pushed it to Myer's neck. Myers face red, pushed back.

A gun fired.

The man dropped, dead.

Myers scrambled to stand.

Eri lowered her weapon.

"Thanks," Myers said, winded.

She knocked shoulders with him. "What are friends for?"

They ran further down the wall. A man jumped out and pulled Eri to the ground. A second later four or five encased them. The group fought them off. Laura kicked a man in the face, then flipped around to stab another in the stomach. A man jumped on her back, then wrapped the crook of his arm at Laura's throat. It was hard to breath. Laura gasped, ready to pass out. She ran backward as hard as she could, ramming the man into the wall. His hold lightened enough for Laura get a second wind. She yanked the man off her back and tossed him against a tree. He seemed dazed. Laura located her pistol on the ground. She snatched it up and held it at the man's head, ready to fire.

He glanced up.

Her heart stopped. *Harding?* Her partner for the last two years. Did she fire? Could she fire? She knew his story. Where he came from. He never wished for this life either. Did it end here?

"Black, what are you doing?"

"I can't do this anymore. They tried to have me killed."

He shuffled back and stood.

Partner or no partner, no way did she trust him. She kept the gun trained at his chest.

"You know there is no escape," Harding said. "They'll find you and when they do, you're dead."

"We know. That's why we brought a camera," Laura said.

He raised an eyebrow.

"Yeah, we filmed the facility. We showed their dead newscaster. And we will all be interviewed." She relaxed her hand a bit. "We will expose them. Then we'll all be free."

He stared at her, unbelieving.

"Say something."

"It's suicide."

"Don't you get it, Harding? I was sent on a death mission this morning. I wasn't supposed to return. I would have been dead either way."

"I know."

"You knew?"

He dropped his gaze to the ground. "I was told to stay back. When they told me who your teammates were, I knew it was over."

"And you didn't warn me?"

He bit the inside of his cheek and frowned. "What did you think would happen? You know the consequences of fraternizing with other agents, let alone a recruit."

No way. "It was you? You told on me?"

Harding stared at her, but didn't answer.

Her heart hurt. This man she trusted with her life betrayed her. "Why?" her voice cracked.

He met her stare. "Isn't it obvious?"

Apparently not. She didn't know this man at all. How could she read his mind? "No, enlighten me."

Eri whispered behind her. "He likes you."

Harding peered past to Laura at Eri, but said nothing. The girl must have spotted another assailant and ran away.

"So you liked me and couldn't have me, so you sent me to die. Is that it?" Tears streamed down her face. Years of having Harding as a partner, not once did she pick up on this betrayal. What kind of agent was she that she couldn't even see what was in front of her all along?

"It's not like that."

She stepped forward, her eyes blazing. "Then what's it like?"

"Come on, Laura." He turned away and paced back a few steps. "I didn't have some school boy crush on you. You know me better than that."

"I'm not so sure." She rested her free hand under her other elbow, keeping the gun trained on him. "So, what is it then?"

He faced her. "I help you...they kill me."

Unbelievable. So he didn't like her, he was just selfish. "Harding, this is your chance to help me stop them. Then you don't have to worry about that any longer."

He jammed his hands in his hair and paced. "I can't."

"Why? Why can't you?" She lowered her gun.

"You hate this organization as much as I do. You've never been fully committed. This is your chance—to be free."

Myers and Eri ran to her side. Blood trickled from Eri's nose, but she was smiling.

"You okay?"

Eri giggled. "I'm having fun. Who knew I'd be so good at this?"

Harding glanced at Laura.

S.I.U. did. That's why she was here.

"Harding, I'm not going to shoot you unless you try to stop us. Understand?"

He nodded.

"But it would be better if you'd just come with us."

Harding held up his hands and walked backward. "I have nothing to go back to."

"But you'd be with *us*."

Myers touched her shoulder. "We need to go. I can see Charlie running this way. He'll get caught if we don't hurry."

Laura hated to leave her partner, but what could she do? "Fine. Suit yourself. Good luck to you, Harding."

"You, too."

Laura gave him one last look and then ran after her team.

****

"Just hurry up and film the body!" Bryce saw a dog sniffing their way.

"I'm done." Charlie snapped the camera off. "Let's move."

Bryce didn't need to be told twice. He scooped the body over his shoulder and sprinted in the direction of the wall.

"Are you really going to carry him out of here?" Charlie said, breathless.

"I'm sure going to try. He should be buried."

An agent ran their way.

Bryce aimed his gun.

"Don't shoot! It's me, Harding."

Bryce slowed. "Why should that stop me?"

"Because I won't harm you."

"Charlie, grab him."

Harding shook his head. "No, you can't take me. I just…"

Charlie snagged the man's arm and pushed him forward, but Harding held his ground.

Bryce held a gun to his head. "Walk."

The agent exhaled through his nose and started forward. "You realize having a hostage in this place means nothing. They'll shoot you to get to me."

"I don't care. Keep going." Bryce didn't entirely trust the man. He didn't want to hurt him; after all, he was Laura's friend. But he couldn't leave him untouched either. The simplest solution appeared to take him with them.

"I promise not to rat you out. I just want to go back to my barracks and forget this night ever happened."

"Don't we all," Charlie said.

Along the path, bodies lay around their feet. Laura and her team were doing as they said, clearing the way. The rock entrance lay ahead. He hoped Laura would give some indication on how they were supposed to get through it.

"You know you're trapped." Harding crossed his arms and glanced at Bryce. "You guys are not even worthy of a badge. You'll never make it out of here. You're fighting agents with tons of experience."

Charlie flipped around and pointed his gun at Harding's face. "Shut up, Agent Harding. The great news is we don't have to be afraid of you anymore."

"Charlie, settle down," Bryce said.

"Fine. But make him shut up."

Harding laughed. "You guys are pathetic."

Charlie raised the camera and cold cocked Harding in the side of the head. The man fell back, but stayed coherent. He looked to jump up and finish the fight. Bryce cocked the gun by his head. "Don't even think about it."

Harding narrowed his eyes. "He will pay for that."

"Are you sure we have to take him with us?" Charlie said, shaking his fist.

"No, I suppose not." Bryce pulled back and slammed his pistol against Harding's head. The agent dropped to the ground. "Don't tell Laura."

Charlie grinned. "Not a chance."

****

Denise shivered, not from the cold, but from the sound of feet coming out of the jungle. She removed the gun from her jacket and pointed it toward the noise. Slowly, she pulled the hammer back. Her arms shook in anticipation. They ran closer. Her heart thundered in her ears. If she missed, she couldn't run. Fear took over. She readied herself to fire.

"Denise?"

She dropped the gun. "Myers?"

And then he was there. Hugging her. Kissing her. She closed her eyes and let his soft lips envelop hers. He brushed her cheek with the back of his hand. "I was worried about you."

She smiled. "Same here."

He kissed her again, slowly, lingering. His breath warm and inviting. "Do you think, when we get out of this hell on earth, that you'd be willing to go on a date with me?"

"Only if I can have a rocking dress."

He kissed her forehead. "I would love to see that."

"I bet you would."

"You probably have some fine legs."

She batted his arm.

He laughed and kissed her again.

Laura cleared her throat.

Myers sat next to Denise and faced Laura.

"We need to keep moving. Help Denise up, grab the gear, and let's go."

How Denise hated that she couldn't help. It wasn't like her to just sit back and watch people around her do their thing. She liked to be a part of the action. Myers took her in his arms and they began running.

"Where are we going?" Bryce asked.

"I spotted a flat bottom boat by the plane crash. It's not the best boat, but it will hold all of us."

Leaves from the trees crashed against Denise's face. Several most likely left a mark. Despite the hour, the air was tepid and moist. Myers sweated against her, making her hotter. She suddenly began to feel claustrophobic. "Let me down."

He looked at her, but didn't stop. "What?"

"Let me down. I can walk."

He shook his head. "Not fast enough."

"Then I need a break."

He eyed her. "You're not even the one walking."

"I'm getting motion sickness or something. Please."

A concerned look washed over Myer's face. He stopped and set her on a log.

Laura doubled back. "We can't stop."

"She needs to," Myers said. "I think she's getting sick."

"Just give me a moment." Denise held up her hand. The spinning in her head slowly decreased.

"Fan out," Laura said. "Cover the perimeter."

Myers tucked a strand of Denise's hair behind her ear. He really did love her, she could tell. And he wasn't alone. Her heart soared whenever he was near.

Laura knelt next to her. "Let me see the wound."

Denise shifted so her left side angled up.

Her gentleman diverted his eyes. *He's so cute.* Denise smiled.

Laura lifted the shirt. Blood seeped through the dressing. "Did they give you any antibiotics?"

"I did," Myers said. "But it may only be for dogs."

Denise snickered; Laura did not. "I know you're sick, but if we don't keep moving, it won't matter. You'll be dead."

Her compassion was overwhelming. Denise knew arguing with the agent was pointless. The woman's mind worked like a robot. The enemy could probably drop a dozen rounds in Laura and she'd still come at them.

"I'm better. We can go." Denise wrapped her arm around Myers neck.

He lifted her as Laura rounded up the team.

Denise relaxed her head against his strong chest. His heart beat fast in her ear. No matter the danger, she felt extremely safe in his arms. If today were her day to die, at least she'd be with him.

****

A Workstar 770 lay just down the bank from where they stood. The boat was wide with a cabin for the captain in the middle. The sides had rust, and there didn't appear to be any slats to sit on, but it looked seaworthy.

Laura hesitated running to it. It was very likely that S.I.U. had planned for this and was guarding the beach from the jungle.

"What are we waiting for?" Charlie asked.

"I'm not sure this is the right move." Laura crouched back to the group. "Charlie, you said your uncle is a senator, right?"

"Yes, and we have to get him this tape."

Laura tapped her index finger to her lips. "I don't know what awaits us down at the water. We don't have enough man power to scout out the danger."

"Maybe one of us could start down and see what happens," Myers said.

"You mean bait?" Denise said.

He nodded.

"No way. That's a dumb idea." Denise tried to sit up, but winced and fell back. "Agent Black, please don't let him do that."

"I didn't say it had to be me."

The group all looked at one another. Myers was right. Someone had to be the bait. But who?

Bryce stood. "I'll do it."

Laura heart plummeted into her stomach. She leapt to his side. "No!"

His eyes met hers and softened. He caressed her

cheek with his finger. "Somebody has to do it."

"But not you," she whispered.

He stepped closer to her so his nose almost touched hers. "Why not me?"

"Because, I…" Her heart pulsed in her ears. "I…"

"You what?"

A force she couldn't explain drew her to him. Suddenly, she didn't care if he ran back to his girlfriend. For this instant, he was here. He cupped his hand around the back of her head. She placed her lips to his and kissed him. A chill ran through her nervous system.

"Eri, no!" Denise yelled.

Laura and Bryce broke away.

Eri ran down the beach toward the boat.

"Oh no," Laura said.

"We have to stop her!" Charlie readied his weapon, his eyes scanning the trees.

Laura cocked her weapon and ran after her. The team didn't hesitate. Within seconds, they were all there.

Eri glanced over her shoulder. "No, you guys need each other. Go back. I've got this."

"Fight, live, die together. That is what we've trained to do." Charlie came alongside her.

Laura smiled, holding back tears that once again threatened to break her. She had done it. Trained a group more worthy than anyone graduating out of S.I.U. Too bad they would never have the chance they deserved.

Like a bee, a bullet zipped onto the beach, hitting Charlie's arm. Blood splattered onto Eri's vest and she screamed. He fell to the sand, clutching the wound.

"Get him in the boat, now!" Laura fired.

Everyone jumped in and ducked down, while shooting crazily at the tree line.

Bryce managed to get the boat engine started. Myers helped pushed it back and they were off.

Three S.I.U. agents ran from the jungle down to the beach, firing.

Laura swung around and fired rounds into each of their heads. They dropped to the ground like paper targets.

"Wow," Bryce said, with a dumbfounded look on his face.

"I'll say." Eri's eyes were wide. "You are the queen, Ms. Black."

Laura smiled, then looked to Bryce. "Take us home."

Chapter Twenty-Seven

"Charlie, you okay?" Laura asked, once they were all settled.

He nodded, pulling at his blood-spotted sleeve. "The bullet just scratched me. It stings, but it's not bad."

"Eri, check it out," Laura said, then looked at the jungle, ready for more shooting. The air was remarkably calm. Finally, she buckled to the bottom of the boat and sighed. She started to close her eyes, when a voice rang in the distance. "Did you hear something?" Laura peered over the side of the boat.

Harding waved his arms over his head from the shore.

"Don't go back," Charlie said. "It could be a trap."

Laura glanced over her shoulder at Bryce. He stared straight ahead, his hands on the ship's wheel, no expression visible. "Bryce, he's my friend."

"Your friend?" Bryce looked at her, surprised.

"Yeah."

He laughed. "Well, your friend gave me this cut under my eye."

"It was his job. You can't blame him."

"Not sure about that, but if it'll make you feel better." He started to turn.

She smiled.

"Wait, no." Charlie shook his head animatedly. "Are you guys nuts? He's one of *them*."

Harding continued to jump up and down, yelling her name. He was finally brave enough to leave S.I.U.; how could she abandon him? "If it was one of you, I'd go back." She glanced to the shore and exhaled. Maybe she wouldn't have to. Harding had started swimming. Laura walked to the back of the boat and tossed out a line.

"I have a bad feeling about this." Charlie pulled off his beanie and rubbed his head.

"If I'm wrong, you can be the first to toss him overboard," Laura said.

"Yeah, well, I did hit him with a camera."

Laura looked at him.

He smiled sheepishly. "He asked for it."

Together, Myers and Laura pulled him in.

"Thanks." Harding swung his last leg over the side and dropped down to the fiberglass bottom. He wiped water from his eyes and then winked at Laura. "I guess you convinced me to leave."

"I'm glad. You won't be sorry. Ten minutes of freedom, and you'll be convinced it was the right decision." She walked back to the bow where Bryce steered the boat. She leaned like she was nuzzling his neck and whispered, "Keep an eye on Harding. I don't trust him."

"I thought he was your friend."

"He's an S.I.U. agent who didn't want anything to do with this a few hours ago."

Bryce glanced back at him and then to her. "Understood."

****

The boat crept along the blackened sea like an eerie horror film. Water lapped at the sides in the darkness. Fog hovered low, blocking any moonlight. Myers tried to sleep, but when he closed his eyes he envisioned over and over the nightmare they'd just lived. Visions of Denise suffering filled his mind. Images of her taking her last breath. So much blood. Tearful good-byes. Of course, she still lived. His eyes shot open, fearful that this time the ending had changed.

Suddenly, an arm came around his throat.

Myers panicked. *Am I dreaming*? He gasped. No. He tried push against his assailant, but the grip was too tight. Gulping to fill his lungs with oxygen, Myers kicked. Swung. Batted at the arm around his throat. Lightheaded, he started to falter, unable to breathe.

The man's hold instantly relaxed as his body dropped with a thud.

Myers scrambled away, coughing.

"Are you okay?" Laura asked, lowering the paddle she must have used to clock Harding over the head.

Myers swallowed. His throat hurt but he was alive. He nodded and then looked at the culprit.

Harding lay unconscious on the ground.

"Let's tie him up."

"Why don't we just drop him overboard?" Myers said.

"Better to know what your enemy has planned for you." Laura yanked a rope off of a life preserver and tossed it to Myers. "I knew he was a traitor. Now, we can interrogate him and find out what his mission was."

"Obviously to kill me." Myers scowled, tying the knot probably tighter than needed.

Laura reached in Harding's pocket and withdrew a

knife. "No, I think it may have been to kill us all. You were sleeping so he probably thought he'd start with the biggest and work his way to the others. You're lucky he didn't break your neck."

Myers touched his throat. It still hurt.

Laura cupped some water in her hand from the floor and sprinkled it over Harding's face.

He blinked.

"Welcome back," she said.

He jerked his bound wrists in some vain effort to be free and glowered. "Untie me."

"Ha. Not likely." She knelt next to him, with the knife close to his cheek. "Why are you on this boat? What's the mission?"

Harding glanced away, smug.

"Yes, I know. 'Don't tell the enemy anything.'" Laura had been taught the same mantra for years, but she obviously didn't care. She squeezed his cheeks, forcing him to look her in the eye. "But I wasn't aware that *I* was the enemy. You let me go back at the compound, and now you've come to kill me. Why?"

He stuck his tongue in his cheek, not meeting her gaze.

"I want an answer. And you know, I'll have no problem doing what I have to do to get it." She let the knife graze his arm, just enough to prick the surface layer, revealing a small amount of blood.

He winced.

"It doesn't have to be this way, Harding."

His eyes narrowed as he finally looked at her. "I can't believe you've allowed these kids to ruin your life. You're so stupid, Black."

Laura pushed his chin, forcing his head back, and

then let go. "I'm stupid! These kids didn't ruin anything. S.I.U. ruined my life. These kids *saved* it." Her voice rose with apparent frustration.

He didn't respond.

"You're hopeless. I should let Charlie push you overboard."

Charlie stepped forward, obviously ready for the command.

Harding diverted his gaze away from her.

"Fine. We'll deal with you later."

Myers lay back next to where Denise slept. He wondered what Laura was thinking keeping this man alive. Right now, Myers would have happily taken him out. And that disturbed him. Had S.I.U. changed him that much? How could taking a life ever seem like the right thing to do? He stared at Harding. The man held a hardened expression, lost, as he stared out to the inky sea.

God protect us all.

****

Bryce squinted through the lifting fog. A sliver of green blanketed the horizon. "Land!"

Laura joined him.

"What do we do when we get there?"

She sighed. "We get fake passports and fly to Washington."

He looked at her. She made it sound so simple. But it wasn't, was it? "Will this work?"

"It has too."

A little while later, the boat ran aground on some coral. Eri and Laura hopped into the water first. Charlie pushed Harding out and then followed with gun in hand.

Myers carried Denise as he slid over the side.

Bryce was the last out. The turquoise water sloshed around his waist. It felt warm, but horrible in his boots. He sprinted the best he could to the beach.

"I can't get over how beautiful it is." Eri kneeled to the white sand and allowed the granules to sift through her fingers. "I wish we could spend more time vacationing here."

"You can disappear wherever you want later. Right now, we have to keep moving." Laura touched her back. "Let's go."

Eri nodded.

Bryce followed them up the embankment to a sidewalk filled with tourists and locals. A group of Latin men, wearing turbans and flowered shirts, played calypso drums. Children with dirt smeared clothes and faces approached them with hands out.

A little boy tugged on Bryce's pants. "Chicle?"

Bryce shook his head, but didn't look at him. For some reason, he needed to keep his focus on Laura. He felt somehow responsible for her. Why, he wasn't sure. In a fight, she could hold her own. With his wounded shoulder, she'd probably even do better. Still, he needed to watch over her. Ensure she was safe.

"Keep moving," Laura said to the group. As the crowd increased, it was obvious she worried they'd be separated. She positioned herself behind Harding, hiding his binds, and nudged Charlie more to the man's side.

"How are we going to get passports without money?" Bryce whispered in her ear.

Her stern expression said it all. They weren't going to pay. Their trip to America would come at a high price for some man, because they'd likely take it by force.

****

Laura ducked out of a dark smoke shop and met her companions across the street. "We have an appointment in ten minutes. Let's move."

The group followed her east, toward the jungle. The sun had dropped below the horizon, yet the air remained warm. Laura retied her jacket around her waist and glanced back at Bryce. His skin looked pale and hot. Sweat beaded on his forehead and his eyes lay at half-mast. Earlier, without him noticing, she'd touched his skin. Without a doubt, he had a fever. Any female instinct she possessed said stop and let him recover. But her S.I.U. training won out. Their best chance of survival didn't include a break. They had to keep moving. She knew that. She prayed it wouldn't kill him. Or Denise. Both of them were in desperate need of medical care.

Bryce caught up to her and gave her a tight smile. "You okay?"

She nodded. "I'm hoping we can rest and clean up while he prepares our paperwork."

"What's the plan?"

She grimaced. He wouldn't like it. No one would. Since they didn't have any money, they would have to take the paperwork by force. Maybe if she could convince her team that these were bad guys—thugs destined for prison. But she looked at the kids in her party and knew it wouldn't matter. All of them, except Eri, were criminals. Criminals with a conscience, but criminals just the same.

"I'm not sure you want to hear the details."

"Promise me no one will die," Bryce said.

"I will do my best."

He grabbed her arm. "Laura, please."

She locked eyes with his. This man was not her equal. How could he ever really love her? Not kill someone. That was his biggest concern. Did he have any idea how many people she had killed in the name of survival? Could he still care for her if he knew? "No one will die."

He nodded as if the matter was settled.

"Oh, no!" Charlie patted his pants like crazy, then fell to the dirt, and checked the bag. His eyes met Eri's. "Tell me you have it."

Laura came alongside him. "What's missing?"

Embarrassment shadowed Charlie's eyes. "The S.I.U. tape."

Laura's heart sank. Their freedom—gone. "Where did you see it last?"

"On the boat," Charlie said.

"We'll have to go back," Eri said, stepping up to the huddle.

The bamboo shack they were there to find lay about thirty yards ahead. "This guy may not wait for us."

Harding laughed.

"What's so funny?" Myers said, sticking a gun in the man's face.

"Your precious tape is at the bottom of the Atlantic by now."

Heat rose up Laura's spine. "What did you do?"

A hideous smirk flashed on his face. "Let's just say all you did was for naught."

Eri began to cry.

Laura didn't blame her. She felt like sobbing a few buckets herself. Without thinking, she punched Harding in the face.

His body sailed through the air, landing on a pile of wood. He appeared to be knocked out.

"I'm done with him. Leave him there to rot." Laura waved her finger at the hut in front of them. "That's where we're going. Eri, you'll come with me. Myers, you stay back with Denise and Harding. Charlie, you and Bryce keep guard."

"Remember not to kill anyone," Bryce said.

"Why do you think I'm taking Eri? The queen of Judo will keep things civil."

Eri laughed.

Bryce tapped Charlie's arm and they walked ahead, scoping the jungle.

"So, what do we do?" Eri asked, as they crept toward the door.

"We don't have the money to pay for this, so I'll try to negotiate. If that doesn't work, then we'll take the guy out of play."

Eri's eyes went wide.

"Not kill him. Knock him out."

"But then how will we get the documents?"

"I know how to do them. I've had plenty of practice. I just need supplies."

Laura wrapped on the screen door.

Shuffling came from the other side, then the silhouette of a thick man came in view. Laura gulped. He may be a bigger challenge than she thought.

"Yeah?"

"Javier sent me," she said.

"How do you know Javier?" the man said in

233

English with a country drawl.

Javier had warned her that this would be the question to get them in. She hoped she got this right. One word off, and the appointment would be over.

"Well, the other day two Mexicans stumbled into a bar. One of them had on a red hat and the other a yellow hat. I was intrigued by this, so…" She paused for a moment, trying to remember the next code color. "I opened my green notebook and approached them. Javier was the man in the yellow hat, and he wanted me to buy from a man in a blue hat, a Texan named Mike."

The screen door creaked open.

The two girls passed him and walked into a "dump." The floor was littered in papers, food, and beer bottles. Flies buzzed around the room, and the air reeked of cigarette smoke and wet dog.

"Sit on the couch," he said.

Laura grimaced at the stained, flowered material.

"Do we have to?" Eri hissed in her ear.

"You can shower once we're in the United States," Laura whispered back.

Eri sat timidly on the edge.

"So, what brings two gorgeous ladies out here in the jungle this late at night?" Mike lowered his corpulent frame in the love seat across from them and lit a cigarette.

Laura stared at the orange burn as Mike inhaled. "I think we'll keep that to ourselves. Just know it wasn't our doing and we need to get back to the U.S."

"Just the two of you?"

Laura shook her head. "There are four others outside."

Mike glanced back at the door. "Planning an

invasion?"

"I didn't want to intimidate you with our whole team."

An amused expression appeared on his face. "Well, they'll all have to show sometime. I need to take yawl's photo for the passports."

"Right." Laura motioned with her hand for Eri to get the rest of them.

Eri left.

"I ask for five thousand up front. That's pretty good, considering what you're getting."

Laura didn't flinch. "What are we getting?"

He scratched the few hairs left on his head. "Well, Javier said you needed passports and a way to the States, correct?"

"Yes."

"Well, I can do the paperwork, and my cousin owns a private plane." He looked toward a roast-infested kitchenette. "I can even feed you, if you like."

She swallowed against the bile that thought brought. "No, that'll be okay."

"So, business first."

Laura peered back to the door. *Where are they?* She couldn't have this discussion without back up. She'd have to stall. "Business, of course. Once my assistant returns, we'll be able to conduct that."

He stared at her, his eyes revealing nothing. She wondered if he was used to people trying to take advantage of him. Would he be ready for this? She hoped not.

The door squeaked open.

Laura visibly exhaled.

Mike stood.

Charlie's eyes followed Mike's frame rise, and he noticeably gulped.

Bryce and Charlie looked like rag dolls next to the man. If Myers weren't holding Denise, he'd have been their best chance at intimidation.

"Well, looks like we're all here," Laura said, with a nervous giggle. It wasn't like her to panic. She took a big breath.

Mike nodded and stuck out his hand, obviously wanting money, not a handshake.

"About that." Laura glanced at Bryce, then Eri. She hoped they understood. "We don't have the five thousand just yet."

Mike slowly withdrew his hand, and his smile with it. "Then I'm sorry, but I can't help you little lady."

"I know this isn't your usual way of doing things, but if you could just hear us out."

He pointed to the door.

The team exchanged glances. Then all eyes were on Laura for some sort of signal. Not that she knew what to do here. She couldn't kill him; that was already decided. But to bring down this mammoth without that option could be a problem for them all.

Laura cocked her gun.

The sound of clicking echoed behind her as each of the group did the same.

Mike laughed.

Not the response Laura had anticipated.

"You think you can just waltz in here and take something like that by force. It doesn't work that way."

"And why not?"

Mike sneered. "Because, missy, I'm untouchable."

"How so?" Laura snickered, then waved her gun

around the room. "You have five guns on you. How do you plan to duck?"

He snapped his fingers and a dozen red laser-beamed dots streamed through the windows, landing on Laura's chest. "Like I said, I'm untouchable."

Air seemed to suck out of the room. Laura labored to breath. She lowered her weapon, but kept her empty hand raised in surrender.

"Look, we didn't come here to hurt you or to get hurt." Bryce stepped forward with his hands up. "We need papers, and we're desperate. If you knew the people we're running away from, you'd understand."

"S.I.U." Mike licked his lips.

Bryce glanced at Laura.

"You seem surprised." Mike let out a throaty cackle. "Well, don't be."

Laura closed her gaping mouth. *How did he know about them? Was this a trap all along?* "You work for them?"

He pursed his lips, obviously considering his answer. "Not exactly."

"I don't understand."

"Tell your men to lower their weapons, and I'll explain."

Laura nodded to her team, and then faced back. "Explain."

"They have been expecting you. I was contacted this morning to prepare for your arrival."

Her heart sunk. Behind her, she sensed panic. But she didn't turn to console them. She couldn't. "So, are you ordered to kill all of us?"

He shook his head. "Nope. I get paid a big, hefty sum to return you."

"How much per head?"

"Five hundred K."

"We're worth that much to them?" Eri asked.

Mike shook his head and pointed at Laura. "No, only for her. We're supposed to kill the rest of you, but I think we can work a deal."

Laura blinked, trying to stay upright. "You're saying they want me back."

"Yes."

Bryce stepped to her side. "No. You can't have her."

She touched his elbow. "It's okay."

He met her eyes. So much warmth poured from them. "I won't lose you."

"If it means you can live, then I'll do it."

"There has to be another way." He looked away to Mike. "Tell me there is another way."

"Not unless you can come up with more than fifty Gs, son."

Chapter Twenty-Eight

Bryce stared at the man who wished to keep the owner of his heart hostage. No way could he do it. He'd rather die than see someone keep Laura. "Can you give us a minute alone to say goodbye?"

Mike shot his eyes around the room. "Leave your guns on the porch, and I'll let you have the living room."

Bryce and Laura handed their guns off to Charlie. He mumbled something to Myers as he stepped outside to comply.

"Just remember, you're not alone." Mike laughed and exited to a room in back.

The group stood in a circle, similar to a football huddle trying to figure out their next play.

"So, tell us Obi-wan how to get us out of here," Charlie said to Laura.

"You don't. You let them have me, then you get away."

"No way! Not an option." Heat escalated in Bryce's chest. Already a fever made him hot, but now his fury brought his temperature up to dangerous heights. The room seemed to spin. He held his head, trying to stay conscious. "That isn't the only alternative here."

"You have something else?" She glanced back at

the closed bedroom door. "Because from where I'm standing, I see a gorilla with a gang. There isn't a chance in this world that we can bring him and all his gunmen down."

"The question to ask is why does S.I.U. want you and not us?"

She dropped her gaze to the floor.

"You know, don't you?"

"It's my fault," Charlie said, walking next to them.

Bryce looked at him. "What did you do?"

Laura held up her hand. "Charlie didn't do anything wrong. It was me."

"What?"

"About a month ago, when you all first started talking about escaping, I downloaded all of the agency files from the network."

Bryce cocked his head to the side. "I don't understand."

Laura and Charlie exchanged glances. She had leveled with Charlie, just in case something went wrong. "I carry all their records inside my body."

His eyes went wide, as they traveled down her torso. "Where?"

She pulled her T-shirt up, revealing a one-inch scar on the left side of her navel.

Bryce stared with his mouth open, shaking his head. "Are you nuts?"

"Apparently." She offered a tight smile.

Myers laughed.

Everyone glared at him. What could possibly be funny about any of this? If it were Denise, he would hardly be laughing. No, he'd be furious. Sort of like Bryce at this moment.

"What's your problem?" Bryce snapped.

Myers rubbed his hands together and grinned. "This is so simple I can't believe you all don't see it. Just pull the files out and hand them off. I'm sure the S.I.U. would still pay for them, and then Mike can let us go."

Bryce glanced back at Laura. "What do you think?"

She crossed her arms and scowled. "Not an option. I don't want to give them up."

Not the answer he was looking for. He squeezed his eyes shut, but thought better of it when he started to sway. His eyes met hers with frustration. She could be so difficult sometimes. Didn't she see that her life depended on this decision? Something he wasn't so easily ready to trade. "You're keeping them is obviously not a choice here either. If they get their hands on you, then they get the files anyway. I'd rather not have to go back there to rescue you."

"They won't know where to look."

"I don't think it would take them long to find out."

"Just copy them," Charlie said.

Mike stepped out of the room and coughed. "So, are ya'll ready to do the exchange?"

Bryce crossed to him, hoping to remain calm. Wasn't going to be easy. Though typically he was a pretty passive man, right now he felt like ripping the man's head off. "What if we could guarantee you'd still get the money, without having to take anyone prisoner."

"I'm a businessman. I told ya'll, I just want my cash."

Just what Bryce wanted to hear. He smiled at Laura. "Then we have a plan."

****

Laura cringed at the unhygienic environment she was about to expose to her insides to. The dining room table, though wiped "clean" by Charlie three times, still looked like a playground for germs.

Bryce must have read her mind. He took off his jacket and poured tequila on it. "Here, lay on this. It'll be wet, but a little more sterile."

"I'm not a drinker, but in this situation, I could probably use the anesthetic. It's pretty deep."

He handed her the bottle.

She took a swig and gagged as it burned her throat. *Foul stuff. Who could drink it for fun?* She put her lips to the opening and shot back more. Her body began to relax.

Eri entered with a charred knife. "I held it in the fireplace for a good minute. Practically scarred my hand, so I think it should be good."

"Let's do this." Laura climbed on the table and created a bikini top by stuffing her shirt in her bra. She hoped it wouldn't take long for them to dig the chip out.

"You know you're crazy." Bryce kissed the top of her head.

"Maybe, a little." She smiled.

He took the knife from Eri. "Hold Eri's hand and brace yourself."

Laura closed her eyes and felt Eri's hand slip in hers. She squeezed it in anticipation of what was coming.

The cold edge of the blade touched her skin. She flinched, though it didn't hurt yet.

"Ready?" Bryce asked.

"Wait." Laura's eyes shot open. "I'm going to

scream. Put something in my mouth."

Eri walked to Charlie and snatched off his beanie.

"Hey!" Charlie said.

She laughed and walked back to Laura. "Here."

"Charlie, Myers," Bryce said over his shoulder.

"Yeah?" They came in the doorway of the kitchen.

"Hold her down."

The two men stood on either side of her and put pressure on her arms.

"Here we go." Bryce poured some alcohol over the scar, then readied himself with the knife.

Laura took a deep breath and nodded, her eyes wide. Should she close them? Maybe a good idea. She let her lids ease shut.

A sharp pain shot through her stomach. She screamed into the beanie. Everything went dark.

****

Laura heard muffled voices. She struggled to open her eyes.

"I think she's coming around." Sounded like Charlie.

"Laura? Can you hear me?" Bryce said.

She blinked.

Bryce and Charlie leaned over her, but they weren't in the house. Trees towered overhead. The air felt cool and moist. Something lulled underneath her. She was mobile.

"Where are we?" She tried to sit up, but winced and laid back.

"We're in a boat off the coast of Florida. We should be there shortly."

"Florida?" Laura pushed herself up, her curiosity fighting against the pain. "How?"

"He let us go. We promised to send him money once we got to the mainland if he'd help us." Bryce tucked a piece of her hair behind her ear.

"And he believed us? How is that possible?"

Charlie bit his lip. "We had to bargain with your copy of the data. He knew we really wanted it, or it wouldn't have been in your stomach. He held it as collateral."

She squeezed her eyes shut and exhaled. "If he doesn't return it to us…"

Bryce touched her arm. "He will. We just have to get our hands on some cash."

Charlie smiled. "Which Myers has all figured out. Don't you, man?"

Myers winked. "Don't worry, Agent Black. I've got you covered."

Laura sighed. She'd learned quickly that she could trust her team. Now, not only with her life, but also with her future.

****

A thrust of adrenaline shot through Bryce's system. He wasn't sure if it was excitement or fear, but he prepared himself. A Coast Guard ship slowed on the starboard side of their boat.

"Laura, wake up," he said, nudging her side.

She sat up and glanced around, her eyes stopping at the white vessel.

"What do we do?" Charlie whispered behind her.

"We tell the truth," she said.

Bryce raised an eyebrow. "Really?"

A smirk formed on her lips. "Well, sort of."

The coast guard called over to their ship, announcing that one of his men would be boarding. A

244

plank was slid across, and a moment later, a young man dressed in a white coast guard uniform crossed to their boat. "I need to see all your passports," he said.

Bryce pulled them from the backpack Leo had given him and handed them out.

The young, clean-shaven sailor inspected the documents, then each of their faces.

Bryce's stomach twisted. He silently prayed.

"Okay, everything looks good." The coast guard nodded and re-boarded his ship.

The team waited in silence until the ship pulled away, then everyone cheered.

"We did it!" Laura leapt in Bryce's arms.

He hugged her tight. Within minutes, they'd be back in the United States. His heart soared. He searched her eyes. A force pulled him to kiss her. Slowly, he leaned forward and caressed her cheek.

She glanced away to the port that neared.

His heart plummeted into his stomach. Though they'd endured so much fear, his biggest worry was losing Laura once they reached the mainland. She had no reason to stay with him. Nor did he believe she would. Suddenly, he wished they'd stayed at the compound. Maybe there he would have found a way to love her.

Myers ran to the bow, grabbed a rope, apparently ready to jump on the pier.

"He looks like he knows what he's doing," Denise said.

Bryce let his gaze drift from Laura to Denise. "You're awake."

She looked at him and nodded. "I'm feeling much better."

"Okay, folks, here we go." Myers leapt onto the dock and tied them off. It didn't take but a minute for everyone to follow. People talked about kissing the ground before, and at this moment, Bryce completely understood the trite expression. He was home.

"I need to think of where to go. They're not going to let us escape with our lives. Leo may only care about money, but S.I.U. will want us dead." Laura dug in her backpack for a map. "Give me a second."

The reality of any freedom just sank into the wooden planks below his feet. They may have made it to America, but it was obvious they were still in a cage. Bryce glanced around. Palm trees lined the walkway, two girls wearing bikinis road by on a pair of bicycles. A group of teenage guys ogled them from a few feet away. An elderly man and possibly his wife wore Hawaiian-print shirts and big smiles. They took pictures of the scenery around them, oblivious to anyone but each other. Little kids danced in some showers just off the beach, while their moms watched from a few feet away. Life to these people seemed so simple. Happy. Carefree. How long had Bryce been away from that sort of bliss? Without a watch or calendar, he didn't even know. A lump formed in his throat and he swallowed against it. Sure, he was tired, but getting emotional at this moment seemed the wrong move.

"What now?" Eri asked, coming alongside them.

"We have to keep moving," Laura said. "Come on."

The group followed down the street. The smell of fried fish wafted through the air. Bryce grabbed his stomach. *When did we last eat*?

"Man that smells good," Charlie said.

Myers touched Laura's shoulder. "Can we eat?"

"We don't have any money."

It was true. They had the clothes they were wearing and a few supplies. That was it. No food. Only some water. Bryce's stomach rumbled in complaint. He yanked Laura's arm and pulled her into an alley. "Listen, we have to eat and get cleaned up. We can't go storming the news studio like this."

She glanced down at her dirty black jacket and then to the dirt and blood-smudged team. "You're right. Ideas?"

"We sell a gun. That would at least get us a hotel room and a meal."

Laura laughed. "Why don't we just steal both?"

Still he didn't understand her. The woman had a soul. He'd been given glimpses, but her usual response made him wonder. "We don't want any trouble here, especially if we're going on the news. Don't you think the people we rob would recognize us once we're on TV?"

"Not if we wear masks," Laura said.

She was serious. He shook his head, exasperated. "Look, no violence, okay? Let's just sell a piece and go from there."

"Whose gun?" Laura crossed her arms and leaned to one hip. "Yours."

"If necessary, yes."

Denise hobbled forward, gun extended. "I'm not much of a soldier right now anyway…use mine."

Bryce snatched it up. "Thanks."

"So where do we sell it?" Charlie asked.

"The nearest gun store or pawn shop. Let's go."

****

After the team had each taken a shower and eaten some pizza, Laura gathered them around the hotel beds to discuss strategy. "We can't stay here long. As soon as the sun peeks out, we're on our way to the studio."

"What do we say?" Eri asked.

"The truth. All of it."

"But we don't have your evidence yet?" Eri glanced at Myers.

Myers held up his hands. "Look, we'll get it. We just have to find some way to make some money."

"How much?" Laura asked.

"Ten thousand."

Great. Laura exhaled. "Fine, we'll cross that bridge eventually. In the meantime, we'll tell the station we have evidence coming."

"That may be the wrong move," Bryce said, from where he sat in the hotel corner chair. "Once we expose them, they'll be gone. Underground."

Everything in her knew Bryce was right. Funny that he'd figured it out. "Yes, most likely."

Charlie popped his knuckles and stood. "So, what do we do? Are we completely screwed, or what?"

"We pray," Eri said.

Everyone looked at her at once. No one talked. Especially Laura. She didn't pray. What a ludicrous idea. "I think in theory that's a nice idea, but…"

Bryce stood and nodded. "She's right."

Laura stared up at him. "You aren't serious."

He responded by grabbing Eri's hand.

Eri grabbed Denise's hand, and around the circle, everyone joined hands.

When Myers reached for Laura's hand, she flinched back. "I-I can't."

"Agent Black, come on."

She shook her head and stood. "You guys are nuts if you think a little time praying to who-knows-who is going to help you win against this evil villain. They're going to kill you. All of you. And no higher power is going to save you."

In a voice almost inaudible, Eri said, "We're here, aren't we?"

Myers gently took Laura's hand and closed his eyes. A second later, Eri reached for her hand too, completing the circle. They began to pray.

As they prayed, Laura couldn't deny the peace she felt. A weight from all the wretched things she'd experience seemed to dissipate into the rug. *God, if you're real, then save me from this life. Save us all. 'Cuz we seriously need a miracle.*

The room stilled.

Laura looked up.

Everyone removed his or her hands; Bryce kneeled by her. "Are you okay?"

She wiped at her wet eyes and smiled. "Better. Yeah."

Chapter Twenty-Nine

Laura bought everyone clothes from a thrift store down the street. She ran a hand over her "new," white poplin shirt and faced her crew. Bryce looked amazing in a dark-blue polo shirt and jeans. It was the first time since she met him he looked normal and happy. "Ready?"

"Yeah," he said.

Everyone else nodded in agreement.

They loaded backpacks over their shoulders and walked into the twilight. The sky was gray, anticipating the sun on the horizon. Only a few cars were out, and most of the city's lights were off. An airport shuttle waited for them in front of the lobby, idling. Myers had discovered the shuttles were free from the hotel, and the news station was only blocks from the airport. It was the perfect mode of transportation.

The team climbed aboard and sat facing each other as the door slid closed.

Laura felt lighter than she had in so long; in some ways, she felt it put her at a disadvantage. She didn't know how to act. How did she function if they came under fire? Could she shoot someone now? Take another man's life, if needed? Before she'd built a wall to protect her heart from compassion and guilt. Last night in the hotel room, that wall crumbled to dust on the brown, shag carpet. What was left now was an uneasy feeling in the pit of her stomach. Unlike any other time in her life, she found herself praying. *You're going to have to help me through this, because honestly I feel like a fish floundering on dry land.*

The van stopped at the first terminal.

Bryce nodded at her.

She returned his nod. "Let's go."

They piled out the doors and onto the curb. Passengers rushed past them to hail cabs or meet their rides. Laura didn't feel like staying at the airport longer than it took to get a bagel and go. It was likely S.I.U. would have secret agents waiting for them to board a plane. It was an illogical decision they would expect.

"Come on, let's get a bite and get going."

They were in and out of the coffee shop in ten minutes, eating their breakfast as they walked toward the airport entrance. Myers had somehow confiscated a wheelchair for Denise. Laura didn't want to know how.

Dodging a few cars, they crossed the street and ran for the main road.

A yawn slipped from Laura's lips. She took a sip of her water and tried to find a second wind. She was exhausted and dreaded the long walk. She hadn't had a decent night's sleep in over a week, and her body rebelled.

Bryce met her pace. "You okay?"

She smiled, reassuring. "I just need a nap, that's all. You?"

"A trip to the doctor would be good."

She glanced down at his side. Fresh blood stained the side of his shirt. "Are you in pain?"

"I work to block it out."

She nodded. Something she'd done many times in the field. Desperate situations meant desperate measures. Wasn't that what Greenstone preached a million times. He was right. In the field, people do what they have to do to survive.

"I promise. We make this happen, and we'll get you some care. All of us."

Charlie looked at her. "Thank you, Agent Black. For everything."

Thank me? That seemed odd. She belonged to an organization that almost killed them. But she did try to save them. She only hoped, in the end, she'd succeed.

They trudged along the freeway, for what seemed like hours, especially when the Florida sun lifted, bringing with it the day's humid heat.

Like Santa on Christmas, Eri pointed and yelled, "I see it. There!"

They all peered ahead, expectant. Sure enough, a warehouse lay ahead with a white TV sign posted on top next to a tall antenna tower. Laura closed her eyes and grinned. They'd made it. She exhaled and looked back to the building. *Now to get in.*

Charlie brought his hand to the back of his waistband and clutched the handle of his gun; probably assuming force would be the only way in. Normally, Laura would have done the same. But today, she actually wanted to avoid violence. She touched Charlie's arm. "Let's go to the office first and just see what happens."

She spotted a door to the warehouse just inside the gate. They just had to find a way on the other side of the chain link fence. They walked around until they spotted the entrance. Instantly, she knew there might be trouble. A guard eyed her from a shack.

"Now what do we do?" Myers whispered.

"Be cool," she said back. Sauntering with her most alluring smile plastered on her face, Laura approached the man. "Hello, sir."

He didn't return her smile. "Can I help you?"

"My friends and I have traveled a long way to talk to someone in your studio."

His eyes traveled to her team, then back to her. "I'm sorry, but I can't allow you to go inside without authorization."

Not good. "This is a news station, is it not?"

"Yes, among other things."

"Well, we have some pretty big *news.* Trust me, these people are going to want to hear our story. I guarantee it." Laura glanced at Bryce and took a deep breath. "If you don't let us talk to them, we'll just take it over to Channel Six." She hoped he bought her bluff and that there was indeed a Channel Six.

The guard stared at her, no hint of emotion on his face. Laura tried to read his eyes, but he gave her nothing. He looked away and grabbed a phone, then pivoted his shoulder so she couldn't hear.

Bryce slid his hand around the small of Laura's back and whispered in her ear. "What happens if he doesn't go for it?"

She leaned her head against his shoulder. "Then we let Charlie pull out his gun."

Charlie must have heard that. His hand slowly reached behind his back. She prayed he didn't act prematurely. She held her hand down low, motioning for him to wait.

The guard turned back to face her as he hung up

the phone. "Someone is coming out."

Charlie relaxed his arm.

"That's great," Laura said. "Thank you."

"Just wait over there." The guard pointed to the side of the fence next to a white brick wall.

Her crew moved next to the spot. Luckily, they didn't have to wait long. A man, dressed in a brown, button-down shirt and jeans, walked around the corner and stuck out his hand. "Hi. My name is Ian. I get stories for Bruce Canten."

Like I know who that is. Laura fought the urge to roll her eyes. It didn't matter. "Great. Then we have something important to tell you."

In that second, the world seemed to slow down. Colors ran together and sounds were distorted. But one thing was clear. Gunfire.

Everyone dropped to the ground, except Myers who covered Denise and the chair with his body. Laura low-crawled behind the brick wall and gasped. The guard lay in a pool of blood inches from her position. She ducked behind the shack, cocked her gun, and glanced around. Another shot rang out.

Eri screamed.

No! Laura frantically searched for the shooter.

"There!" Bryce pointed up.

Laura searched the roofs across the street. Something reflected in the sun. Another bullet grazed the dirt, less than a millimeter from Bryce's leg. "Find better cover!" she yelled, trying to stay calm. They didn't have a gun powerful enough to reach the sniper, but that didn't matter. Most likely gunfire would bring the police and maybe the news crews out. They needed that. "Fire at him."

"It won't reach."

"I know. Trust me. Just fire."

Bryce, Charlie, and Laura began shooting. Glass broke in several of the cars and house windows across the street.

The sniper fired a few more rounds and then seemed to vanish.

Laura held up her fist and everyone stopped firing. She crawled forward, in search of Eri. "Status report."

Myers lifted his head off Denise just enough so Laura could see his eyes. "We're good."

A second later, Charlie rolled from behind a wheel with a thumb raised.

"Bryce? Eri?"

A flood of personnel, cameras, and reporters rushed behind them. At once, a newsperson introduced her report. Laura worked to block them out in search of her other two team members. "Bryce?"

"He's across the street," Charlie said, pointing.

Sure enough, Bryce crept up a stairway that appeared to lead inside the apartment complex. Laura would worry about him later. She needed to find Eri.

"Charlie, where's Eri?"

A worried expression slipped to his eyes. Together, they moved forward. Shell casings and broken glass covered the pavement, mixed with blood. She prayed none of it belong to her new friend. "Eri?"

"Excuse me, miss."

Laura glanced up at a microphone held by a woman with big hair and a cheesy smile. *You've got to be kidding me.* "Not right now, please. I'm trying to find—"

"Found her," Charlie said from beyond the brick

wall.

Laura stood and ran to him.

The reporter and crew followed in mob fashion.

Eri lay crumpled on the ground, covered in blood.

Oh, please, no! Laura bent down and flipped her over. The red liquid saturated her body and face. A sob choked Laura's throat.

Charlie pulled his beanie over his face, sobbing.

"She's not dead," Denise said. "Right?"

Laura glanced at Denise, then back to Eri.

Eri's eyes opened.

"Thank God." Laura took a sigh of relief, thanking her newfound protector. "Where are you shot?"

"Um…" Eri passed a hand down her body and shook her head. "I don't hurt anywhere."

There was too much blood. Laura glanced around, trying hard to understand. "Can you stand?"

Eri lifted up, using the palms of her hands against the sidewalk. Underneath her was the reporter's assistant, Ian. Blood oozed from a hole in his skull. Instantly, the frantic crowd silenced with gaping mouths. This was one of their own.

"Oh, no, Ian," the woman reporter said, then yelled to the camera man, "Turn it off. Someone go get Bruce."

"We have to get this footage, Marta," the cameraman said.

Marta leapt between the camera and Ian. "You film Ian like that, and I'll personally see that you're fired."

A second later, a good looking man broke through the crowd, then paused before bending next to the body. "Ian," he wept. "What happened?"

No one spoke for a moment, and then all eyes fell

on Laura.

Police sirens roared around the corner.

"We've got to go," Charlie hissed.

"No. This is why we're here. We may not get another chance like this to tell our story."

"They will lock us up," Eri said.

Laura shook her head, defiant. "This is why we're here. We didn't do anything wrong."

"Just what did you do," Bruce asked, now facing her, face stern, arms crossed.

"We just came here to tell you our story, and our story followed us." Laura licked her lips, letting her gaze fall on her battered crew. How she wanted them to see real life again. To not be locked up, but taste freedom. But more likely, they were right. Time in prison was sure to follow.

Chapter Thirty

The six young adult criminals turned agents turned criminals, now sat at a police conference room table in silence, waiting for questioning. On one side of the room was a two-way mirror. On the other, a white board with facts from their story. The cops entertained it, so far. One of the reporters had been allowed to listen, though Bryce didn't know why. It didn't seem like an act of protocol. Usually an ongoing investigation was closed to the press. But Bryce didn't mind. That was exactly what they wanted and what Laura had asked for.

"So, you're saying this organization recruited all of you to be assassins?" Swift said, looking away from the white board.

"Try kidnapped," Laura sneered.

Bryce reached over and squeezed her hand. Surprisingly, she didn't pull away.

"And you were a part of this S.I.U. for almost a decade."

She nodded.

"I see." Swift glanced at the mirror for a moment and then stood. "If you'll excuse me for a moment."

When he'd gone, Charlie stretched his arms out on the table and leaned forward. "I told you we should have just contacted my uncle."

"The Senator?" Laura nodded. "I told the sergeant about that…"

"Charlie's right. We should have gone straight to him." Myers exhaled through his nose, shaking his head in obvious annoyance.

"What do you think will happen to us?" Charlie whispered.

Myers groaned. "Simple. All of us, except Eri, and maybe Bryce, are going back to prison."

Charlie peered at Laura. "Is that right, Agent Black? Even you."

"Especially her." Myers pursed his lips. "Laura killed people for nine plus years."

"Shut up, Myers," Bryce said through clenched teeth. It was no mystery the cops were listening in on their conversation. All they needed was a scapegoat, and Bryce wasn't about to let Laura be it. "We haven't done anything wrong. We escaped. They followed and shot those two men. Not our fault."

"But what about her…" Myers said.

Bryce slapped the table. "I mean it, man. Shut up."

Myers held up his hands in mock surrender. "Fine. But I'm not going down for her. For any of you."

What? Right now, Bryce wanted to reach across the table and yank Myers by the throat. It wasn't Laura's fault they were here, but it was her help that got them out of the company. *How can he turn on her?*

"Charlie, if you get a phone call. You contact that uncle of yours, okay?" Laura said.

The door opened and Swift entered again. "I need you all to come with me."

"Are we getting out of here?" Charlie asked.

"Let's go," was all the detective replied.

They all glanced at each other and stood.

Laura let go of Bryce's hand and followed Swift out the door.

Bryce stayed close. No way did he want to lose her now.

They walked down a white hall to a pair of metal doors. The cop pushed them open and led them into a parking garage. A black van was parked just outside the entrance.

"We need to get you out of here. A death threat just came into the station." Swift opened the side door. "Get in. We'll take you somewhere safe."

Everyone clamored into the vehicle and Swift slammed the door shut. The space fell dark. There weren't any windows on the sides, and the ones on the back were tinted. A veil of some kind blocked the view of the driver. Within seconds, the van moved. They were on their way—once again, not of their own choosing. Once again, not free.

****

When the van stopped, the door opened and a metal can hit the back wall. The door slammed closed and locked.

"Don't breathe," Laura said and then held her breath.

Smoke hissed from the grenade. She didn't know what it contained. Her eyes began to water.

"I can't hold it," Eri cried. "I think it's all right, it's just—" And she fell silent.

Bryce and Myers coughed.

Charlie and Denise were silent.

How long can I hold my breath? She began kicking at the door, to no avail. Her lungs burned and she began to lose consciousness. Unable to hold her breath any longer, she gulped in a lung full of tainted air.

Laura blinked. She'd been moved and her hands were tied behind her back. She tried to struggle, when a syringe poked into her neck. She tried to react, but her muscles lay like rubber. Beyond her will, her eyelids closed.

When she opened them again, panic raced in her chest. The team sat in a circle, each strapped to a metal chair, arms taped behind their backs, gags in their mouths. Laura glanced around. They all stared back at her with the same worried expression. *Lord, help!*

The door opened and Swift entered. The apparent arrogance on his face sickened her. "Well, it's wonderful to see our guests are now awake." He walked behind Laura and held a knife to her cheek. "I'm going to remove your gag. If you scream, I'll butcher that pretty face of yours. Understand?"

She nodded.

"Good." He pulled the rag out and let it fall around her neck.

Laura sucked in her cheeks, trying to moisten her parched mouth.

"Now, as you can guess, I'm a sleeper. S.I.U. has had me stationed in the States for quite some time now." He walked around so she could see him. "I have to say, I'm not real happy with you right now. I had a life—children, a spouse, a job—that I loved. Now, it's all gone." He stared over their heads, his jaw locked, his eyes hard. "Why? Why couldn't you just complete the training like everyone else? No, you had to be stupid. You had to go running your mouth." Swift plowed his fist into Myers's face.

Myers let out a muffled scream. Blood trickled from his nose. His brow furrowed; he was ready to fight.

"Stupid kids. Don't you realize how big the giant is?"

"Take them down with us, and you can go back to whatever life you want," Laura said.

He laughed. "Yeah, right. You really are clueless, Black."

"It's possible. We have proof to stop them."

"Yeah, and I have a lunch date with the President at the White House. Want to come?" He pulled down the rest of the team's gags one-by-one. "Greenstone is on his way. He asked that I wait to kill you until he gets here. I can only assume he wants to witness the bloodshed of his traitors in person."

"Greenstone is coming here?" If Laura was even a little afraid before, now she was terrified. Not just for herself, but for her team. "Swift, come on. We can help you."

"Shut it, okay." He spun around in a circle, pointing the knife at eye level. "You're all dead. Understand?"

The door opened and an agent entered. Laura recognized him instantly.

Agent Harding.

Chapter Thirty-One

Laura didn't know if she should smile or cry. Harding had helped her before, but the fact he was here now meant they intended for him to be the one to pull the final trigger. It was Greenstone's way. He would want someone close to Laura to kill her.

"Give us the room," Harding said.

Swift nodded and laughed. "See you all in hell."

"No you won't," Eri spat back.

Thankfully, she was right. If today were indeed their last, then their destination would be to their Maker, not His adversary. Ten minutes in a hotel room had determined a different conclusion to her story. She was thankful for this group, if for no other reason.

The door slammed closed.

The clopping of Harding's dress shoes echoed in the hollow room. He walked toward her with a smug look on his face. She feared he would enjoy this too much.

"I know you're angry, but..." she started to say.

He slid a revolver from his coat pocket and flashed it in front of her face. It came complete with silencer. "I've been sent to kill you. Greenstone will be here within the hour to see that I've done my job well."

"You're really going to kill us?" Charlie's voice wavered.

"What did you think would happen?" Harding said, facing him. "You all ran off half-cocked with some stupid plan to bring down the organization. It isn't possible. You all know that, right?"

"Why isn't it possible?" Laura cried. "We have proof they exist. That's everything."

Harding reached in his pocket and held up a familiar thumb drive. "Like this one."

Her heart collapsed into her stomach. The freedom she longed for now wedged itself between Harding's thumb and index finger. "So you confiscated it from Mike?" All hope was gone. She closed her eyes and exhaled. "Do you have any idea what I went through to get that out?"

Harding knelt in front of her. Usually, she could read her partner, but not today.

"Rumor has it…you cut yourself open to conceal it. Pretty clever. Probably would have worked if you didn't have to babysit these kids."

"Just shoot me and get it over with. I can't take this torment."

"Take the torment," Charlie said. "I'm not ready to die."

Neither was Laura. But she didn't know what else to say. Some S.I.U. agents were like vicious cats that played with their food. They liked to prolong the suffering of their victims. Harding was no exception. Several times, she had scolded him for it in the field.

"You left me to die," he said.

"I had to. You betrayed us."

He stared at her a moment, then laughed. "Are you kidding? You betrayed me first."

"I know," she whispered. Her gaze dropped to her

knees. If only she could have confided in him, accessed his possible involvement early. "If I had talked to you first, would you have come willingly?"

"Yes."

She looked back at him, unsure. "Really?"

He shrugged. "Maybe. But you didn't give me a chance."

Regret enveloped her. "I didn't know who to trust. I'm sorry."

"Me, too." He stood, leveled his gun at her head, and pulled the hammer.

Laura cringed.

The gun clicked, but didn't fire. "That was a warning."

She peeked out from behind her eyelids. "You meant to misfire?"

He held up a clip. "It helps to load it first."

"I'm glad you didn't forget one was in the chamber."

He tucked the gun in his belt and walked behind her.

"What's going on?" Charlie asked.

Harding unbound her hands and then moved to Eri. "I'm getting you all out of here."

"But why?" Laura asked. "Why now and not back on the boat?"

Harding looked up from where he worked on Bryce's ties. "Let's just say I grew a conscience."

Laura reached out and hugged him tight. Never had she been so happy with someone. He winced and pulled back. She eyed him suspiciously and then noticed blood on his shirt. She cautiously lifted it. Deep gashes covered his back. Apparently, he'd been beaten.

"I don't understand." Though, suddenly, his reason for helping became clear.

"They didn't believe I didn't run with you. Beat me until I lay in a puddle of my own blood. Then stuck me in the pit overnight. I had so many bugs eating on my skin that, when they dug me out, the doctor didn't think I'd make it through the night." He lowered his shirt again. "I've never done anything but serve them. But this was my wake-up call. Never again will they lay a hand on me. Not on me, or my friends." Harding handed out the files and then a DVR tape.

"What's this?"

"The tape of the compound. I kind of stole it from Charlie on the boat."

Charlie's mouth dropped open.

Harding looked Laura in the eye. "You do what you need to do."

"What about you?"

He jammed his magazine in his gun and cocked it. "Greenstone and I need to have a talk."

She kissed his cheek. "Thanks."

****

Bryce checked around the wall and then waved the group past him. The media now surrounded the news station like a horde of wasps, buzzing about the latest story. He wasn't sure what their team's purpose was. Returning to the crime scene sounded like a ridiculous idea. Cops lingered in every direction. The reporters were sure to rat on them, since it was assumed they were the criminals behind this heinous act.

"Stop," Laura said, holding up a fist to Myers.

"I thought you wanted us in front of those cameras? You made me drop off my girlfriend at a hospital and we don't know what might happen to her. I want this done and over with."

She shook her head. "Not like this. We go in there, and we're putting our lives at risk again."

Bryce walked to her side. "What do you have in mind?"

"We need to kidnap one of those camera teams. I don't care which network, just get us one."

Myers and Charlie exchanged glances. They were obviously okay with the plan.

"How about the Hispanic lady in the purple suit." Charlie pointed to a woman giving her intro a few feet from their position.

Laura scoped out the area and nodded. "Yeah, they're the ones. Close enough to the tree line, so no one should notice."

"Let's do it." Charlie slapped Myers's back and ran into the bushes behind him.

Myers followed.

"You think this will work?" Eri asked.

"It better," Laura said.

Bryce watched the reporter lower her microphone. The cameraman clicked his equipment off and brought it down to his waist. They were totally clueless to what was about to happen. The story of a lifetime.

****

Laura withdrew her gun, but made sure it stayed on safety. There was no real need for violence. She just wanted them to listen. So far, the hysterical cameraman and too-tough-for-nails woman had yet to help them. Until they calmed down, this would not work.

"Just keep watch, Charlie." Laura waved for him to leave the hotel room. "The rest of the team will be back with supplies shortly."

"Good luck," Charlie said sporting a black eye as he passed Bryce through the outside door. A shiner he acquired while trying to tie up the woman.

The gun needed to be visible. She assumed it was their only chance to get what they wanted. In most cases, it worked. "Hi, I'm Agent Laura Black, formerly an employee of the Secret Intelligence Unit. Not that I expect you to know what that is. But we'll get to that." Laura shifted on the mattress so her knees faced the reporter's knees. "I'm sorry for all of this. It was the only way we could think to talk to you."

The woman spat at Laura's feet and then started spouting expletives in Spanish.

Bryce backed against the wall and crossed his arms for support. He seemed to be waiting for Laura's signal. Not that she planned to have one. She could handle this just fine.

"I understand you're upset…if you'll just let us explain," Laura said.

"You're holding us hostage with a pistol. That's explanation enough."

Tears flowed down the cameraman's face; his body trembled. Maybe the gun wasn't the right approach after all.

Laura tucked it in the back waistband of her jeans. "If we had come to you in that parking lot, the cops would have arrested us, and you'd never get our story."

Her eyes perked up. "What story?"

"What's your name?"

She raised an eyebrow, obviously not used to people not recognizing her. "Barbara Billings."

"And his name?"

"He's Michael Dunn."

"Nice to meet you."

Barbara huffed.

"And this is Bryce Chappelle."

Bryce nodded to the two captives.

"I'll introduce you to the rest of the team later. Now if you did any digging, you'd find that all of us are supposedly dead."

Barbara now seemed to be listening.

"The six of us were recruited by an organization, posing as the U.S. government, who actually has ties to several terrorist cells. Their sole purpose is to train assassins to take out the enemy. Whomever they deem that may be." Laura had clearly piqued their interest. She sat across from Barbara on the other bed and crossed her legs. "It is their recruiting methods that are most disturbing. They prey on the forgotten people— orphans, delinquents, those who won't be missed."

Michael coughed.

"Would you like some water?"

"Please," he croaked.

"Bryce, can you get him a glass of water?"

"Sure." He crossed to the bathroom, and a second later, she heard the faucet turn on.

"As I was saying, they only trained those society had deemed dead or unnecessary."

Barbara studied her for a moment, probably assessing the validity of her statement. "And you are one of them?"

"Yes. I was recruited as a young teen."

"It doesn't seem possible."

Of course not. What sane person could possibly dream up such a ridiculous idea? But there it was. Their founder was hardly sane. "In 1989, a former C.I.A. agent, Mel Greenstone spent some time in Africa with a militant leader. He learned about how they would go from village to village and collect orphans to fight in their Army. Greenstone was intrigued. He returned from his trip wanting to start a black ops unit like none the U.S. Government had ever seen before." Laura sighed. "However, for obvious reasons, he wasn't able to convince several high-ranking officials to implement his plan. So, he decided to take matters into his own hands. With a few financial backers and a couple of rogue soldiers, he created S.I.U.—the Secret Intelligence Unit."

Bryce untied Michael's wrist and handed him the water. The guy took two timid sips and handed it back. Bryce returned the man's bindings, disposed of the cup, and then returned to his post.

Barbara stared at her, her expression emotionless.

"He felt young people without a real future would now be given one as the next generation of soldiers." Something he often said in board meetings. Anytime one of his backers had doubts, he rationalized it with those very words.

"This is an interesting story, but without facts, I can't—" Barbara started to say.

Laura reached in her front pant pocket and pulled out the thumb drive. "How about proof? Do you have a computer in your van?"

Chapter Thirty-Two

Bryce's heart raced at a million miles a second. They were finally on the brink of hope. The day would come. Life would finally make sense again. Freedom. So close.

Michael pulled the network van into a dirt lot and turned off the engine. "I think this should be safe."

Barbara poked her head between the two chairs and nodded. "This is perfect. Let's set up."

Bryce jumped out of the passenger seat and ran around to let the team out. They piled out, excited for what was to come. This was it. The moment they had fought to achieve for almost a week.

They were led into an abandoned warehouse. Inside were several wooden tables and metal chairs.

"What was this place?" Bryce asked.

"We used to do training and classes here before the new warehouse was built." Barbara tossed a rag at Charlie. "There should still be an active line running in here. We use it now and then for testing equipment."

Charlie began to set up. Barbara had given him a laptop among other stuff. He was like a kid without a spending limit. A big grin hadn't left his mouth since they'd climbed in the van.

"Okay, we should be all set on our end," Michael said, then turned to Laura. "Are you ready?"

She took a deep breath and nodded.

"You can join me here," Barbara said, pointing next to her.

Laura glanced around the room. "Won't your people know where we are?"

Michael looked over the lens. "I'm keeping the angle high. It could be any warehouse in the world. I promise. And the good thing about here, there isn't any ambiance. When you have trains or boats, people can pinpoint your location by process of elimination. Trust me, this is the best place for us."

Bryce believed him. He faced Laura and nodded reassuringly.

A cell phone ring cut through the air. Barbara snapped it open. "Yes?" She looked up and met Bryce's eyes. "Go on? And we have footage?" She smiled. "And you'll feed it? Good, because we're ready to roll."

Bryce wanted to jump and scream. *This is it*.

Barbara ended her call and grinned. "We are going live. And even better, before we even got here, teams of U.S. soldiers surrounded the compound on Escondido Mona. Within the hour, S.I.U. will hopefully be no more."

Eri dropped to the ground with her fists cupped to her chest. Bryce knew how she felt. Tears welled in his eyes. He glanced at Laura. She worked to blink back the tears, dabbing under her eyes. "What a mess I'm going to be on camera, huh?"

"You look beautiful," Bryce said.

"We're live in five," Michael said, before counting down with his fingers, then pointing on one.

"Good evening. I am Barbara Billings with a

special exclusive report." She motioned for Laura to join her. "With me, I have Agent Laura Black. As you look at her, you will see a young woman who had to endure the torture of almost a decade at the hands of a mad man."

Bryce had agreed to watch from the monitor in the van. Laura said his presence would make her nervous.

As Barbara explained the history of S.I.U., outlined by Laura earlier, images of the compound, the training facility, several cadets, and classified documents faded in and out across the screen. A headshot of Greenstone flashed in the center of the monitor.

"Yes!" Bryce pumped his fist. Now everyone would know his face.

Charlie came behind him and slapped his back. "This is it, man."

"Agent Black, tell me about Mr. Greenstone." She placed a microphone under Laura's nose.

"For over two decades now, Greenstone has been destroying the lives of children and the countless lives of those he's ordered them to kill. He's an evil man, and he must be stopped," Laura said. "He believes he has a right to kidnap orphans, delinquents, and others society may deem forgotten, but we are humans with rights. I never wanted to be a part of his program. I just wanted a family. A future. He stole that from me and countless others." Her voiced wavered and she stopped talking.

Barbara looked back into the camera. Her expression stoic. "As you can see, I haven't told you where we are filming. This is for the protection of those who risked their lives to bring us these secrets. Since they have tried to bring this to light, they've had their lives endangered numerous times, including the shooting in front of the TV studio earlier today."

A chill swept over Bryce. The reality of this moment made his head swim. But even more, this was a powerful piece. Even if he hadn't experienced it firsthand, it would choke him up. With the right amount of people, this thing would end.

Barbara wrapped it up with some final thoughts, and then said, "Back to you in the studio, Jim." She lowered her mic and looked at Laura.

"Thank you," Laura said.

"I hope it works." Barbara hugged her, then collected her stuff and Michael, then waved and exited through the sliding door.

Bryce frowned. "If it didn't work, we just painted a huge target on our backs. They know we're still in the city."

"When will we know if we're safe? When can we go home?" Charlie asked.

The look on Laura's face said it all. Never. This was it. A new life. "I'm sorry," she said, then looked away.

"So that's it. All this, and we're still running?" Myers's face grew red. He spun around and punched the wall. "Unbelievable. This is not what you promised, Agent Black."

"What did I promise, Mr. Luther?" Laura spun on her heel to face him, jaw clenched, ready for a fight. "I never promised you anything. Nothing. It was you guys who wanted out. I was perfectly ready to stay in my cage for the rest of my days. I had my life mapped out."

"You mean your death," Charlie said.

She swung her gaze to him with piercing eyes. "At

least I wouldn't have to worry about being shot in the back. I would know when it was coming. So, don't you dare blame me for anything that has happened. I did what I could. I risked everything. You're alive because of me."

"She's right." Bryce walked forward with folded arms. "I'd rather be running, than stuck in that prison. She got us out. We owe her that."

"Whatever." Myers grabbed his jacket. "I'm going to see Denise."

Laura cocked her gun. "You can't do that."

He turned around slowly. "You better get that gun off me, Black, or so help me."

"Or you'll what?"

Without warning, he rushed her. Their bodies collided, sliding across the floor. The gun skated to the wall. Myers swung. His fist hit hard against her jaw. She kneed him in the groin. He groaned. She swung again. He shoved her off.

Bryce jumped in and pulled Myers back.

Eri grabbed Laura.

"Stop it, man!" Bryce yelled. "This is stupid."

"No!" Myers leapt from his grasp and ran for the gun.

Laura beat him to it.

"Stop!" Eri fired her pistol into the air. "Both of you knock it off. This isn't helping."

"Great, Eri. Notify the cops, why don't you?" Charlie said.

Myers spit blood to the floor. "This ain't over."

Laura picked up her gun and shoved it in her waistband. "You should have rotted in prison."

"Maybe so. But then so should you."

They glared at one another. The tension as thick as lard.

Bryce didn't know what to do. Of course, if this got ugly, he'd be on Laura's side. No matter what. Though he'd grown to like Myers, he loved *her*.

"You know this is lame, Myers. Why are you fighting Black?" Eri stepped in front of him, so he was forced to look at her. "We have a powerful organization after us. They could be anywhere, and you're bickering with our leader. Really?"

"She won't let me go see Denise." He glanced around Eri, meeting Laura's gaze again.

"I'm protecting you and her."

"Or yourself."

Laura let out a deliberate sigh. "Your face has been plastered all over the news. If you go walking into Mercy, they will have you in jail so fast your head will spin. Worse, it will lead *them* to her."

That made him pause. He turned around and paced a few feet away. "Then what do we do? You don't expect me to leave her there. Because I can't."

Laura walked a few paces toward him. "Of course not. She's one of us. If you'll stop trying to hit me, I'll tell you my plan."

Despite himself, a smile slipped. "Deal. Lay it on me."

****

Later that afternoon, Bryce entered Mercy hospital with an enormous basket of flowers. A reception desk lay just ahead on the left. He walked to it and smiled at the elderly man behind it. "Excuse me. I have a flower delivery for a Ms. Krueger."

The man typed something on a computer keyboard

and checked his monitor. "She's on the third floor, room 302B."

"Thank you." Bryce walked to the elevator. The door opened and he stepped in. Once it closed, he texted Laura. "I'm in."

When the elevator reached the top floor, he stepped out. A few feet away, he spotted Charlie behind a newspaper. He was there as back up.

Laura walked by wearing scrubs and winked.

Bryce didn't wait. He walked to the room at the end of the hall and ducked in.

Eri was there.

Laura followed a moment later with a wheelchair.

"Hi guys," Denise said groggily, obviously not fully awake.

"Did you bring it?" Laura asked.

Bryce turned the plant upside down and dropped a syringe on the sheet. "Are you sure about this?"

She nodded. "Trust me. It only gives the appearance of death, he'll only be in a deep sleep." Laura scooped up the needle and crossed to the man in the bed next to Denise. She lifted the end of the IV and injected the toxin in.

Within a minute, nurses and doctors rushed in the room. Amazingly, Laura was right. They were so occupied with the "dying" patient that none of them seemed to notice the group move out the door with Denise.

They took the elevator down and met in the garage. The tires screeched as Myers squealed to a stop in front of them. "Get in."

"We need to find a place to regroup," Laura said after they were all settled.

"How is she?" Myers yelled over his shoulder.

"I'm okay," Denise said. "The doctor seemed positive about my recovery. But then, they didn't expect the Calvary to pull me out."

Eri pulled a plastic bag from under her shirt and handed it out. "Now the rest of you can clean up."

Laura reached inside and pulled out antibiotics, butterfly bandages, and gauze. She looked at Eri and smiled. "Good girl." Her gaze shifted to Charlie. "Were you able to get a lap top and the supplies I asked for?"

"Of course. The doctor had everything we needed."

"You guys are the best," Laura said.

Bryce grinned. "We were trained by the best."

Their eyes locked, and for the first time in days, the desire to kiss her returned. He didn't know what future they had together, but he prayed for it. He needed her in his life.

"There it is!" Charlie said, pointing to the warehouse they'd holed up in earlier.

Myers swerved.

The team braced themselves against the inertia.

"Sorry, hold on."

The van braked hard and they piled out.

Bryce grabbed a pair of duffel bags and followed Laura inside. He pushed some junk off the wooden tables in one fluid motion, then swung the bags on the table, and unzipped the first one. Inside was food and clothes. He handed them out. "First, we get comfortable, then we can work."

Laura frowned, but didn't argue.

After everyone was dressed, patched up, and full of canned ravioli, they pulled out the hardware Charlie had boosted. Between Myers and Charlie, they were able to get online through satellite feed, then they used search engines to find the information. "I found something."

The group gathered around the tiny computer screen. A newscaster stood in front of the familiar compound. Flashing lights, helicopters, and a heavy police presence could be seen in front of the S.I.U. gates.

Bryce squinted. A figure was being escorted to the back of a police car. "No way! Greenstone. Did you see him?"

Laura slapped a hand over her mouth, her eyes filled with tears. "Yes," she rasped. "It's him. I thought he was here."

Myers glanced to Laura, then to Bryce, then back to the screen, then to Laura again. "What does that mean?"

Laura fell to her knees. "We're free."

****

What now? Laura wasn't sure. There were no guarantees. It was conceivable S.I.U. sleepers could have been activated before this happened. The six of them could be on a watch list somewhere, but they couldn't live their lives in a warehouse. If they did, they'd be no better off than they were before they left.

Myers cuddled with Denise on the cement floor, whispering, making her giggle.

Eri sat on the table swinging her legs.

Charlie paced a few feet away, cracking his knuckles.

Bryce watched her.

It was time. She had to let them go. "If everyone will give me a second, I'm going to be honest with all of you."

They all stood and faced her.

"You'll need to watch your back. I wouldn't suggest going home anytime soon, just to be safe, but…" She grinned. "It is time for you to live your lives. Whatever you want that to be. We have our new passports, compliments of Charlie."

Charlie bowed.

"We have money, thanks to Myers." Not that she wanted to know how he got it. He swore it was legit, but she had her doubts. "So this is it. I think it is better if we split up for now."

"Sick of us, are you?" Myers said. "I'm sorry for hitting you."

She touched his arm. "You were protecting Denise. I get it. No, that's not why I'm saying this at all." Never had she felt this close to a bunch of people. She'd miss them enormously, more than they could possibly understand. "You'll always be my friends. And if you get in trouble, we've developed a protocol. Charlie is setting up a website that fronts as a dating service. If you get in trouble, you log on with this special code." Laura handed out cards Charlie had prepared earlier. "It will look like you're placing an ad for a date, but it will actually be a signal to the rest of us."

Denise crossed to Laura and hugged her neck. "Thank you for everything."

Tears clogged in Laura's throat. "Ditto."

Everyone joined in a mass hug. Tears flowed, leaving not one dry eye. Laura owed them more than her life. She owed them her soul. Because of them, she'd found not only freedom from captivity in this life, but from the darkness that was sure to follow her into the next. She would miss them greatly.

Denise and Myers were the first to suggest leaving.

Bryce shook both their hands, then the couple turned to Laura.

"I know I've been a jerk, Agent Black, but I am really grateful for everything." Myers stuck out a hand.

Laura took it and he pulled her into a hug.

"Thank you."

Tears welled in her eyes. She nodded and stepped back.

Denise hugged her next. "You're an amazing woman. I believe God put you in our path for a reason. Thank you. Thank you."

"You take care of one another, okay?" Laura said, looking from Denise to Myers.

"You can count on it," Myers said. "She's not getting out of my sight. And you'll have to make it to our wedding."

Laura laughed. "Really?"

Denise put her hands on her hips and smiled. "Oh, really? We're kind of young, no?"

Myers kissed her forehead and laughed. "We've got time and anything is possible. Black said to do what we wanted to do. I'm dreaming, baby."

"Play your cards right, and you just might get your wish." Denise kissed his cheek, then looked back at Laura one last time. "Bye, Laura. You are the queen."

She waved. "Bye."

"Later," Charlie said.

Eri walked them out.

Charlie packed up his stuff and swung his bag over his shoulder. "Well, I've never been one for long, sad goodbyes, so…"

Bryce stepped forward and stuck out his hand. "Thanks, Charlie."

Charlie dropped his bag and shook it.

"Yeah." He waved at Eri as she came back in, then to Laura. "Bye, Black."

"Bye, Charlie," the two girls said together.

He nodded and sauntered out the door.

Eri didn't make any indication she was leaving.

"What about you, my friend? Where will you go?" Laura said.

Eri smiled. "I would like to go home to my family when it is time, but in the meantime, if it's okay, I'd like to stay on with you."

"Of course." Laura smiled.

Charlie stepped back in the room. "Well, if she gets to stay."

Bryce and Laura laughed.

"You're welcome to stay as well," Laura said.

"Cool." Charlie dropped his bag and clapped. "Because, honestly, you guys are the closest thing I have to family now."

"Ditto," Bryce said, and then turned to Laura.

Her heart ached for what he might say. After all, he had a fiancée waiting for him back home. Now was the moment of truth. She wouldn't blame him if that was his choice. Life with her would never be easy. With his girl, Shawna, he could disappear. Be a normal married couple somewhere. Maybe start a family someday. Could Laura really expect him to give all that up for her? "You know, you're free to go."

Bryce glanced at Charlie and Eri, then back to Laura. "Yeah, I know."

"Shawna is waiting."

He visibly flinched. "I know that, too."

It hurt Laura to say Shawna's name. Why couldn't he just leave? A second more, and she may pull her gun and force him to stay. "So, why don't you go?"

"I can't."

Laura raised her eyebrow. "Why not?"

He reached out and cupped his hand around her cheek. "Because I'm madly in love with someone else."

Her eyes watered again. Never had she experienced so many emotions in one setting. "You do?"

"With all my heart. I love you, Laura Black."

She opened her mouth to speak, but no words came. He wrapped his arms around her and pulled her into him. His lips touched hers. Slowly, they kissed.

She felt it everywhere, making her head spin. Finally, he pulled back and looked her in the eye. "I'm not leaving without you ever again."

"That's good," she whispered, "Because I love you, too."

"Excuse me," Myers said from the doorway.

Laura glanced away from Bryce. "Yes?"

"I was just wondering…if no one is leaving…"

Laura laughed. "I insist. Please stay."

Myers led Denise back into the warehouse. What would she do with them? They were like puppies who needed a mother. *I guess I'm it.* "So now what?"

A big smile crossed Charlie's face. "Ever thought of starting a business that encompasses all our skills?"

They all looked at each other, no one saying a thing. Laura let a grin slowly slide on her lips.

Maybe, just maybe, God did have a plan for their lives. "You may be on to something, Charlie."

A word about the author...

Kimberlee Mendoza is the recipient of the Sherwood Eliot Wirt Writer of the Year for 2007 for all of San Diego County. She is currently an English professor at San Diego Christian College, University of Phoenix, and Landry Academy High School.

She is also the Creative Arts and Youth Pastor at San Diego Hope Church, a cover artist for Wild Rose Press, and an author of over a dozen novels.

Mendoza has published a non-fiction book on human video and several plays through Meriwether Publishing. She is a graduate from Longridge Writing Group, has a BA in Human Development, and a MA in Humanities.